The Foursome
A Love Story

by

Vern Turner

Other Fictional Works by Vern Turner

Meadows and Minefields (Summer Solstice, 2020)
A Hero's Journey (Summer Solstice, 2020)
The Ten Arms of Durga (Mirador, 2020)
Demon Slayer (Mirador, 2020)
The Medalist (Mirador, 2021)
The Immigrant's Grandson (Savant, 2022)

Contents

Preface

I grew up in northeastern Ohio, where many fine people lived, loved, worked and played. There were even a couple of Presidents who came from my neck of the woods. Not many prodigies in any field emerged from my time there or from the period covered in this book. One must understand that the social environments between the white suburbs and the inner city of Cleveland, Ohio were as different as chalk is from cheese. The suburbs all around Cleveland were the direct result of "white flight" from the city to the country. The Second World War arrested that move, but once the boys (and girls) returned home from war, the cookie-cutter neighborhoods would soon spring up like mushrooms.

My family did what most white families did in 1954 – 1960, and later: They sold their homes to the black people who were often used as fear generators in previously all-white neighborhoods. The tired phrase, "Well, there goes the neighborhood", was not a throwaway comment. The fear stemmed from black people's lives and property being assumed to be not as valuable as the white people's. Thus, property values would plummet – at least according to the real estate and construction contractors promoting this ruse.

This story is truly a love story centered around my love for the game of golf. It also intends to be counter-intuitive to racial animus, the white flight described above, and the inherent racism that permeates the United States. My intent is to show what real possibilities look like when racism, bigotry and fear are defied by strong people. It also intends to illustrate how love can grow and become the great enhancer of personal strength, courage and perseverance. The four main characters in this story push back against those self-destructive human traits that poison so much of our society. It was my intention to use this sort of bifurcated love story to make the point of how social harmony can be made to work.

I know "foursome" is a golf term. But unlike a golfing group with the same title, this foursome is not in competition with one another. They bond together to form a loving, caring and hugely successful unit to show themselves and their communities the possibilities that are available.

Chapter 1

Dumb Luck

To say that Bill Bannock got lucky would be an understatement of great proportions. That's because it also involved unspeakable tragedy. Just as he turned thirty, in March 1963, his parents were killed in an auto accident on an icy back road in northeastern Ohio. It wasn't far from where he grew up, but the weather along the lake was always shitty, especially in winter. And this particular tragedy followed a late winter ice storm that glazed everything. Bill's mother had a dental appointment that day and she was adamant about keeping it. Hell, they had all learned to drive on ice. It finally caught up with his parents though, and they died while trying to dodge an oncoming, out-of-control car that was sliding sideways toward them.

Bill had been living in his own apartment in one of the new high rises along Lake Erie's shores, but now had to handle the estate – such as it was. He worked at the same factory his father and mother had for most of their lives, but Bill's collar was white, theirs blue.

Perhaps it is presumptuous to say that it took his parents'

deaths for him to realize how lucky he was. They were good, hard-working, salt-of-the-earth folks who believed in God, telling the truth and promoting fairness for everyone. That's how they raised him too. Bill's father often came home from work complaining about how some of his co-workers talked about black people as if they were undeserving of human status. After growing up alongside so many white kids that came from shattered, bigoted or violent homes, Bill knew that his home life was a symphony of love and harmony by comparison. Bill Bannock was lucky.

But his good parents were now dead, and he was the only child of Harry (not Harold) and Helen Bannock. Here was their only son, Bill (not William) Bannock, now forty years old and rich beyond anything he ever deserved. He was lucky. Real lucky...

With his parents' life insurance policies and the sale of their little brick house, he walked out of the lawyer's office with a check for just over $50,000. Not bad money for 1963. He was just 30 then, but felt like he had just inherited a fortune.

Then, while drinking a beer with his buddy Clayton Ambrose the week after the estate settled, he learned about this company that was making these copying machines that would end the life of the mimeograph clunkers and the volatile chemicals that went with them.

"I read about this company in the Wall Street Journal, so it has to be the right company to invest your money in," he said. "Why don't you go and buy as much of that stock as you can while it's still cheap? I'm gonna go buy a thousand shares tomorrow. My broker says it's a can't miss."

"What's your broker's name and number? Lemme give him a call and talk to him myself."

The broker's name was Sam Stewart, and he talked Bill into investing about forty of the fifty thousand dollars into this company that was going to take the investment world by storm.

It did.

He also successfully encouraged him to invest in a business machine company that was venturing into things called computers.

The day after his thirty-fifth birthday in March 1968, Bill's office phone rang and Sam told him that his two stocks had just split again after splitting three months ago. The stocks were going up the value ladder like a bat out of hell.

"How much are my shares worth now, Sam?"

"Well, your original investment of twenty-five thousand shares in that copying machine stock at a buck sixty per is now sittin' at a hundred thousand shares worth about five bucks apiece. The computer company stocks are doing that well too. This is because they split last year as well. Have you been getting those quarterly reports? You were smart to roll most of the dividends back into more stocks. It helped with your taxes too. If you hadn't done that, your dividend payment would be... um... about a buck ten per share per year averaging the two. To save you the trouble, after my cut, you'd be lookin' at getting checks totaling maybe a hundred and fifty thousand dollars a year before taxes. You're rich, my boy! Why are you still working?" That sum was more than triple what Bill was making flying a desk.

"Holy shit, Sam! I had no idea. Could I just roll half of the dividends?"

"You could, and that would be the smart play. I mean, sixty or seventy grand a year will buy you a lot of golf balls."

Bill hung up the phone and just made it to the men's room without peeing his pants. Then, he turned around and puked his guts out into a commode.

Quick calculations showed that at just a constant rate of

growth for his investments, he'd be a millionaire before he turned forty.

"HOLY SHIT! I didn't plan on this. What am I gonna do for the rest of my life? I'm sure as hell not gonna be making my pants shiny sitting in that office chair forever. I think it's time to get serious about my golf game again and maybe use my education for something other than working for a company that builds torpedoes. But doing what?

Chapter 2
Getting Some Game

Bill Bannock grew strong during his teen years, but remained supple due to stretching routines he learned from his physical education teacher at school. He lifted some weights and did pushups every day. Whenever he could, he'd run a few miles to keep his legs in shape. He kept practicing golf, of course, and after his 16th birthday, broke eighty for the first time. His father's pride in his son's golf game expanded along with Bill's lowering scores.

Bill signed up for the high school golf team and, over the three years he played for the team, won almost two-thirds of his matches. He was never good enough to play as first player, but he was a reliable team point most times.

The golf coach at Bill's high school was an eccentric science teacher named Chester White. His science classes were always entertaining and interesting. In class, he was jovial and constantly told little jokes. But at golf practice, he was serious without being dour, attentive without being suffocating, and knowledgeable without being pedantic. He *knew* about golf.

What Bill learned from Chester White was the *game* of golf, not just the physical expression of hitting it where you wanted to. To Chester White, golf emulated life. He lectured his team about integrity and character. He'd say things like, "It's easy to cheat at golf, but if you do, you show the world how shallow of character you are and how little respect you have for yourself and the game. The game is there for us, but never lose sight of who puts it out there. All those grounds crews and superintendents maintain the golf courses for us. So, when you hear that old saying, 'don't forget to smell the roses', it means that you should enjoy that special time with nature while you're on the golf course as well as extend respect to those who keep the courses in playing condition. I know it sounds like preaching, but being out on the golf course is a kind of religious experience, a kind of reverence that only exists for us."

When they were out on the course, there were moments when each of the players just stood quietly and watched a bird or a squirrel doing what they do. The smell of freshly mown fairways always created a special atmosphere that made it hard to concentrate. Sometimes, if they were lucky, they would see a deer jump out of the woods, or a raccoon waddle across a fairway and look back at them with masked diffidence.

After one of Bill's tournament wins where he was the low round player, Harry Bannock was over the moon and kept pounding Bill on the back.

"You've got some game, my boy. Your consistency and your putting were what won you the match today. If you were old enough, I'd buy you a beer."

Coach White called an all-hands meeting and congratulated his players profusely for adhering to their games and not getting too far ahead of themselves. Bill kept hearing White's words: "Honor those who help you. Be humble, because next week somebody just might kick your ass."

Bill Bannock played good to very good golf, but was never good enough to play as first man. The thing that bugged him and his dad was that he seemed to have hit a scoring floor. Oh, he broke par occasionally, but he just couldn't get below a "2" handicap. No matter how much he practiced, there were always the putts that lipped out, the perfectly hit approach shots that bounded over the greens and the odd and freaky bounces into hazards or out-of-bounds. They often joked—sort of—that the golf gods just kept laughing at him and occasionally flipped him their middle finger. It was frustrating, even though Bill would be categorized as being in the top 2% of all amateur golfers in the country.

When Bill went to Ohio University, he discovered that he wasn't even good enough to make the team. All the players there, from freshmen upwards, were "scratch" players; no handicap needed. Bill ended up caddying for his roommate who *did* make the team. They played together at times, but Bill just couldn't lower his scores. Still, his love of the game acted as his personal muse in life. It was a healthy pursuit and kept him fit and engaged.

For Bill Bannock, the message from the golf gods was: *"Two handicap. Our allocations for 'scratch' golfers has no room for you."* Alas.

After college, Bill was left with the consolation prize of being feared by the local players. None of them would even play a skins game with him or otherwise bet, no matter how many strokes he gave them. He was in golfer's no man's land. Then, just after his 40th birthday, his world of golf—and everything else—changed forever.

Chapter 3

Her Name Was Alice

Bill Bannock was still considered pretty good-looking by Jackie English, his latest former girlfriend. At just over six feet, he weighed a fit 185 pounds. He had medium brown hair that had just begun showing signs of graying. He was also blessed with good eyesight, so no spectacles interfered with his bright green eyes. They remained uncovered for all the world to see. Bill was developing a healthy set of wrinkles at the corners of his eyes, but otherwise, his clean-shaven face looked younger than its calendar years. A twice-weekly boxing regimen provided a discipline for him to remain trim. He also jogged a few miles along the shore of the lake when the weather permitted, so his muscles remained reasonably taut throughout the year.

During the second week in May 1973, Bill went to Willow Creek for his weekly golf and betting exercise with the only guys who still thought they could beat him. Money changed hands between the four of them so that, at the end of the season, the net gain for any of them was close to zero. The weekly winners bought a beer for the group after the round. Handicaps were, of course, part of the game. The "high stakes" were five dollars for the winner of each nine holes and ten dollars for the winner of the match. All of the men were well off enough to not have to work for a living, so this weekly event was the highlight of their week. The betting was just another way for the guys to needle each other. *Serious* money would have given Bill's pals the *yips* so badly that they wouldn't have been able to take the club back.

The three other players had names. Harry Holcomb had a four handicap and sometimes beat Bill for low gross. He was a retired real estate broker who co-owned a Cadillac dealership with Lonny Shell, another player. They both kept getting rich peddling those Cadillacs to other real estate brokers, and anyone else who wanted to drive that well-known status symbol. Lonny was as ostentatious as Harry was nondescript. He always wore something pink... bright pink. Once he showed up dressed entirely in pink, including shoes. The other three guys wouldn't play with him that day for fear that some bomber pilot might see him as a target. Lonny's game was generously defined as occasional contact with the ball. That meant the small ball. He spent most of his rounds brushing dirt clods off his clothes from previous shots. The other three men teased him about thinking that the BIG ball was easier to hit, and that he gave the maintenance crews job security.

Finally, there was Frank Goscz. It was pronounced "Goosh". They called him "Eye Chart" for obvious reasons. He admitted to his Polish heritage and didn't mind being called "Polack" along with other colorful adjectives.

This Wednesday in May, in the eastern suburbs of gritty Cleveland, was one of the few glorious days with perfect temperatures for short-sleeved shirts. The low humidity kept sweat to a minimum, so savage color clashes in Lonny's shocking-pink shirt armpits were small. The jovial group had a 10:28 tee time this particular morning. Bill arrived about an hour earlier to warm up and putt some.

Bill hauled his clubs out of his car and walked past the bench where kids would sit hoping to caddy for some geezer for money, enabling them to pay for the cigarettes they smoked while waiting for the next loop. Bill often hired one of the kids as he liked walking and didn't care to share body odor with a cart mate, especially on such a beautiful day as this. Harry and Frank chose to ride together in one of the new electric golf carts. These things were Willow Creek's latest capital project and caused them to raise the green fees by a dollar for each nine holes. Capitalism run amok... Lonny walked the course with a pull cart for his bag.

Today, the only kid sitting on the bench was a brown-skinned girl who seemed to be all arms and legs.

"What's your name, young lady?" Bill asked.

"Alice. Alice Morgan, mister."

"Are you here to caddy today?"

"Yessir. Are you here to play today?" she said, smiling a dazzling smile with impish dimples.

"I am. I need a caddy. Do you know how to do this? Are you willing to walk fast for eighteen holes, rake traps, replace divots and such?"

"Yessir. My rate is ten dollars for the round plus any tips you might feel generous enough to add to that."

Alice Morgan had none of the speech affectations that most of the white guys who had been insulated in the suburbs expected to hear from a person of color. That politically correct term wasn't yet used in 1973. Other less elegant adjectives were part of the white guy lexicon for non-white people in suburban Cleveland.

Her diction was perfect white guy diction. Her eyes were perhaps the largest Bill had ever seen, but they fit her pretty face perfectly. When she stood up, she was just a little shorter than him, so she almost looked him straight in the eye. Her skin tone was of a medium shade, maybe a little darker than coffee with one cream. Her arms and legs were lean but showed muscle. But it was her face that was captivating. Her smile was perfect and infectious, making it hard not to smile back.

"How old are you, Alice?"

"Sixteen, sir."

"So, you've done this before?"

"Yessir. I caddied for my daddy before he got killed. He started me out caddying up at Highland Park, where all the colored folk play."

"I'm sorry to hear about your father. Was he killed in the war? You know, Vietnam?"

"No sir. Some street punk tried to mug him at a bus stop down on Cedar Avenue. My daddy fought back and the punk shot him dead. The police (She didn't say 'Po-leece'.) never caught the mugger. Momma and I have been trying to keep food on the table for my little brother and us since. I kept going up to Highland Park to caddy, but the money was hardly worth my time, and the men were really rough. So, last year, Momma started driving me out to the suburb courses where I could make better money and not worry about getting pawed on. She didn't want me to be cleaning houses or babysitting either, so she looked into this kinda clean, outdoor work. I like it because I get to be in the fresh air and sunshine, and away from the nastiness around where I live.

"Sorry for goin' on like that. Do you still want me to loop for you today? I've never been to this course before, so I have a lot to learn. Are *you* willing to accept that?"

To say Bill was a bit flabbergasted by this girl's poise and straightforwardness would be an understatement. "You bet. I like to teach and coach too, so let's go out there and whomp my boys over there."

"Did anyone ever tell that guy that pink doesn't look good out here?"

That cracked Bill up and he planned to save that line for the beer call after they played the round. Alice grabbed Bill's bag and toted it right over to the driving range and got him a bucket of balls. She found a spot with good grass and waited for him to come over after he finished needling the guys. As Bill was stretching, Alice took a towel off the starter's bench and wet half of it. A dry towel always hung from Bill's golf bag.

His warm-up routine began with a few easy wedges, then 8-iron, 6-iron, 4-iron, 2-iron, 4-wood and driver. Then, he went back down to 9-iron through 3-iron, 3-wood and a few sand wedges. After thirty balls, he was ready to go over to the putting green.

Alice told him he had as good a swing as she'd seen. "Do you warm up like that all the time?" she asked.

"I do, and I follow the same routine when I have a full practice too. I just hit more balls—maybe a hundred, or so.' Do you play at all?"

"My daddy had me hitting balls when I was younger, so I know the basics. Nice clubs. When did you get the *Tourneys*?"

"About three years ago. I gave myself a Christmas present. I finally retired the Wilson Staffs my dad bought me. Still have 'em. They were my first adult set, and I have trouble getting rid of them for sentimental reasons."

As they walked over to the first tee, she asked, "What's your name? I should know who I'm caddying for." She said it with a mischievous grin and a sidelong glance.

"Oh. Sure. Bill Bannock. Sorry. Bad manners."

"So, you're not married?"

"Nope. Never been. Got a boyfriend?"

"Nah. The boys where I live don't like smart girls. They think I'm uppity and conceited. That's fine with me, though. Most of them are just street thugs or guys that are so full of themselves, playin' sports and such. I'd rather read a good book than fool with them anyway."

"Okay Alice, what's this hole look like?"

She looked at the map on the scorecard. "Three-eighty-five with a slight dogleg to the right. You'll probably want to hit a little fade."

"Hey, Bannock!" Lonny yelled. "No fair getting expert help out here. That's gonna cost you another two strokes on the par fives."

"Lonny, anybody who wears pink golf shoes has no room to criticize anybody.' I give you enough strokes as it is. Just go ahead and kick it around like you always do. Giving you strokes is meaningless."

Harry and Frank laughed out loud. Harry said, "So, is your new caddy goin' to get you to finally break seventy out here?"

"She might. I already feel like she's a good luck charm. Hit away, Harry. You haven't had the honors yet this month.

"Okay, Alice. I'm playing a Titleist three. I have another couple of sleeves of them in the bag. When you get a chance, check out where I put things so if I ask you for something, you can give it to me quickly."

When it was his turn, Bill striped his drive down the fairway, just a little bit left of center, and with the prescribed fade.

"Great drive, Bannock. Did your caddy tell you where to hit it?" razzed Lonny Pink Shoes.

"As a matter of fact, she did. She knows talent when she sees it. And shouldn't you be more concerned with your game than with my caddy?"

As they walked up to the ball, Alice said, "Do those guys

always give you a bad time, Mr. Bannock?"

"They do. Any excuse to needle me. Of course, I've gotta give it back to them, or it's no fun. By the way, it's 'Bill' when nobody is around. But be sure to emphasize the 'Mister' when they can hear you. Now, hand me the eight."

"How far do you normally hit eight?" Alice asked.

"About one forty-five. What's my yardage from here?"

She looked for the 150-yard stake. "About one forty-five to the center. The flag looks to be toward the back, so give the eight a rip."

Bill smiled at her and felt more amazement for this girl. *"This kid knows the game. No retiring violet, she. This is gonna be a fun round."*

Following his caddy's instruction, Bill flushed the eight iron and it bit nicely, six feet short of the hole. "Great shot, Bill," Harry said. "Gotta make the putt though."

"Alice, hand me my putter, then head up to the green and start reading my putt."

She waited for Frank "Eye chart" Goscz to hit up before replacing the divot from Bill's shot. Goscz was always the longest hitter in the group, but couldn't hit anything else.

Alice scooted ahead of the group as Lonny and Bill walked together, letting the two "older gentlemen" ride their way up.

"It looks like the putt is gonna slide to the left a little," Alice said when Bill arrived at the green. "I'd say, inside right lip. It's a little uphill too, so you can put a solid stroke on it."

"Thanks, Alice. Let me have a look." She was right. Bill nodded. She nodded back.

The putt did slide to the left and went straight to the bottom of the hole. He winked at Alice as the guys hooted. She smiled back.

As the round progressed, Bill kept outscoring his playing partners. He was five strokes up on Harry, and approaching double-digit leads over the rest of them as they approached the 18th tee. Lonny kept chirping all the way around and even said some astonishingly tasteless things about Alice even while she was within earshot. Bill scowled at him and told him that he'd be better off concentrating on *his* game instead of him and his caddy. After a couple of holes where Bill was giving him *stinkeye*, Lonny shut up and continued to gouge the earth.

Alice handed Bill the driver at the last tee box and stepped back so she could watch the ball flight – as she'd done all day. The 18th at Willow Creek was a long par five that turned to the left. This allowed Bill to play his natural draw and land his drive 270 yards down range, right in the middle of the fairway. The "gentlemen" opponents all ended up in the rough and not very far down the length of the hole. They were clearly tired and had even stopped needling each other. Bill was three under par and wanted to birdie the last hole for a cool 68 to cap off this excellent round, his best ever at Willow Creek.

Without him asking, Alice handed Bill the three wood, gave him a little smile and stepped away. With that little bit of happiness in mind, he crushed the shot. It bounced once in front of the green and ran all the way back to within three feet of making double eagle. Even Lonny whooped at that shot. Bill tapped in the putt for a three, and carded the 67 with more than a little joy. He'd only gone this low once before, when he was just a kid out of college. Time to celebrate.

Alice took Bill's clubs over to the water spigot and started cleaning them. After receiving all the back slaps he could stand, Bill said he'd meet them in the restaurant in a couple of minutes. "I have to go pay my caddy. She earned a nice tip too."

They agreed.

"Alice, you were great today. You picked up on my game right away. Great job at reading the greens too. You seem to have a knack for that."

"My daddy taught me well. These greens are about the same difficulty as those at Highland Park, so it felt pretty natural. These are smaller, though."

"So, do you have another loop today?"

"I don't think so. Looks like nobody's gotten here in time to play eighteen now. So, I'll call Momma and have her come and get me."

Bill handed her a crisp, new $20 bill.
"Thanks, Mr. Bannock, er, Bill. This will help a lot."

On an impulse he said, "Are you hungry? Let me buy you a late lunch. Wait for me here and I'll come and get you. We'll go to someplace nice." Bill turned and walked away, leaving her looking dumbstruck.

Bill quickly drank the obligatory beer with the guys and told them to save up for next week, when he would set the course record. They all laughed and jeered and told him that his ship had sailed; today was the last hurrah at breaking par.

"We'll see," he said. "Got me a caddy that knows the game now. You assholes are in real trouble."

That brought more jeers and laughs. Bill left to find Alice.

"My car is that dark blue Oldsmobile over there, Alice. What do you like to eat?"

Chapter 4

Lunch With Alice

"Don't think I'm some dirty old man, Alice. I just really appreciate your work today. Besides, I get the feeling that you have more to say about things," Bill said as he pulled out of the parking lot. They headed straight for Jackie's Burger Palace down at the west end of town on Euclid Avenue.

"I do. Momma keeps telling me that nobody else talks about the stuff I talk about. If you don't mind me saying so, I didn't like hearing what Mr. Pink Shoes said about me. We hear that shit all the time when we're outside the neighborhood. Sorry. Shouldn't swear."

"No, Alice, you were right in this case. That kind of mindless talk IS shit. I let Lonny know I didn't appreciate him saying that stuff. Did you notice how quiet he got?"

"Yeah. His game is pretty bad too. Why do you keep playing with guys like that?"

"Good question. Tell the truth, they're the only guys I can have a game with. Nobody wants to be beaten by ten strokes. My reputation is toxic."

"Why don't you join a proper country club? Do you ever enter the city tournaments? You got enough game to be competitive everywhere, I'll bet."

"Thank you for the compliments, Alice, but I don't shoot sixty-seven every day. I'm a two and have been for almost twenty years, no matter how hard I practice. So, what does your mother do?"

"She is a school teacher at Glennville High School. She teaches English and history. She graduated from Ohio State when she was just twenty, then met my daddy. I was born about a year after they were married, so she had to quit teaching for a while. Daddy worked in a factory as a machinist apprentice until he was shot. He was about to get promoted, but..."

"So, your mother has you and your little brother to support, right?"

"Yeah. Benny was born a little more than a year after I was, so she had two growing kids on her hands. I was fourteen and Benny thirteen when daddy was shot. The three of us started working any job we could find to make a few bucks. I caddied for Daddy starting when I was twelve, so I know what to do, and I really love golf."

That's quite a story. I love golf too."

They pulled into Jackie's and got a booth along the windows. It was almost four o'clock, so the place was nearly empty. Jackie herself came over with menus.

"Hi, Bill. Who's your friend?"

"Jackie, meet Alice Morgan, my new caddy. Alice, say hello to Jackie English."

"Nice to meet you, Miss English."

"You too. So, how is it working for this guy?" Jackie said as she directed a thumb in Bill's direction.

"He's pretty good, and he pays well," Alice said with no expression.

Jackie cracked up and asked what they wanted. Bill

suggested that Alice should get the burger platter special. He ordered the same, because it was the specialty of the house and it was *very* special. Jackie marinated the hamburger meat in her own special sauce and the burgers were delicious.

"Alice, what's your favorite subject in school?" asked Bill.

"Well, it has to be English, of course, because Momma teaches it. I'm in her class and she is really hard on me so the other kids don't think she's playin' favorites. Like you, she's very much into fairness and doing the right thing. When she's teaching history, she points out how the cheaters and the really bad people made really corrupt decisions that got a lot of people killed. So, yeah. She teaches integrity in her classes.

"We live in the Shaw High School area, but it was easier for me to ride with Momma to her school. I'm learning a lot from the other teachers there because they know I'm Momma's daughter. They push me extra hard with higher-level work.

"Too many of the kids simply don't want to learn anything. They just want to be 'players' like their daddies, uncles or big brothers. The girls want to be the chicks that these guys chase."

"So, I'm guessing you don't have much social life. Are there any other girls who actually do school work besides yourself?"

"There are a few of us, but we aren't in any of the cliques that the so-called popular kids are in. We don't end up in jail or in *juvie* either."

Bill knew that "juvie" meant the juvenile offender programs in the city of Cleveland. It wasn't supposed to be a garden spot, and from all reports, it was really bad; kids came out of "juvie" much more hardened than when they went in. The system basically made these kids ready to be adult jailbirds. The term *rehabilitation* had yet to find its place in the canyons of inner-city Cleveland, especially where "those people" lived.

"Well, your mother sounds like somebody special. I hope I get a chance to meet her someday."

"How about today? She will be out of class about now and is just waiting for my phone call."

"Sure. After you finish the platter, we'll give her a call."

Throughout the rest of the lunch conversation, Alice Morgan was poised, thoughtful, witty and exhibited rare intelligence for any sixteen-year-old kid. She certainly charmed Bill, not as a kid, but as a person. Yes, she was dark of skin, but her pigtails spoke of retention of youth and her flashing eyes were indeed windows into a good soul. It made him despise the racism that his golfing buddies exhibited. This girl sitting across the table from him was anything but the stereotype that white America had built for "colored" people.

They finished their burgers and Bill talked Alice into a dish of ice cream.

"Oh, man. Bill, you're gonna make me fat. Thanks. It's been a while since I had a meal like this. Momma won't have to feed me tonight," she said, smiling broadly. "I saw a pay phone in the lobby. Better call her."

Bill handed Alice the change for the phone and got up to pay the lunch bill, leaving a ten spot for Jackie's tip. *Gotta keep making the local businesses know you appreciate their work.* Jackie was still friendly with Bill, even though they stopped dating a couple of years ago.

Bill waited with Alice on the bench outside the restaurant until her mother drove up. When a ten-year-old Chevy rolled up the driveway, Alice jumped up. "Here's Momma. Come say hello."

"So, you are Bill Bannock, the golfer. My name is Gerry Morgan. How do you do."

Gerry Morgan thrust a strong-looking right hand out of the car window, and Bill shook it, feeling the power within. She had a striking face that showed sharpish features of both nose and cheekbones. Her eyes were not dark brown, but a deep tan that nearly matched the color of her skin, which was barely a shade lighter. She wore her hair in a loose style, neatly and uniformly packed around her head while framing her face. The handshake lasted a few seconds longer than it should have, but the attractive woman smiling at Bill Bannock kept him from letting go.

"Nice to meet you, Gerry. You are raising a terrific kid. She caddied like a pro. Well, I guess she is a pro. I would like her to caddy for me again. Why don't you give me your telephone number so I can tell her where and when to meet me? Would that be okay with you?"

"Oh, that would be great. Baby, write down our number for Mr. Bannock. She spoke very highly of you on the phone and told me you stood up for her on the course."

"Yeah. Well, some guys are just too thoughtless and rude. I don't care for that stuff."

"Nice to know. Thanks also for treating Alice to some ice cream. That's a rare treat for her."

Gerry Morgan turned toward Alice, took the slip of paper from her and handed it to Bill.

"Here you are, Mr. Bannock. Thanks again for giving my daughter some good work. I try to raise my kids with the values of earning their way. Take care.

They shook hands again, and Gerry Morgan put the Chevy in gear. As she drove out of the parking lot, Alice waved to Bill through the windshield and Gerry smiled as she passed him standing on the sidewalk.

Gerry Morgan. What a captivating smile. Not gorgeous, exactly, but very attractive and pleasing to the eye. Alice is pretty. Gerry is all woman. Okay, wise guy. Now what?

Chapter 5

Taking Stock

While driving back to the 12th-floor condominium Bill owned outright, for some unknown reason he began wondering what the word *dissipation* meant. He'd heard it before, even as a kid in Sunday school. *Dissipation*. It sounded awful. He had to look it up as soon as he got home.

Maybe it means what I'm doing with my life. What do I do with all my money? I don't give much to charity—maybe a twenty in a Salvation Army kettle at Christmas. Every big-ticket item I own is paid for. I'm not a clothes horse, so my stuff is pretty much off the rack. Who are my friends? What do they do with all their money? Hell, I don't even belong to a country club. Alice mentioned that today. My address book is basically blank.

During the winter, when I'm not playing golf up here, I fly down to Florida for a couple of weeks, get sunburned and play a dozen rounds or so, at Doral or some other fancy resort. Then what? Oh, I fly back home between blizzards and watch the endless college football bowl season, the Browns and any other game the networks choose to show. Hell, I don't even have a Monday Night Football buddy. My other season ticket for the Indians often goes unused and I sell it to a scalper.

I hate bars. Too loud. Too smelly. It doesn't feel right sipping twelve-year-old Scotch around a bunch of sweaty guys screaming and yelling at the referees on the tiny TV behind the bar.

He went straight to the dictionary and looked up *dissipation.* While thumbing to the right page, he came across another word he'd heard before, *dilettante.* The definition jumped out at him: *superficial interest in things.*

"Yep. That's me... except for golf, of course," he said aloud.

He found *dissipate* and its extensions. Defining words and phrases like *wasted, scattered, unrestrained, wasteful* and *the indulgent pursuit of pleasure* smacked him right between the eyes.

It was the wake-up call that he'd needed for quite a few years. He didn't feel lonely, exactly, but did enjoy his time alone... for the most part. He'd dated a few women, but as he approached forty, the thrill of the pursuit (of pleasure) lost its luster too. He thought that maybe this was the beginning of what a mid-life crisis looked like.

So that catchy phrase, NOW WHAT? once again entered his frontal lobes.

What was it about meeting Alice and her mom? It was almost like there was a clicking noise one hears when circuit breakers turn on and off. But what was clicking? Were my circuits turning on or turning off?

He took a shower. He put on clean shorts and a polo shirt, and flip-flopped his way out onto the balcony with a cold glass of beer. The sun was beginning to approach the light chop of Lake Erie and glint off of the taller downtown buildings that were almost twenty miles away. Bill drank the beer, watched the seagulls police up more human refuse along the beach below, and began making a mental list.

While on the balcony, the list was without form or real organization, just a collection of trips through his personal asset closet.

This is bullshit! I gotta write this down. That's what I did when I was an engineer. It's what I did when I took all those science and math classes. I re-copied my class notes and studied them. It's time to take inventory and figure out what the hell I will do with the rest of my life. I can't possibly be this shallow. My mom wouldn't allow it.

It didn't take long to write down what he had for experience, education and any talents other than golf. The only thing he was ever really good at, he concluded, was teaching kids at Ohio University how to hit the golf ball and understand the game and its rules. It was gratifying for him to see some guy or girl without the least glimmer of coordination finally put it together and hit that first sweet-spot shot.

"How did that feel?" he'd ask.

"Almost as good a sex," one guy said.

Bill had to agree. "The first one is the hook that makes you want to hit them all on the sweet spot," he'd say.

He made a list of places he could work to teach golf. He didn't want to go through PGA school and watch all those 20-something studs hit it over the moon. The list was, therefore, pretty short. In fact, the only realistic item, it seemed, was school teaching. Chester White was his golf coach in high school, but he also taught the heck out of biology. Bill tried picturing himself as a physics teacher and golf coach at a high school. It was an image that beat the hell out of anything else he was doing or had going for him. He summarized himself as a middle-aged, has-been golfer with a firm two handicap and that wasn't much to get excited about. There were few redeeming qualities here. Dissipation. Yep. *I'm pissing away whatever talent, skills and reason for being at a very rapid rate.*

The next afternoon after lunch, Bill committed the rest of the day to finding out what it took to become a high school teacher and golf coach. He called somebody at Cleveland Public Schools and got a lengthy bureaucratic summation from a gentle-sounding lady named Ashley Jones.

"Oh, well yes, we do need physics and chemistry teachers in many of our schools. There's always a lot of turnover in science, so openings will be posted 1st June every year. This school year ends next week, so everybody will be gone on vacation for at least a month. Do you know about getting your teaching certificate? No? Okay. Find a college or university that offers teacher education courses that will certify you to teach in Ohio. It'll take about a year to get certified, then you have to find a job. My suggestion is to get all your transcripts and letters of reference together and begin finding the program that suits your needs and interests. Feel free to call back in two weeks. I'll be back from Wyoming then. Good luck, Mr. Bannock."

"Thank you, Ashley. See you soon."

Bill had no idea how to begin this process. He kept asking himself – through nearly a half bottle of Glenfiddich – if this was what he wanted to do. Dusk became night. The sun had set on Lake Erie in a blast of colors derived from long light waves passing through airborne industrial waste. The water's surface looked blood red as the sun hid behind the convenient horizon. Wispy clouds continued the light wave symphony of reds, golds and, eventually, black.

The *Glenfiddich* coupled with meeting Alice and Gerry helped him find the mental gearshift he needed to make maybe the most important decision so far... in his dissipated life.

Chapter 6

Ask Somebody Who Knows

Bill Bannock awoke the next morning—a Friday—to the sound of his phone ringing. It rang and rang until he answered it with a mouth filled with cotton balls: "Lo."

"Oh, did I wake you? It's Lonny. I just got a new Cadillac to run around in. I even got a one o'clock tee time. Wanna come play?"

"What? Oh. Wait." He got a glass and slammed down a couple of mouthfuls of orange juice. "So, where did you get a tee time?" he asked.

"One of my clients is a member down at Pepper Pike CC, and he invited me to play along with a guest. So, naturally, I thought of you. Wadda ya say? I know. Short notice."

"Okay. Sure. What time will you come pick me up?"

"I'll be there in an hour. Wear long pants and a clean shirt. It's a pretty fancy club. Bring cash."

"Yeah. Of course. See you in an hour."

Pepper Pike was indeed a fancy club, with a very well-groomed golf course. Putts didn't roll that smoothly at Willow Creek, that's for sure. Lonny's pal was an executive at an insurance company near Canton who smoked expensive cigars and kept trying to sell Bill a policy. Lonny just kept hiding his smiles and giggles.

It's always a surprise when a golfer can play well on a new course. The "sponsor" started giving Bill directions on each hole and which side of the fairway was best. But after he saw Bill stripe some drives, he just pointed him in the right direction. Lonny carded a 91—good for improving his handicap—while Bill missed a 20-footer for birdie on eighteen for a one over par seventy-three.

The sponsor was duly impressed and said Bill should be doing this for a living. Somehow, that rang a bell with him, and it wouldn't stop ringing.

When he got home that evening, Bill dug around until he found Alice's phone number. He called. She answered.

"Hi, Alice, it's me, Bill Bannock. How ya doin'?"

"I'm fine. I'm also in the middle of making dinner for my mom, brother and me. Here. Talk to Mom."

"Hello, Mr. Bannock. To what do we owe this pleasure?" Her melodic voice sent shivers down Bill's back and his knees trembled.

"Well, I've been doing some thinking about what to do with the rest of my life. I know, you're gonna ask me to take it a little slower, right?"

Gerry laughed. "Not at all. Why are you calling Alice?"

"Oh. Well, I actually wanted to talk to you. You're a school teacher, right?"

"That's right. Are you thinking about going into teaching?"

"Well, that's why I wanted to talk to somebody who knows about teaching. I don't know any school teachers except you. Well, I don't exactly know you, but I hope you will give me some advice; you know, an insider's look."

"I can do that. Would you like to arrange for us to meet? Be sure to bring a notepad and pencil or pen. I am, after all, a school teacher," she said, followed by a throaty laugh.

"Exactly what I'm looking for. How about I take you to dinner tomorrow night and you can impart your wisdom then?"

"Sure. I live on Sixth Avenue in East Cleveland. It's close to Shaw High School, but I teach at Glennville a few miles in the other direction. There's a cafeteria-style restaurant up on Hayden Avenue. We can eat there and you'll have a table and good light to take notes. Does that sound okay with you?"

"It does. I'd ask Alice and your son to join us, but they might be bored out of their minds."

"That is correct. You already seem to have an idea about young people, so maybe you're headed in the right direction. Stop by around six, and we'll beat the Saturday night crowd. In this neighborhood, things don't start shakin' until after nine."

She gave him the address and they said their goodbyes. Bill started to get that youthful anticipation reaction with butterflies, sweaty palms and the whole excitement thing. He grabbed a beer, fired up the grill and made a couple hamburgers that had been marinating in Jackie's secret sauce. She gave him the recipe one night after a strenuous bout of lovemaking, but made him promise to never reveal it to anyone. He found himself grinning. *It wasn't because I shot 67 that I'm so excited, is it?*

Chapter 7

Dinner With Gerry

Bill arrived at Gerry's Sixth Avenue home about ten minutes early. Alice opened the door and gave him a smiling greeting.

"Mom's still upstairs. Have a seat. How've you been?"

"I'm fine, but you made me start doing some serious thinking. Don't worry, it's nothing specifically that you said or did, it was just listening to you talk that made me re-evaluate what the hell I'm doing with my life. Pretty heavy, huh?"

"I'm sure you're gonna tell Momma, so I'll get the scoop from her later," she said and followed it with a smiling chuckle at his discomfort.

"Just between us," she said in a whisper, "I haven't seen Mom this excited about a date in years. I can also see that you're acting like a kid on his first date too. Yeah, I can tell. I'm thinking it's chemistry right now. 'So, when are you gonna need a caddy again?"

"How about next Tuesday? You make a tee time for us up at Highland Park. Since I'll be just a single, they'll pair us up. Mid-morning will be good. I'll come get you and we'll go up early to warm up and putt. Man, I haven't played up there since high school. Should be fun."

"Okay, I'll call the starter Monday. He knows me, so he'll

work us in with some good folks. Here's Momma."

'Momma' came down the stairs dressed in a cream-colored blouse and brown slacks that looked very Lauren Bacall; very 1940s. Then, she had the perfectly proportioned body shape, skin tones and projected personality that would make every style period worth a re-visit through her.

Bill's mouth must have been hanging open, because Alice elbowed him in the ribs. "Say something, Bill," she whispered.

"Love the outfit. You look like you just stepped out of a Bogart movie. I didn't realize you were so tall. Hungry? I brought my notepad."

Gerry just looked at him and smiled for a while until his mouth ran out of gas. "Thank you, Bill. Yes, I'm just a little under six feet. Does that intimidate you? I played some volleyball and basketball at Ohio State."

That brought a cackle from Alice who just waved at them, said, "Have a good time," and went into the kitchen.

"No, I like tall women. I enjoy looking straight into your eyes. They ARE beautiful eyes. Let's go."

"Gerry is short for Geraldine, in case you were wondering."

"I was gonna ask later, but thanks for blowing up my opening lines. Now I'll have to be off script the rest of the evening."

"That'd be a good thing, Bill. I hate scripted meetings. When my principal calls them, I try to invent lesson plans in my head while he drones on."

The restaurant was indeed like a cafeteria. Gerry and Bill scooted their trays along the stainless-steel rails and selected their entrees and side dishes. Bill barely noticed what he was picking out from behind the sneeze screen. He wanted to keep hearing her talk as her voice simply mesmerized him. He wondered if it did the same for her students at Glennville.

They found a table for four, but since Bill was going to be the note-taker they needed the extra room.

"So, what made you want to become a teacher?" he asked with the hopes of breaking the ice.

"Well, it goes back to my heritage. My parents emigrated from Ethiopia, so that's why I look like I do. Lots of Arabic influence in our genes. As you know, Ethiopia is fairly close to India and the Arabian Peninsula. Their merchant fleets visited Africa often, and left more than goods behind, as you can see. My husband Lester was pure Alabama Negro, as he described himself. He was quite handsome and strong. The children are a blend of both our genealogies."

Bill suddenly felt that he'd been dropped into a classroom. She just had that air of competence. He realized that he hadn't visited that end of his mental storage locker for a very long time. The boys at the golf course just didn't get much past where their next beer was coming from.

"Anyway, my parents were professionals in Ethiopia and learned to speak excellent English, German and Italian. Dad was a doctor, and mom was the school teacher at their small school. Even back in the twenties, there was unrest and thwarted opportunities for the quality of life they wanted for their children not yet born. They took advantage of a faculty position at Western Reserve that my dad discovered here in Cleveland. They'd let him teach anatomy, but he couldn't practice medicine. Even when mom got a teaching job, the pay was too low to allow dad to study for the Ohio board exams, and then I came along. I was born in 1936, almost two years after they arrived in Cleveland. Their escape from the Italian invasion of Ethiopia before World War II got going was a close call, and their stories were chilling. In case you were wondering, our Ethiopian family name was Ayenew."

"Are they still alive?"

"No. About ten years ago, a drunk driver jumped a curb and wiped them out instantly. They were walking back to their apartment on 105th Street from a Severance Hall concert when they were hit and killed."

"Oh, I'm so sorry to hear that. My parents were killed on an icy road about ten years ago too. Tragic coincidence."

"Perhaps. I don't much believe in coincidences. Anyway, I had graduated from Ohio State by then, had my two babies and started working on my teaching certificate. I managed to finish that and taught some before Lester was shot. His company was kind enough to honor his employee insurance, so I was able to feed my children and myself. Someone I knew at Fenn College— it became Cleveland State in '64—said she owned a duplex on Sixth Avenue, so we moved in there from the apartment Lester and I were renting. It was larger and less expensive too. My kids were sort of latchkey kids, but were old enough by then to do fine while I was at school. They could walk to Mayfair Elementary, just a couple blocks away, and then up to Kirk Junior High when they were older.

"Glennville hired me right away at the first job fair interview I had. I only had to change buses once to get there from home. I didn't buy that car until after Lester died. The kids and I walk up to Goodman's market on Fourth and Hayden a couple of times a week for groceries. We do pretty well.

"Sorry. Got off the subject. Teaching seemed right for me. When I was a T.A., I found that I was kind of a natural. I opened my mouth and out it came. History fascinated me and I wanted to impart it in the context of our times, troubles and achievements. When I got pregnant, I had to put all that on hold.

"That kind of puts the cart before the horse, but now you know how I got here sitting across the table from a seemingly nice man who wants to be a teacher. So, take good notes, Mr. Bannock. They'll be a quiz tomorrow."

They both laughed.

"Gerry, you have as melodic a voice as I've ever heard. It's not like you're singing, exactly, it just has a tone and expressiveness that holds one's attention. I would have loved to have had a class from you. Speaking of which... I'm *going* to have a class with you tonight."

Her eyes shone brightly as she laughed at his lame jokes. She always looked directly at him when she spoke. It was like she knew where every pea on her plate was when they were talking, because she never looked down. Bill noted that these were some serious communications skills. He also came to realize that this was his first lesson in learning to be a school teacher. The next part of the lesson, though, wasn't quite so ethereal or awe-inspiring.

After they finished dinner, they bussed their trays, passed on dessert and returned to the table for the lesson on how to become a teacher in Ohio.

"Alice told me that you graduated from Ohio University with a degree in the sciences. Is that right?"

"Yes. Class of '55."

"Okay. Good. I assume you have a copy of your transcripts, so what you need to do next is make a resume. List all your work experience including your golf instruction. In fact, that will be very attractive to any school that has a golf team. Science teachers are always at a premium because with those science degrees, most of them can make a lot more money in industry than in teaching school. Next, get three letters of reference for your portfolio. If we're still friends after tonight, I'll write one for you to show you what they look like and what your friends and ex-supervisors should say to support you in the best light possible."

She said that last sentence with a twinkle in her captivating brown eyes and an accompanying dimpled smile. It was also evident why Alice seemed mature beyond her years and had that forthright personality that was so attention-getting. After just an hour or so, Bill felt caught in a much larger net cast by a woman who didn't seem to be casting anything except the energy that comforted him, while at the same time compelled him to pay attention to what she was saying.

"Next, you have to acquire an application from a local college that has a teacher education curriculum. I suggest Cleveland State down around twenty-first and Euclid Avenue. That's where I did my work, and I could share my notes and things with you ... if you wanted them."

Oh, he wanted them, alright.

"Right. Well, that should get you started with the bureaucracy. Now, the rest of it is more specific. What should you look for in a school where you'd want to teach, a principal and student body? That's up to you. You have worked in industry for a time, so you know what businesses expect from young people entering the workforce. That's a huge advantage over most new teachers looking for a job. You can straddle both worlds, and you should present that at your interviews.

"Okay. I'm getting ahead of myself. But when you have an interview with the principal or the assistant principal, ask for a tour of the school and look carefully at the cleanliness and infrastructure. Those things will tell you about the 'management' quality. If the school is dirty and light fixtures remain broken, for example, that tells you that the management is not up to snuff. His or her faculty will reflect that kind of carelessness and sloth too.

"Maybe the most important teacher education class you'll take is *Classroom Management.* Every teacher has their own style of controlling the class, of course, but the common denominator is good, solid lesson plans. You *must* keep the kids on task and engage them all the time. The Socratic method of student involvement works great, especially in schools where the kids lack grade-level verbal, reading and writing skills. They must also know that you care so much for their education that the consequences of denying others that learning opportunity will be met with prompt and appropriate action. They will test you, of course, so you have to be consistent with your rules from day one.

"One of my favorite introductory lecture points was: 'What really makes me angry with your behavior is when you make me get you in trouble with the principal's office.' The point is, of course, that the kids need to know you care about them. For many inner city kids, the teacher is their only source of love or caring. It's a shame, but that's part of the burden we teachers have to bear in this society."

Bill had filled four pages with notes as she spoke. She saw his writing pace and adjusted her delivery to match it. She recognized that Bill was taking good notes, and clarified many points along the way.

"Well, that was some dinner date!" he said. "How about if we walk down the street for an adult beverage? It's not nine o'clock yet, so it shouldn't be crowded, right?"

"Sure. Two blocks down Hayden is Eddie's Jazz Club. Do you like jazz? The combo probably won't start until maybe ten, so..."

"I do, but I'd rather just talk with you tonight."

"Yes, I'm enjoying your company too."

As they left the cafeteria and turned west on Hayden, their hands brushed and it seemed the natural thing for them to take hold. Bill squeezed her hand. She squeezed back, turned toward him, smiled and said, "Thanks for dinner. I hope I didn't quash your interest in becoming a teacher."

Bill's heart was doing its long-forgotten two step as he felt her warmth in his hand. "No. In fact, I can't wait to get started. I'll be on the phone with Cleveland State on Monday. Will you be around next week to look at my resume and such?"

"Yes. School finishes for me on Wednesday. I have to have all my grades in and do the other things at the end of the school year, so my head will be down until Thursday. Call me then and tell me how it's going."

"Okay. I'm playing golf on Tuesday and hired Alice. I'll give her a preliminary report."

"Good thinking. She remembers *everything*. The girl must have a photographic memory. She even told me that you play Titleist three golf balls. Amazing kid. Do you think you can teach her how to play golf this summer? I'll pay for lessons."

"I'd love to, and no, you will not pay for lessons. I don't need the money, and I feel a kind of special attachment to Alice. She's as captivating as you are."

POW! It's out. She now knows. What have I done?

As they approached Eddie's, she turned slowly toward him, looked into his eyes with that penetrating yet mesmerizing gaze and said, "Am I? Well, you are quite interesting yourself. You're very different from any man I've known or even gone out with. I like your enthusiasm. Besides, Alice is very suspicious of white men, but she likes you."

She turned back toward the door. Bill opened it and entered into the next phase of his life that guys like him only dream about and rarely stumble into.

There was the familiar smell of cigarette and cigar smoke blended with the stale beer and liquor aroma that acted like a veil in the air that said, 'Jazz Joint'. They found a booth as far away from the pool table as possible. There was, however, a jukebox and a small dance floor.

"So, what kind of music do you like that might be on the

jukebox?" he asked.

"Let's have a cocktail and talk some more before it gets too crowded. You've spent six hours with my daughter and only two with me, so I have some catching up to do. Tell me more about you and your life. You don't seem like someone who is independently wealthy? How is it that you can play golf all the time and not have to work?" she asked with a leering smile.

"I got lucky, and a little bit smart. When my parents died, I sold their little house and just put the cash in the bank."

He then recounted the story about his timely investments and their outcome.

"Before those investment windfalls, I worked for the big company in Euclid that builds super powerful torpedoes for the Navy. I was a manufacturing engineer whose job it was to make those things more efficiently. Not very glamorous, that's for sure, but it paid well. I was able to afford a mortgage on the condo I own on the Lake Shore up in Willowick. It's on the twelfth floor and looks out over the lake. On a clear day, you can see all the way to Ashtabula to the northeast and Bay Village to the southwest. It suits me fine right now."

"Did you ever have any meaningful relationships with women?"

Bill looked at her with some surprise, thinking that this was a pretty bold question. He then realized that they were both on the far side of thirty-five and bold questions tended to cut through the bullshit.

"I have. I got pretty close to the aisle with a woman named Linda once, but when I came home from a business trip, I discovered that she'd used my car to take an ex-boyfriend with her to the drive-in movies. His cigarette butts were still in the ashtray and I don't smoke. That left me with a very raw feeling, so I never let things get too advanced after that. Alice met Jackie English at the hamburger place she owns and where we first met. Jackie was the last real 'girlfriend' I had. We're still friends, but she was looking for true romance and all the trimmings.

"I don't really go out much anymore. I know I should, because the area still has a lot of cool stuff going on. I've always liked the music scene, especially when Motown was really rockin'. Have you ever been to Leo's Casino down around twentieth and Euclid? All the big acts stop in for their obligatory cabaret sets in between sold-out arenas. I got to know the night manager there from playing golf with him in a pro-am, and he gets me good tickets when I ask.

"Sorry. I'm babbling. Don't mean to bend your ear."

"Oh, that's precisely what I wanted you to do. I'm enjoying your story. You seem to be able to bring your thoughts together so the storyline stays solid. If you're going to teach science in high school, you're going to need to exploit that talent with your daily lessons."

Bill had forgotten what they'd ordered, but the waitress dropped two glasses of something in front of them that sat there until Bill drew a breath after his story. They sipped. They looked at each other over the rims of their glasses. They smiled. Bill reached for her hand and found it finding its way toward his. It was just a brief touch and squeeze, but Bill felt a small electrical shock travel up his arm. Gerry's face was simply captivating.

"How come some good guy hasn't snapped you up? Your kids seem more than a little able to take care of themselves. You're very good-looking, smart, learned, and seem to have a solid set of ethics and values. Aren't there any single male teachers who would want to embrace someone like you?"

"Well, I've been at Glennville and Cleveland Public Schools for a while now, but so far nobody has piqued my interest.

I've been asked out a few times – and I've gone. But not much came of those few dates. So, here I still am."

"Here's the qualifying question: Do you like baseball?"

"I think so. Lester took me to a couple of Indians games when we could afford to take the kids too. Lester wasn't much of a teacher, so I didn't learn very much about what goes on. The uniforms were weird, but the crowd seemed enthused at certain times. I just didn't know what was happening. Why do you ask? Do you have something in mind?"

"As a matter of fact, I own two season tickets right behind the Indians dugout. The extra seat often goes empty, but I keep it just in case I want to invite somebody. That said, the Indians are back in town next week. You'll be out of school, so would you like to go? I'll try to get two seats for the kids nearby. Shouldn't be a problem. I know people." Bill then grinned like a raccoon eating pudding out of a hairbrush.

Gerry grinned back, but with a much less severe stretching of facial muscles. "Sure. Pick the game, find the tickets and call me. Oh, I don't have your number. Write it down."

He still had his notepad and wrote down his name, telephone number and address. He didn't know why he put down the address. His hand just seemed to have a mind of its own at the moment. Clearly, he was being controlled by forces previously unknown to him. Taking this woman to a ball game seemed, at this moment, the most natural thing in the world. Then, somebody dropped some coins in the jukebox.

The first song was Stevie Wonder's monster hit *You Are the Sunshine of My Life*. The volume was loud, and they just sort of hummed along. Bill knew most of the words; not bad for a white guy making eyes at a beautiful brown woman in a bar located in a totally black neighborhood. The thing was, nobody seemed to notice or care. He didn't think that would be the case if they were sitting at *The Castaway* in Willoughby near Willow Creek.

The song ended and the dulcet voice of Roberta Flack started singing *Killing me Softly...*

Gerry said, "Do you dance?"

"I do. It's been a while, but I'd love to dance with you."

When Gerry oozed into his arms it felt as if she'd always been there. They danced close together, but not so close that they were able to count each other's buttons.

"Did you know that Roberta Flack was an English teacher before she made a fortune singing?" Gerry said.

"No, but it seems that there is no limit to the talent embodied in English teachers," he said, looking right into those magical eyes. By mutual movement, their lips brushed in a most gentle kiss. She pulled back, lightly laid her head on Bill's shoulder and sang the song to him in his ear. Her smell was fresh and clean without any cheap fake odors.

When was the last time I had a dance like this? he thought. *Answer: Not for a very, very long time. Maybe it was Suzie at one of the college dances in Athens.*

But this was not Suzie.

They continued to glide softly until the song ended. Without letting go of their hands, Gerry walked them back to their booth.

"That was a nice way to end the evening, Bill. I think it's time to take me home. Alice will think that we've eloped or something."

"Sure."

They walked back to the car without saying much, but their grip on each other's hands was firmer than before.

Bill walked Gerry up to the front door. She handed him the key and he opened the door for her. As he handed back the keychain, she wrapped one long arm around his neck and kissed him solidly and tenderly. When the kiss ended, she smiled and said, "Now go copy your notes and get to work. If you're gonna be a teacher, you have to meet deadlines." A big grin followed, and she was in the door.

Bill wasn't sure he remembered touching the steps going down and back to his car. All he DID remember was the sweet afterglow of Gerry's kiss. When he finally found the ignition for the key, he had a burst of *NOW WHAT?* Again. He rolled down the windows as he drove east on Hayden toward Lake Shore Boulevard. The cool air revived him somewhat from his reverie, and he knew he had to start asking those annoying questions about what he'd been experiencing and thinking about for the last few days.

Am I considering this move toward teaching in school because I'm bored, or is it because of Alice and, now, Gerry? This has got to be MY call, and not something to do with currying favor with two very interesting females. This 'thing' may not go anywhere with Gerry, and I would still have to be committed to being a teacher. I admit the personal evaluation I just did was stimulated by Alice's comments during and after our golf day, so I can't argue with that. I've never been one to waste things, so why would I waste my whole remaining life by being a—what is that word—dilettante?

Bill pulled into his parking garage and ascended to the 12th floor. He was almost certain he rode the elevator. It was only 9:30 P.M., so he poured some good scotch into a clean glass and sat on the balcony watching the city lights blink and a half moon rise in the east. He chuckled and thought of that lesson he learned from that young geography teacher at OU: "The moon actually only appears to rise in the east. It's actually traveling from west to east, but the rotation of the Earth is so fast in the opposite direction, compared to the transiting of the moon, that it seems to rise in the east and set in the west."

Stuff like this had always stuck in his head like taffy on a shirt. *Maybe these little nuggets are what I need to write down for when it's my time to teach them.*

He drank a little more scotch. The moon "traveled" westward. His free thoughts swirled around Gerry Morgan like the scotch in his glass.

She is really special, no matter what happens between us. It's about time I started meeting more quality minds and souls anyway. Hell, we're all day-to-day, and you never know when tomorrow will be your last day. At least I broke par a few times in my life.

Chapter 8
The Next Round

Bill awoke from a dreamless sleep with the realization that he had tasks to perform. There was a half-read pulp novel lying face down on the chest of drawers and a pile of laundry begging for soap and water. But first...

After he made a pot of coffee, he piled the dirty clothes into the laundry bag and went down to the in-building laundry room; a nice convenience included in the high building utility fees. It was Monday, after all. He was the second tenant in, so he loaded everything into the other empty washer, slammed in the two quarters and started the machine. He heard the hiss of the water as he walked out and back to the elevator. It took about forty minutes to do the load and another forty to dry them. That left him some time to dig out the paperwork for his upcoming application processing at Cleveland State. With the laundry finished, Bill took his paperwork with him so he could make copies at one of the new super-duper markets that sold everything under one roof. They proudly displayed one of the biggest models of the copying machines from the company that was making him rich. After laundry, he drove down to the college to pick up the application, prospectus, and whatever else he'd need to get this ball rolling.

He parked his Oldsmobile on Euclid Avenue, just a block from the Cleveland State University building. Inside, the legend told him where admissions was and he went there to collect the necessary application paperwork, a school catalog, and anything else that might be handy. The lady behind the counter—Lydia Smith, according to her name tag—suggested he visit the head of the teacher education department before he jumped all the way into this venture. Lydia was on the short side, with dark brown skin and a stylized hairdo that complimented her face. She smiled easily and wrote down the department chair's name, phone and office numbers. Bill thanked her, exchanged smiles and headed to the bank of elevators.

He arrived on the 5th floor and walked around like a lost puppy until he found 540. EDUCATION was printed in large gold letters on the door. He went in and was met by someone named Mabel Jordan. She looked to be Bill's age and had the most incredible head of red hair he'd ever seen.

"May I help you?"

"Yes. My name is Bill Bannock and I'd like to speak with, uh, Dr. Emmitt Donohue. Is he available?"

"What does this concern, Mr. Bannock?"

"I'm looking to apply for the teacher certification program. Miss Smith downstairs suggested I have a chat with Dr. Donohue before deciding to do so."

"I see. Let me ask him if he has a few minutes."

Five minutes later, Mabel and Emmitt Donohue emerged from an office in the back of the room.

"I'm Emmitt Donohue. How may I help you, Mr. Bannock?"

"Well, with the help of a new friend who is a teacher, I decided to investigate becoming a science teacher myself."

"I see. Come down to my office. I have a meeting in a half hour, so I have time to speak with you.

They made their way into his office, where Emmitt Donohue continued to speak.

"What made you decide to pursue this course, Mr. Bannock? You're not exactly fresh out of college."

"No, sir, I am not. I worked in industry after graduating from Ohio University. I'm sitting on a degree with double majors in physics and chemistry. I made some very good investments almost ten years ago and sort of retired early. I did a self-evaluation last week and decided that I have at least another quarter century of productive life left, so I thought about teaching. I used to coach a golf class at OU, enjoyed it and found out I was pretty good at it.

"My former company builds these super deadly torpedoes for the Navy, and I no longer wanted to be just another cog in the great war machine. Now, I'd rather do something positive for my country and maybe the world. Is it a noble calling I'm looking for? Maybe. So, before I get started on this path, I suppose I should ask if a forty-year-old should be pursuing teaching as a career?"

"Well, Mr. Bannock, I have to say that we don't see too many folks like yourself walk through that door. The perspective that I think you bring is quite different from most of the young men and women who want to become school teachers. Most of them have never really been out of the classroom. They go from kindergarten right through twelfth grade, into college, graduate, go back to college for their teaching certificate, then right back into the classroom as a teacher. That's what I mean by a different perspective. Do I have that right about you?"

"Well, after eight years of flying a desk in a major manufacturing firm, I certainly know what the business world expects from the kids coming out of school—both high school and college. We loved to have high school kids work in our shops after they'd had the great vocational classes at most of the schools around here. The college graduates that upper management wanted were people they thought would be able to meet the future expectations and challenges of both existing and shifting markets, products and financial machinations. I know that was a mouthful – the company line, you might say – but my job required me to work with the factory employees more, actually, than with the white-collar workforce."

"It sounds like we're speaking along parallel paths, Mr. Bannock, but how could you tailor your experience and lessons to a sixteen-year-old who wants to either play pro sports or have babies?"

"Good question. I don't know. What I DO know is that what kids learn in school will have a cumulative effect on who they will be as citizens and that would be my job: show them how the physical world works. If a kid doesn't know how or why their dad's car works or doesn't, that kid will be more likely to make poor decisions when it comes to buying a car or having one repaired. My dad had me crawling around under our car when I was just a kid. I took auto shop in school and learned the smaller details. Then, in physics classes, I learned about the mechanical aspects of how an engine and mechanical systems work. Chemistry taught me about fuels, lubricants and reactions that are helpful and harmful.

"I know I'm just thinking out loud, but it seems to me that putting complex topics into practical or everyday terms is the secret to effective teaching. It worked for me and I remember how and why it worked. Is that what you mean by perspective?"

After a lengthy pause, Emmitt Donohue looked over the top of his glasses. "I see you have the application and some of the other bits of information from downstairs." He reached down and retrieved a sheaf of papers from his desk drawer.

"Here is the summary of classes you'll need to take to prepare for your certification exams. In case you hadn't come across it yet, there is one semester of student teaching required after you finish your in-class curriculum requirements."

"How does that work?"

"Right. Well, you find a mentor-teacher who is willing to let you teach his or her classes—preferably in your major field— for a semester. You will do all the things a regular teacher does, including making your own lessons and exams. Your mentor will supervise everything you do and write a final evaluation. If you do well in all phases—including passing your 'certs'—the state of Ohio will impart upon you the legal right to teach your specialty in our public schools.

"Mr. Bannock, please send your application and transcripts directly to me as soon as you can. I want to review them with my faculty advisors and see about getting you started right away. We have one class this summer session – *Classroom Management* – and if you're serious about being a teacher, this class will be the one that usually makes or breaks that decision. When schools resume classes in the fall, you will spend time observing how different teachers manage their classrooms as well as attending the classes taught by our faculty.

"Thanks for coming in to see me, Mr. Bannock. I'll look forward to reviewing your application materials."

Bill drove home as quickly as he could, filled out the application, inserted it into a large envelope along with copies of his other credentials, and addressed it to Dr. Donohue. He guessed at the number of stamps he needed. There was a mail slot on the first floor, so he trotted down the stairs for the sake of burning off excess energy.

Tomorrow, he had a golf game with Alice Morgan on his bag. She'd called before he left to run his errands and said their tee time was 9:40 A.M. Bill told her he'd pick her up at eight. It sounded corny, even to his own jaundiced sense of irony, but tomorrow would begin his next round ... in life.

Chapter 9

Learning About Other People

Before going to college, Bill Bannock lived most of his life in the typical white person's bubble. Nobody in his extended and immediate family had any activities or relationships at any level with anyone darker than Mediterranean. You know, Italian, Greek, maybe the odd Spaniard... It just wasn't on the agenda, as far as he could tell. When he was a boy, the adults used to talk about 'the coloreds' all the time. The gist was mostly not favorable. Words like "lazy", "shiftless", "immoral" and "deadbeat" were thrown around as if those doing the throwing really knew what they were talking about. What else was a kid supposed to learn about brown and black people? All of his family lore about non-white people was voiced in disparaging tones. The teachers in his all-white schools never talked about colored people at all. White bubble.

Then he went to college and started meeting brown and black people, first in classes, then in sports. Holy crap! Colored people spoke real English, wrote and spoke coherent thoughts, wore laundered clothes, etc., etc. After the first couple of months at college, the shock of this realization wore off to the point where Bill actually enjoyed partnering with a brown or black person on a class project or in a lab. The new personality perspectives, senses of humor and lexicon he found delightfully enlightening. Cloying questions started nibbling away at the perceptions of his place in the world as it was juxtaposed against the tapestry of all the different kinds of humans that roamed the globe.

Shock and amazement! White people were the distinct minority among all the races. There were more Chinese living in China than there were white people in all the Caucasian countries combined! Same with Africa. More black people lived in that continent than there were white people in the entire world. Then, there was the big one: Louis and Mary Leakey discovered a fossil in Tanzania, in 1957 that had both human and ape-like characteristics. That discovery kicked off another review of the fossilized human-like creatures from one to two million years ago originally discovered by Raymond Dart in South Africa in the 1920s.

MY GOD! Humans evolved in Africa! Eve was an African! All modern humans are descended from an African population of ancient, human-like forms. When he introduced that bit of science at a family gathering one day in the late 1950s, he was met with looks of incredulity and the subject was quickly changed.

"But LIFE magazine had a feature article on those discoveries. It must be true."

Silence.

"So, do you think the Indians will win the pennant this year?" was the deflecting response.

It occurred to him at the time that something was terribly wrong with the equation of humanity as seen from inside the white bubble.

He had just landed a job in a defense plant that was important enough to exempt him from the draft. The draft board thought that he was sufficiently serving his country by building things that blew the shit out of hundreds of people at a time, instead of just one or two. We were in the 'cold war' after all, and beating those Russkies at everything was everyone's sworn duty to God and country.

And so, Bill Bannock returned to the bubble... Except that he wasn't entirely "bubbled" anymore. Bill's company employed brown and black people. He interacted with several non-white factory floor workers in order to learn different manufacturing methods and implement new ones that were safer and more efficient.

Some of those jobs included observing the black female workers at what was affectionately known as the "burr bench". These women used very high RPM, air-driven hand drills with stainless steel and carbide attachments that cut away the burrs left by the machine tools that cut shapes and grooves. You could hear the noise from the burr bench area from a long way off, because when you spin a small cutting tool at 10,000 RPM and place it against sophisticated metal alloys, the highest-pitch harmonics imaginable are the result. There was no such thing as required hearing protection during that era, so after working on the burr bench for an eight-hour shift, one's ears rang and rang for hours afterward. Then, you got to do it again the next day.

He met a few black men machinists. Clearly, they were the cream of the crop since only a few percent of all the hundreds of machinists were brown or black. These guys graduated from some of the inner-city high school vocational programs and could make their lathes and millers sing to the tune of very close tolerances and precise output. The work quality these guys produced was as good as any from anyone else. Bill knew this because he'd seen the quality control charts. So, why were they paid 25% less than the white machinists of the same seniority? More questions for outside the bubble...

Nobody asked those questions while inside the bubble.

When he "retired" from manufacturing engineering, the bubble once again wrapped its loving arms around him. He wasn't doing anything that would pull the filmy curtain of the white bubble aside for him to see the rest of the world. Hell, he was playing golf, watching sports on TV and drinking good scotch whiskey and premium beer. He traveled to warm-weather resorts where the black and brown people carried his bags and bussed his tables. Golf was part of the all-white world he inhabited.

When he first played at Highland Park golf course, it was in the high school Greater Cleveland Conference championship. All the golfers were white. The guys working the practice range were not. All the office staff, starters and pros were white. The women waiting tables, the men tending bar and mowing the greens were not. Golf for Bill Bannock, in those halcyon days, was purely a white man's game. He didn't know any different. The bubble was, in many ways, a kind of one-way mirror. White people inside could look out and see whatever they wanted to see and thought nobody out there could see them.

Bill picked up Alice at eight sharp. She smiled that radiant smile and hopped into the seat next to his.

"Good morning, Bill. How are you this morning?"

Her perfect diction and greeting were so heartfelt as to make him smile. "I'm pretty good. How are you? Did you have a good weekend? What do you do if you aren't caddying?"

"Well, that day I caddied for you was the day after I finished my last year-end exam, so Mom drove me out to Willow Creek *early*! Mostly, I read and clean the house for us. And yes. I had a nice weekend. Mom decided that I should rest up for our game today. Are you all rested up too?"

"Oh, sure. Be sure to tell your mother that I filled out and mailed in the application to Cleveland State. Oh, and here is a copy of my résumé and transcripts that she asked to see. Be sure to give them to her when we're done today."

"Can I look?"

"Sure."

"Wow. You took some really cool-sounding classes. What's *differential equations*?"

"It's a kind of advanced math that my guidance counselor insisted I take as part of my science degree. I almost flunked it, but managed to squeak out a 'C'. Hardest class I ever took was *physical chemistry*. Another low 'C'. Soon, I'll get to teach that stuff to the unsuspecting youth of Ohio." He laughed ghoulishly while Alice looked at him with a lopsided grin, one that said she wasn't sure he was kidding.

"Well, here we are. Let's play golf!"

He opened the trunk lid so he could change into his golf shoes and Alice could take the bag of clubs over to the practice range.

"Bill, there are two sets of clubs here. Are these the old Wilson Staffs you told me about?"

"Yep. After we're done playing, we'll take 'em over to the range and see what your daddy taught you."

"Really?! I haven't hit a ball for two years. Are you sure this is a good idea?" she asked with those big, brown eyes as wide as ever.

"We'll see. Now, go get me a bucket of balls while I check in and pay the green fees."

The young man behind the counter checked Bill in with the tee time Alice had called in. "Okay, Mr. Bannock, those three gentlemen over there are who you will be playing with. They would be Mr. Holcomb, Mr. Davis and Mr. Davis's son, Chester. You'll be called to the first tee in about thirty minutes.

Enjoy your day."

Bill walked over to the table where his three playing partners were having coffee and finishing what looked like good pastries.

"Good morning. I'm Bill Bannock, and I have been assigned to play with your group."

They stopped eating and drinking and just stared at him for long seconds before Louis Holcomb spoke up by introducing himself.

"Are you any good?" asked Louis.

"I get by. I just love to play golf. Are you considering asking me into a game?"

"Nah. We just don't want to have to stand around waiting for somebody to take a hundred strokes. If you can keep up, we get around here in just under four hours. Think you're up for that?"

That caused everyone to chuckle.

"Well, I brought my own caddy, so I shouldn't hold you back. Look, I gotta go hit a few balls and stroke a few putts. See you on number one."

The way they looked at Bill made him feel like he was a white invader in their little group. He felt he'd just have to play his way into their hearts. That thought brought a rueful smile. *Wait until they meet Alice.* He laughed out loud.

"What's so funny?"

"Oh, nothing. Just a funny thought passing through. Let me stretch a little first. What club do I always start with?"

"Pitching wedge. I got a towel wet, so I'm ready to keep everything clean."

"I would expect nothing less. You're smart and know how to focus. I'm looking forward to our practice later. I met the three guys we're with this morning. Mr. Holcomb and two Mr. Davises."

She handed Bill the wedge and he took a few warm-up swings. "They didn't look all that excited about having a white guy in their midst. We'll just have to go play really good today."

"Yes, we will. Do you ever not play great?"

"Oh yes. More often than I'd like. Eight iron, please."

After hitting a couple dozen balls, they walked over to the putting green about twenty yards from the first tee. Bill stroked a few putts to get the feel for the green speed, though the greens out on the course were often mowed differently. It was always a good idea to at least make a few good strokes with the putter.

Bill and Alice walked up to the first tee when their group was called by the starter. When Holcomb and the Davises saw Alice, they stared, open-mouthed.

"This your caddy? I hope you're payin' her good," said Chet Davis.

"I do pay her good money, and as you'll see, she's worth it. She reads my greens for me too."

"Uh, huh. Well, you go ahead and lead us off, uh, Bill." The three men chuckled.

Alice handed Bill the four wood and a Titleist 3. The first tee at Highland Park was highly elevated. The fairway at the bottom of the hill turned left about 220 yards out and headed up an equally steep hill to the green perched at the top. Where the flat part of the fairway ended before turning left, there was a little creek at the base of the hill. Bill's tee shot landed precisely where it needed to and stopped rolling about five yards short of the little creek.

Without a comment, his playing partners hit similar shots. They were carrying their own bags and looked pretty fit. Alice strode ahead to where Bill's ball lay and got the yardage.

"Do you men play here often?"

"Yep. Every chance we get," answered Louis.

"Do you work a night shift or are you retired?"

"Me? I'm a security guard at the Sears in Shaker Heights. My man, Al drives a bus in the afternoon shift, and his son Chet goes to Cleveland State when school's in session."

"I just enrolled in the teacher education program at CSU. I might run into him there. My first class starts in two weeks. 'Chet, do you mind if I ask you where you went to high school?"

He gave Bill a baleful look and mumbled, "Glennville. Why you ask?" There was a little edge to his voice.

"Well, my caddy Alice's mother teaches there. Her name is Gerry Morgan. You know her?"

"Yeah. She taught my English class when I was a junior. Why you askin'?"

"Just curious. Mrs. Morgan helped me decide to go back to school and teach science someday. Alice will be starting her senior year in September. I don't mean to intrude, just making conversation during a friendly golf game."

Chet just shrugged and walked away from Bill toward his own ball.

Louis and the two Davises hit their shots up the hill with Chet's being the only one to land on the green. Bill hit a perfect eight iron and saw it land in the vicinity of the flag stick, or at least that part that he could see. When he got to the top of the hill, he saw that his ball was three feet from the hole.

After replacing the divot, Alice hurried up to the green where Bill was repairing his ball mark. He walked over to her and she handed him his putter.

"Do you want me to read that putt for you?" she whispered with a quick wink and small smile.

"I think I can handle this one. Thanks for the offer," he

teased back.

The rest of the round played out, and Bill's playing partners never asked him to join in their game. They weren't bad players, each with a swing honed by their own methods. Louis won the bets with a 79 while Chet came in second at 81. Alfred Davis struggled all morning and finished with an 88. Bill's 74 was close to his handicap, and only Louis gave him a nod and said, "nice playin".

"Thanks, Louis. Why were Al and Chet so unfriendly? We're just playing golf. Let me buy you a beer."

"Yeah. Sure. I'll have a Miller. Al and Chet gotta go home. We ain't around that many white guys. Most white guys make a point of not playing with us, if you know what I mean."

"Yeah. I know. I played with three guys out at Willow Creek who were actually rude and crude to Alice last week. It was like they didn't see her or care that she had feelings too. My daddy raised me to respect everyone without prejudice, but we mostly lived inside the white bubble. I don't think I ever met a black person until I went to college. So, I get it."

'So, did you pick up Alice at Willow Creek?"

"Yes. Her mother dropped her there to caddy. She said that the loops she got up here didn't pay that well, and too many of the gentlemen drank too much and tried to uh, make her feel physically in danger."

"I know. Too many guys think women are just there for playin'. Too bad she so pretty. Lotta guys can't see past that. You say you met her mother? What's she all about? She think it okay for her daughter to be caddyin' for some white dude?"

Bill laughed. "Her mother is very nice... And pretty too. Alice used to caddy for her father here at Highland Park, so she learned the game doing that. A couple of years ago, he was shot and killed down in town, so they've been just trying to make ends meet since. Alice has a younger brother too, so..."

"Man, I hate stories like that. Well, you seem like a good guy. Now go pay that girl some real foldin' money. You takin' her home?"

"I am, but first, we're gonna go hit some balls. I'm thinking of trying to get her a golf scholarship somehow. She's as smart as they come, so maybe getting some help with an academic scholarship to go with the golf will get her to a better place. Do you think that's a good idea?"

"That's good thinkin'. I hope you can make it happen. We gotta keep tryin' to get over, one life at a time."

Louis Holcomb and Bill shook hands. He then went over to the range where Alice was waiting with the Wilson Staffs.

Chapter 10

A Prodigy Emerges

Bill was seriously impressed as he watched Alice Morgan swing the golf club. Her flexibility was that of a warm rubber band. Even with a seven iron, her backswing went way past horizontal. He coached her up because she would lose the plane of the swing by going too far back. She was able to generate significant club head speed, hitting that seven iron almost 140 yards. She looked like a natural.

Alice already knew about grip, stance and alignment, so all Bill needed to coach her on was tempo. Once she found a groove for timing, she started hitting everything pure.

Holy crap! Do we have ourselves a prodigy here? Let's see if she can putt.

She could putt. Once she figured out the pace of the green, she started making putts and skimming the hole from every distance. Sure, it was a flat practice green, but her stroke was simple and, most importantly, consistent. After about a half hour of Bill drooling over her inherent, natural ability, they went back to the practice area where they could look at her short game. Bill coached some technique and, after a few shots, she started grouping her shots together around the hole.

"Well, Alice, I am very impressed with your abilities. We'll have to do this again sometime soon."

As they drove back to her house, they stopped for late lunch near her neighborhood. Just about every brown face in the restaurant glared at them unsmilingly.

"Folks around here aren't used to seeing white faces, least of all one with a brown girl sitting across the table. Just be cool and don't make any sudden movements," she joked.

They both laughed out loud. The hostile looks stopped.

When they arrived at the Sixth Avenue house, Gerry came out to greet them. "Did you guys have fun today?"

Alice answered, "We did. Bill smoked three guys, then he gave me some golf lessons and bought me a late lunch. I'll probably skip dinner."

As Alice started walking toward the side door, Bill called her back. "Hey. You forgot something." She looked at him with a blank stare. "Go get your clubs out of the trunk," he said with mock seriousness.

"What? Really? You're giving me those Staffs?"

"Yes. I couldn't think of a better place for them to be. Oh, and I forgot to pay you for the loop." He popped the trunk lid and Alice zoomed over to pull out the clubs and the basic carry bag that he'd used for years. As she came back around the car, Bill stuffed two twenties into her hand and thanked her for such a good job.

"Well, Mr. Bannock, is my little girl worthy of such gifts from a stranger?"

"Actually, she is, to the first part, and I hope to improve on the second part. The girl is a natural. If you have a minute, I'd like to talk to you about some things regarding my newest, best caddy."

"Okay. C'mon in. I just made a fresh pitcher of iced tea."

Bill proceeded to make suggestions about scholarships and Alice's golfing potential. Gerry listened intently and asked him the most important questions: "Do you think we can get her ready in time for college? Her grades are good enough for academic scholarships, but they won't pay for all that is needed. Do you know of any colleges or universities that have a women's golf team that would accept a girl of her color?"

"Great questions. I will do some research into women's golf teams. By the way, I sent in my application stuff for teacher ed."

"I think I asked you before, but why did you leave such a good job?"

He told her that he just got fed up with making devices of such destruction. "I didn't know it five years ago, when I quit working, but I think I see my future a little better now. I guess I had some intuition about doing something else in life. Meeting you and Alice sure helped that process along.

"Right. Now, I'd better get along and start researching those women's golf teams."

"Okay. Good. Why don't you come for dinner with me and the kids, Thursday evening? We can discuss those details you discover. Bring a bottle of red wine. We'll be having a roast. See you around six on Thursday?"

"Okay. Great. See you Thursday."

Chapter 11

An Enjoyable Evening

As directed, Bill arrived at six on the dot. Gerry greeted him with a big smile.

"I'll put the wine in a cool spot for now. May I get you a glass of iced tea?"

"You may," he said, while admiring her outfit. The apron was one of those backyard barbeque things that said *'Hug the Chef'*. Gerry was wearing light blue Bermuda-length shorts that revealed a portion of her nicely shaped and muscled legs. The short-sleeved top was a pale peach color that perfectly complimented her complexion and shorts. The apron wasn't able to disguise her other shapely attributes.

"Do I have permission to hug the chef?"

"Of course. I was hoping you'd notice," she answered with a defiant look.

The apron didn't offer enough padding for him not to notice how good she felt in such close quarters. She pulled back, gave him a quick kiss and said, "Gotta finish making the salad. Talk with me while I'm slicing the tomatoes."

"Did you have a chance to review my paperwork?"

"Yes. Interesting, but not great college grades. Looks like

good science classes. Your work history is *very* impressive, however. How did you learn to do all that stuff? Alice thought your classes looked pretty cool; hard, but cool. I think she wants to talk with you about astronomy."

They laughed.

"Yes, seeing stars is the first sign of a curious mind," he said lamely. "Is there anything I can do to help? Are your plates and dinnerware in the dining room? I could set the table. My mother taught me how when I was seven. I never broke a plate in all those years."

"Sure, but don't you want to know about my last day at school?

"Oh. Right. Sorry. I'm having an attack of trying-hard-to-please and being a good guest. My mom's training imbued me with an advanced case of the pitch-in syndrome. I can't help it."

"Well, you can *'pitch in'* by listening to me babble about grades and such. I had to crunch final grades for one hundred and forty-three of our beautiful children before I could actually think about coming home for the summer. We all had to prepare our rooms for the annual deep cleaning by the maintenance crew. Glennville is an old school but has held up pretty well. Chipped tiles and broken furniture are typical maintenance issues. This might sound weird, but one of my pet peeves is that our fluorescent light tubes have varying shades and colors. Some are bluish, some are pinkish and some are white. I guess I tend to like consistency in things I have to look at every day."

This last remark was followed by a look over her shoulder that said, "I'm talking to you, Buster."

Being sensitive to such clues, Bill walked up behind her while her hands were in the water cleaning the lettuce. He slipped his hands under the apron and felt the warmth coming from her abdomen.

She leaned back into his arms and said, "I see that you still remember how to respond to inviting looks." She turned around and wrapped her long, dripping arms around him and kissed him deeply with an open mouth. The water dripped from her hands down the back of his legs, but he barely noticed.

"You always smell so good and fresh," he said. "Great kiss, by the way."

"Hm. Kissing says so much about compatibility, doesn't it? I'm glad you like the fragrance of my shower soap. By the way, you kiss nicely also. It's been a while since I kissed somebody with such, uh, serious intent. I'd like to do more of that, but I have to finish cleaning the lettuce. Sorry about dripping water on you."

"What water?"

With a cackling chuckle, Gerry Morgan turned back around and kept putting lettuce fragments into the large salad bowl. "If you want, you can set the table for four. I sent Alice and Benny to the store so I could have a few minutes with you to let you know that I was glad to see you. Do you feel welcome in my home?"

"I do. The woman of the house is warm, intelligent, affectionate and quite beautiful. So, yes, it is a welcoming atmosphere into which I've walked. Sorry. Don't mean to sound so stilted. It's been a very long time since I've felt so welcome in the presence of a woman. I have to also say that you make me mind my grammar."

"Not to worry, Mr. Bannock. I'm off duty now. Just relax and be yourself. I like yourself. Somehow, I expect that we'll find ways to get our points across. Let me get back to work. We can distract each other later."

Bill set the table with a setting on all four sides. "Where are the water and wine glasses?"

"They're in the breakfront in the corner. Wine glasses on top, water glasses next shelf down."

Here I am, forty years old and playing house with a woman who makes my knees weak. I've NEVER played house before. What do I do when the kids come home? What do I do with this beautiful person when the kids go to bed? Are you thinking of some kind of commitment here? This isn't some casual pick-up game, is it? Well, she said to relax and be myself. I think I can remember how to do that.

Alice, and who Bill supposed was her brother Benny, came loudly through the rear door.

"I saw your car, Bill. Good to see you dressed in something other than golf clothes," Alice chided.

"Thanks. I do own shirts with long sleeves. Good to see you too. Is this your brother?"

"Yes. Benny, say hello to Bill Bannock, my part-time boss and instructor," she said, flashing Bill a big grin.

Benny just looked at him. Bill reached out to shake his hand. Benny took it without a word and walked past everyone into the back part of the house.

"Well, that went well," Bill said.

"Benny is suspicious of strangers ever since daddy was shot," Alice said. "I think it really affected him in not good ways. Just give him some time to get to know you. After all, you're gonna be my golf instructor, right? When do we play next? Are we gonna play a round together?"

The excitement in her voice made Bill feel more important than just being a dinner guest.

"Well, that would be a good thing. How about a couple more lessons and then we'll give it a try? How about we have you caddy for me on Tuesday, my usual golf day, and then we'll practice. I'll come get you early in the morning. We can pack your sticks too. How does that sound?"

"Perfect. I'll be waiting on the porch. Should I have a cup of coffee waiting for you too?"

"Sure. You're becoming a full-service caddy."

"Alice, go tell your brother to wash up for dinner," Gerry said. "You do the same. The roast comes out of the oven in five minutes. Bill, will you help me put the salad bowl, dressing and salt and pepper on the table?"

Bill realized that he shouldn't be surprised to be in the presence of high organization. As soon as the salad bowl hit the table, the two siblings took their chairs. Benny took some salad and passed the bowl to his mother, counter to the normal direction of clockwise. Gerry gave him a glare. His move made sure Bill got the bowl last.

"I forgot to ask, Bill... Do you say grace before meals?"

"No. That was never part of our routines and I never got that involved with church or religion anyway. My parents said they believed in God, but rarely went to church."

After everyone finished their salads, Alice bussed the dishes and brought in the roast and vegetables.

"Bill, would you please carve the roast for us?" Gerry asked

He mumbled something and picked up the carving set to slice the roast into as many pieces as it allowed. He passed the platter to Benny who silently took it and served up his portion. Gerry passed the bowl of vegetables to Alice—the proper direction—and the serious dining began. A few pleasantries passed between Alice, Gerry and Bill as they continued between mouthfuls of the delicious roast. Finally, Benny broke his silence.

"What you doin' here? What you want with us?"

"I was invited to dinner by your mother. Alice has caddied for me a couple of times and I knew she enjoyed the game. Did your father ever try to interest you in golf?

"Don't talk about my daddy. He none of your business!" Benny said in a loud voice.

Benny! How dare you insult my guest?!" Gerry said with a sharp tone Bill hadn't heard from her before.

"What you doin' bringing some white guy home? Daddy would be mad."

"Lester isn't here anymore, Benny. And it's my business whom I befriend. I would appreciate it if you displayed the manners you've been taught. You're embarrassing me with your truculence."

Benny just glared at Bill, picked up his plate and took it to the kitchen. He disappeared without saying another word.

"Don't worry, Gerry. I understand. Wounds take time to heal. He won't always be in this much pain. I'm impressed that he understood the word truculence." That broke the tension and everyone laughed a little.

"Too bad Benny is going to miss the freshly baked peach pie Momma made!" Alice said in a loud voice directed toward the back rooms. A door slammed.

After a slice of the best peach pie Bill had ever tasted, everyone bussed their own dishes. Gerry started filling the sink with warm water and dish soap. Alice said it was her turn to wash, so the adults were relegated to wiping dishes and putting them away. Gerry let a salad plate slip from her grasp, but before it hit the floor, Bill's left foot shot out and caught it in the middle, preventing it from shattering.

"Nice catch!" Gerry said.

After that, the three of them chatted amicably and the chore continued without anyone noticing the time.

Alice asked her mother if it was alright for her to watch her favorite TV show in the living room.

"Sure, it's almost eight, so go ahead."

Gerry poured the last of the wine into two glasses and

motioned Bill toward the back door. They sat in a glider that faced away from the house and into the small, fenced backyard. The glider had an awning and a rear curtain. The color pattern was faded badly, and it squeaked when pushed back and forth. The seat was barely wide enough for both of them, and Gerry's hips touched Bill's when she sat.

"I'm really sorry about Benny. He's been really angry about everything. He's gotten into a couple of fights at school when some of the less well-mannered boys teased him about his father's murder. Down here in the city, it's kind of how it goes. Lester's killing was not an isolated incident, so the dark shroud of violence seems to hang over everyone living here. East Cleveland has become an increasingly violent town. I'm trying to figure out how to get us out of here to a safer area where black and brown people aren't discriminated against or impoverished. The crime is so suffocating.

"Sorry. Didn't mean to go on. I've been trying hard to put Lester behind me too, because my kids need me to be on an even keel." She finished her wine and set the glass down on the small table in front of the glider.

She turned toward Bill and put her nearest arm across the back of the seat. "I don't know how to explain it, but when you showed up at the window of my car, it felt that things were about to change for me. Alice fairly gushed over the phone when she called to have me pick her up. I don't know how she knew, but she felt some chemistry too.

"So, Mr. Future-Chemistry-Teacher, what do you think about all that?"

Being at a rare loss for words, Bill slipped his left arm behind Gerry's back and pulled her close. They kissed tenderly and sweetly. Her lips felt like perfect cushions against his. Their tongues naturally found their way to each other. He circled her waist with his right arm then slid his hand up to the soft mounds lying patiently beneath her blouse. Gerry murmured a small noise from her throat but didn't push his hand away. He felt the hard spot in the middle of her breast and caressed it gently with his thumb.

After a minute, Gerry pushed back, her breath coming in deep rhythm, as was Bill's.

"Oh, dear, Mr. Bannock. Whatever shall we do now?"

"Good question. I feel like following my instincts with you. I gotta say, I haven't felt this kind of magnetic attraction to a woman for a very, very long time... Maybe never. You are exotic beyond anything I've ever imagined or fantasized about. I feel very comfortable in your presence. Being myself, as you instructed, has been a mystery for a long time. Being BY oneself for so long really doesn't help define who or what that 'natural' person is.

"That said, I feel your feelings as I hope you feel mine. I'm glad I met Alice first, because she reflects what her environment has been. She's a great kid, really, really smart and has had some very good parenting. Gerry, I'm really drawn to you. The issue of our racial differences is moot. I don't see you as someone of a different race. That's for society to deal with. But I'll tell you that if we keep doing what we're doing here, I'm gonna have to find a way to drug your kids."

Gerry laughed at that. "Yes. We may end up being lovers, but if we do, I want it to be without having to look over our shoulders at what we think society will say ... or my kids. Now, we better take a little walk around the block and cool off before going back inside.'

Chapter 12

The Walk Around the Block

"Let's tell the kids we're going for a walk," Gerry said. Alice was embroiled in some TV program that Bill didn't recognize. Not that it would have mattered since he only watched sports shows. She gave them a wave as they walked out the front door.

"Aren't you going to tell Benny about us?"

"Alice will tell him if he asks. He's probably just sulking or reading some comic book. He's only fifteen, so all sorts of conflicts are visiting his poor psyche these days. You're just another log on his glowing fires. I'm really sorry you had to endure his rudeness."

They walked down the front steps and started slowly walking up toward Hayden Avenue.

"So, you're going to become a science teacher... Do you have any thoughts about where you'd like to teach?" she asked.

"Not really. The one thing that will make my selection easier is to have a golf coaching opportunity too."

"Sure. Of course. But please don't be like most of the coaches I see trying to teach a regular, academic course. They are so distracted by their sport or activity, that they give short shrift to the subject they're being paid to teach. That cheats the kids out of things they should know."

"Good point. The only example I have of that is my old biology teacher from high school, who was our golf coach too. I only discovered how good he was when I took my freshman biology classes at OU. Seventy-five percent of it was a repeat of what old Chet White taught us. Besides, I already know how to teach golf."

"Good. I don't know you that well yet, but I'd hope you would be that kind of educator and not just some jock coach."

"I like the *'yet'* part. I'm pretty sure my drive to do things right will save me from being just a golf coach who, oh by the way, shows up for classes. I will apply my focus from boxing and golfing to the classes I teach too."

"You haven't told me about you being a boxer. Really?"

"I never competed in Gold Gloves or anything like that, though my trainer said I could probably do okay. My dad wanted me to do something that would build my strength. Training for boxing did that. In six months, I packed on about forty pounds of muscle. Of course, I started out as the proverbial ninety-pound weakling, so the added muscle was quick to appear. It was the next twenty-five pounds that took some time to add on. All the weight and gym work helped improve my power for golf. It was quite a shock to dad and me when, after I'd been boxing and training all winter, I started ripping my drives another thirty to forty yards further than the previous year. I had to make many adjustments to the newfound strength and power. Boxing also improved all my reflexes. Catching that plate on my foot was a display of that... at least what's left over after I stopped boxing. The lore says that a boxer never loses his punch once he retires. I hope I don't have to test or prove that adage."

"My, my. Am I consorting with a fighter?" Gerry teased. "I hope you're gentle with me. I'll know not to make you angry."

They laughed.

"Good thinking. I'm not very good at being angry as it happens so seldom. Do you get angry? You seem like such a gentle soul."

"Lie to me. Cheat. Treat my kids poorly and you'll see the wrath of God coming from a very high place. Now you know the limits. Am I a forgiving person? Up to a point. Actually, I've only been that close with Lester where trust was ever on the table. So, what you see in me is something of an ingénue when it comes to affairs of the heart. I don't have a lot of experience."

"Well, I don't either for that matter. I grew up in a typical white, suburban neighborhood. My folks were not from the *some-of-my-best-friends-are-colored* crowd, but they avoided discussions about race during family gatherings. I don't see you as anything but a beautiful woman who is smart, classy, warm and happens to have brown skin. I know that everyone's muscles are pink and everybody bleeds red blood. I can tell that you aren't a zebra or an alligator, so there you have it."

"Thanks for not comparing me to a zebra. I only have two hoofs on the ground," she said in mocking response.

Bill jumped at the bait: "That's not what I meant. I guess I mean that if we appear together in public and get stared at, I honestly don't care. I am more concerned that the black and brown people would be discriminating against ME when we are together."

"Well, there is that element, of course. I have few friends as my job and my kids keep me pretty much away from any social scene. Oh, what game are we seeing next week? The Indians play who?"

"Oh, right, uh, I haven't picked a game yet. I'll do that and get tickets for the kids. Do you think Benny will want to come?"

"Well, Lester had him playing catch since he was very small, and he played in Little League too. I'll ask him. If he doesn't want to go with us three, the lady upstairs will make sure he's in and the doors are locked by nine."

"I'm feeling very comfortable with this conversation," Bill said. "It reminds me of how my parents interacted when planning outings. Are we already that compatible? Your thoughts?"

"Yes, it is making me feel a little weird to be so comfortable around a man who isn't a colleague or even a casual friend. We still haven't put in the necessary time, and we really do need to venture out and see how the rest of the world perceives us. Maybe they'll just shrug and not pay attention. I guess neither of us has that much family to worry about. Do you still have relatives?"

"I do. I have an uncle—brother of my dad, and an aunt—sister of my mother's. They have kids too, so I have some cousins. I see them at holiday gatherings or at the weddings of my cousins. All four grandparents have passed, so it's just that collection of people very different from me.

"This conversation seems to be heading toward a place a little past just friendship. Does this mean we are an *item*? Are we a new couple trying to find our way? I apologize for letting my stream of consciousness get ahead of where we are. My heart is screaming at my brain to say things that are way too early to say."

Gerry stopped walking. She looked Bill in the eye—as always—and laughed. "Yes, I can hear your heart making noises. I'm flattered and pleased. My heart is saying things too. I love the way you hold me, and you kiss wonderfully.

Clearly, I am more reserved than you are, so my brain is holding the reins tightly right now. I have two kids to think about and you have none. That's a big issue."

She then took both of his hands in hers. They were standing in the shadow of one of the big sycamores that shaded them from the street lamp just to their left. She just looked at him in the dark. He looked back. She then dropped his hands and cradled his face with hers. She kissed him sweetly with a rare tenderness.

"I think you are a good man, Bill Bannock. I want to know more about that goodness and what we're really doing besides fighting off hormonal and emotional surges caused by way too much time away from being in love with someone."

With a husky voice, he said, "You're right. I agree. If we were sixteen or something, I'd ask you to be my steady girlfriend about now. But your last point is the most important one. We HAVE been away from loving someone for a long time. We've gotta tiptoe through that minefield a little more, but tiptoe through it I feel we should."

"Very well said, boxer. Thank you for seeing things clearly... or as clearly as we can right now. Now, walk me back home. Let's talk with Alice for a while. Maybe Benny will break his self-imposed exile and join in. You never know."

Chapter 13

A Bad Day at the Golf Course

On the Tuesday Alice and Bill went to Willow Creek for his weekly event with the guys, a new low was set for him. It had never occurred to him before that all the staff and players at Willow Creek were white. This day would underscore the overall attitude of that suburban whiteness forever more in his mind and deeds.

It started with Bill sending Alice up to the clubhouse to buy him a cup of coffee and get a bucket of range balls. They'd gotten there about an hour earlier than normal because he wanted to work on his tempo without feeling rushed. A few minutes later, Alice returned to the range with a shocked, tearful look on her face. No balls. No coffee.

"What's wrong?"

"The man inside said they don't serve niggers. I tried to tell him that I was getting coffee and range balls for you, but he just told me to tell you to get those things yourself."

Bill walked back to the clubhouse and confronted Bailey Worth, the manager. "Hey, Bailey. What's up with throwing my caddy out? Didn't she tell you that the coffee and range balls were for me?

"Yeah, but we have a strict policy about serving those kinds of people. Next thing you know they'll be swarming this place and driving all the good customers away. Know what I mean?"

"Actually, Bailey, I *don't* know what you mean. I had no idea you had a racial policy here. When did that happen?"

"It's been part of Willow Creek's management policy to not serve those people. I think the previous owners put that in place in the fifties, and the new owners didn't bother changing it."

"Well, you DO know that racial discrimination is against the law, don't you? That stuff all went through the courts in the sixties. You knew she is my caddy. Why did you act so rudely to her? She's just a kid, for Christ's sake."

"Yeah. Well, I was gonna tell you to not bring her around here anymore. I got complaints from just that one time she caddied for you. I gotta take care of my paying customers. Here are your coffee and range balls. On the house. Just don't bring that darkie around here anymore."

By now, the flames were licking out from under Bill's collar. "Sure thing, Bailey. While we're at it, please don't add my name to the course record plaque. After all, Alice was my caddy for that round, and we wouldn't want to sully the club's reputation with that knowledge, now, would we?"

Bailey gave Bill a dark scowl but kept his mouth shut. It was good that he did. It took Bill some minutes to cool off. Alice just looked at the thunderstorm that was Bill when he came back out to the range. He looked at her and just shook his head. It took him a while to get into the practice he'd intended and finally started hitting solid shots to the spots he targeted. But this incident in the clubhouse was just the beginning of a bad day.

Bill's three playing partners trickled in and started

warming up and putting. He said hello to them and stood there watching them try to hit shots. Alice stood patiently next to Bill while he waited.

Lonny, wearing his trademark bright pink golf shirt and shoes, piped up and said, "So, you brought your caddy along again. Did you drive her here, or did she take a bus?"

"I drove her here, Lonny. Her mother and I are friends, so it was easy to do a favor for her."

"Oh, so her momma is your friend, eh? So, are you now sampling some dark meat? White ain't good enough anymore?"

"What did you say?"

"I asked if you were finding dark meat better than white. Whatsa matter? Won't white women go out with you any..."

From out of the blue, Bill landed a very quick right-left punch combination to Lonny's big, bigoted mouth. He went down in a heap, groaning. Bill's fists stung a little, and it looked like he'd broken Lonny's nose and jaw.

Lonny tried to speak, but found that he couldn't. Good thing. Bill would have hit him again. Harry and Frank came running over.

"Why the fuck did you hit him, Bill? What'd he say? That's not like you at all."

Still trembling from the adrenaline dump, he stammered: "He insulted my caddy and her mother and me with filthy, racist remarks. I couldn't let it pass."

"Shit, Bill, I think you broke his jaw," Harry said.

"Yeah, well, after Bailey kicked Alice out of the clubhouse this morning, he told me to never bring her around again because it was policy and bad for business. Did one of you assholes complain about Alice being my caddy?

"No, Bill," said Frank. "It wasn't us. I think one of the women's league ladies said something to Bailey earlier."

"Yeah. Well, that does it for me and Willow Creek. I'll never spend another dime here. Have Lonny send me his hospital bill."

He turned, motioned for Alice to follow, and they went back to the car. '

'Bill, you sure have some quick hands. That pink fool was on the ground in a blink."

"Did you hear what he said?"

"I did. Those are the creeps we call *honkies* down in the neighborhoods."

"I've heard that expression, but what does it mean?"

"Well, it comes from seeing white guys come cruising into certain parts of the neighborhoods where the prostitutes hang out. They drive by and honk their car horn when they see some girl they like. They don't get out of their car, of course, so the girls just get in. It's pretty sick."

"Christ! What a country! At times like today I feel embarrassed to be white. I don't feel bad about decking Lonny. His smart mouth has had it coming for a long time. He's been bad-mouthing black people ever since I've known him. This time he got too close to me with his bullshit."

"Bill, you're not like those guys. I'm kinda proud of you that you stood up for Momma and me. You are true of heart. So, I guess golf is out for today, huh?"

"Yeah. I'm still shaking a little and I can't get rid of what Bailey and Lonny said within an hour of each other. Let's go have an early lunch and catch a matinee movie."

When he took Alice home, she insisted that he come in for a glass of tea.

Gerry greeted them with a big smile. "So, how did you two play today?"

"We didn't play. That guy who wears pink started mouthing off to Bill about me and you in very crude terms.

Bill decked him, one – two."

"Oh dear. Bill, what did this guy say that was so bad that you hit him."

"I'd rather not tell you the words he used, but they were of a strong racial and sexual nature that insulted you, Alice and me. On top of that, the clubhouse management wouldn't even serve Alice a cup of coffee I asked her to buy for me. When I confronted him, he told me that 'those people' weren't wanted in the clubhouse.

"So, it was a very upsetting morning. I took Alice to a movie instead. The popcorn and escapism were what we needed after the incident."

"Oh, my God! Do you think he'll sue you?"

"He might, but I don't care. It might be worth it to expose his bigotry in open court. Guys like that can't afford to have public stuff like this occur. Bad for business, you know. I'll probably have to pay for his hospital bill because I think I broke his jaw."

"Dear God! Sit down and let me get you a glass of tea. Welcome to the world we inhabit."

Gerry brought Bill the tea and sat across from him in the living room. "While I'm flattered that you stood up for Alice and myself, I worry that this might be a recurring theme if we continue to see each other."

"You don't have to worry about any of that. I will be much more selective with whom I play golf and who I consider to be friends. As I've said, I really don't have people I hang out with. I've probably shared more meaningful words with you and Alice in the last couple of weeks than I have with any of my friends or relatives in the last year. The conversation quality is certainly better too."

That brought a smile to her face that washed away Bill's worries and angst. He didn't feel prideful in what he'd just done, but didn't care much for the insults hurled toward the woman he thought he was falling in love with. Sometimes, reflexes just don't have time for detailed analysis.

Unknown to Alice, Gerry and Bill, Benny's face peeked around the corner of the hallway entrance. He listened to the conversation with great interest.

Why would some white guy stand up for one of us? he thought. *Is he real, or is he just trying to impress my mother? Maybe I should cut him a break to find out.*

Chapter 14
Advancing on All Fronts

Lonny Shell didn't sue Bill or press charges for hitting him and breaking his jaw in three places. To keep from going to court, he paid Lonny almost $3,000 for medical bills and bought a new Cadillac from his dealership. Having done that financial penance, he signed over the Olds to Gerry and even tried paying for a year's insurance for her. He soon discovered the world of finance for people not white was a different kettle of fish. The motor vehicle department didn't have any trouble with the transfer of title as long as she could sign her own name. The insurance, however, required that the company run a check on Geraldine Morgan, widow of Lester Morgan. Both Gerry and Bill had to appear at Bill's insurance agent's office to sign her up. The agent, Mr. Jeff Alston, started questioning Gerry's background and her remaining debt from her husband's funeral almost three years ago.

"Well, Mrs. Morgan, you know that banks really don't like to offer credit to a single female who is head of the household. From that point of view, we need to be assured that you will be able to pay your monthly premiums, or we will be forced to cancel. I see that you haven't been insured for the current vehicle that is still in your husband's name. That puts you in a high-risk category and your premiums, if we accept your application, will be accordingly higher."

Bill butted in: "What if I co-sign for the insurance policy? I am worth a lot of money, have no appreciable debt, and have been a client of this office for ten years."

"Why would you do that? Are you intending to marry this woman? We need to have some reasonable assurances here. For all we know, you might just disappear after a few months and Mrs. Morgan here might not be able to pay the premiums. Then what would we, or she, do if she got into an accident?"

The agent couldn't have been more than twenty-five and had the pasty complexion of someone who rarely saw the sun.

"What are the premiums for the basic collision and liability policy?" Bill asked.

He was quoted a number that was 50% higher than what he was paying on the brand-new Cadillac.

"Really? You already know that her teacher's salary isn't that high. She has two kids. She doesn't go anywhere except to school and the grocery store, and you want to charge her more of what you know she has little of. How do you get away with that? Let's talk to your supervisor."

Gerry had a look of angry defiance and clutched Bill's leg in a grip that spoke volumes. Bill's facial expression wasn't too keen on being pleasant either.

"How do you do, Mr. Bannock? I'm Irving Smith. How may I help you?" said a tall, lean, middle-aged man in horn-rimmed glasses.

"I am here with my good friend to help her get auto insurance for the car I just signed over to her. I bought a new car and Mrs. Morgan's current vehicle is in need of extensive repairs and service. I'm independently solvent and am extending some generosity to this dedicated professional educator and mother of two. Can you help me and Mrs. Morgan obtain a fair and reasonable insurance rate for the Oldsmobile that I've owned for two years? It's paid for and all its service records are part of the file. I've been a client of this office for ten years. Why is your agent here, uh, Mister Alston, telling Mrs. Morgan that her premiums will be half again as high as mine for the same vehicle upon which you charged me a reasonable monthly rate? We're not here to get a bank loan, only collision and liability—you know, the same as I had with the Olds and have with the new Cadillac. Mrs. Morgan's driving record is cleaner than mine. She hasn't even had a parking ticket. "

"Yes. Well... I see your point." He turned to the blushing Alston and stared at him. Then he stared at Bill. Then Gerry. "You say you will pay the first year's policy premiums for Mrs. Morgan? Why would you do that?"

"Well, she is a friend and I can afford it. Do you need to know anything else?"

"Do you intend to marry this woman, Mr. Bannock?"

"I might, but I don't see how that is any business of yours or how it relates to this transaction."

Gerry was crushing Bill's leg.

"Would you and Mrs. Morgan mind waiting in the lobby for a few minutes while I speak with my agent here?"

Gerry was fairly quivering with fire. "You don't have to do any of this, Bill. My old Chevy will make it for a while longer. It's not worth the aggravation and the humiliation."

"But Gerry, you don't have any insurance on the Chevy either. If some idiot rams you and he or she doesn't have insurance, you're stuck with a pile of junk, or worse, medical bills.

"I'm sorry for taking over the negotiation, but this insurance gouging is bullshit. I didn't stand for this sort of thing when I was trying to negotiate capital equipment purchases and leases at the factory, and I'm not standing for this either. If I have to, I will take my insurance business elsewhere. But these guys are not going to screw you or me. You already own the car, my dear Gerry, and now we will get you the insurance that will make you—and me—sleep better."

"Bill, nobody has ever stood up for me like this. It's very endearing. How can I possibly re-pay your generosity?"

"I'm not asking for any re-payment. My sense of fairness is being jangled by some racist money-grubbers. I can see how they look at us, especially you, with a disapproving eye. I'll bet they have very few non-white clients. I'm realizing more, lately, how the deck is stacked against people like you and how unfair it is. We'll talk more later. Here comes Smith."

"Well, Mr. Bannock, we will underwrite a collision and two-way personal injury policy for Mrs. Morgan and the Oldsmobile for one year. The rate will be the same as you've been paying in the past. You will be asked to pay the full year's premium immediately and we reserve the right to review the policy upon its expiration a year from now. Will that suit you?" He didn't say this with a smile and he kept cutting his eyes to Gerry.

Bill took out his checkbook. "Let's sign the papers."

They returned to Alston's office. Smith did not shake their hands or say thank you, he just walked out. Young Jeff Alston pushed the policy folder across the desk without a word. He pointed to where Gerry needed to sign but didn't offer her a pen. Bill gave her his. He then grabbed the pen out of Alston's hand and wrote the check. When he finished, he threw the pen and the check back at him.

Gerry finished signing the policy papers, gathered up her package, and they both turned and left without anyone saying another word.

Christ! How I hate insurance companies. I just hope to whatever is holy that Gerry never has an issue with the Oldsmobile, because I'm sure these bastards will fight it all the way.

She sold her old Chevy to another teacher for a few hundred bucks a couple of days later, and Bill took them all to dinner to celebrate. It was a very cordial dinner and everyone felt a sense of relief that Bill wouldn't be wasting money on lawyers. Lonny was satisfied with selling him the Cadillac and paying for his medical bills. Bill got the impression that Lonny knew he was being a total asshole.

Benny started talking to Bill that evening. It felt that Mohammed was inching toward the mountain.

"Why you hit that guy, Bill?"

"I hit him because he degraded and insulted Alice, your mother and me at the same time. I was still feeling pretty unhappy after the clubhouse conversation with the manager who refused to allow Alice to buy me a cup of goddamned coffee. That *guy* has a big mouth, an empty head, and has been displaying his jealousy toward me for years. On that day, the release valve on my temper popped."

"Dang! How you learn to punch like that?"

Gerry chimed in. "Benny, you are not speaking in complete sentences. The question should be, 'How DID you learn to punch like that?' Try it again."

"Okay. Having an English teacher as a mother can be a pain sometimes. If I talked proper down on the avenue, I'd get the crap beaten out of me. So, how DID you learn to punch like that?"

"Yeah. My dad insisted that I take boxing lessons when I was about your age, maybe a year or two younger. He wanted me to get stronger, and have a different kind of physical training than just golf. So, I dutifully put on the weight and learned to punch. I never fought competitively, but spent a lot of time sparring with other guys in the gym. Footwork, reflexes, strength, focus... All those things apply to golf too. My dad even bought me a heavy and light bag to work out on when I wasn't in the gym. I kind of enjoyed that as it helped to burn off frustrations and stuff from school... Especially in the winter when I couldn't play golf.

"When Lonny shot his mouth off, I saw red and just treated him like a heavy bag. Two punch combinations are the things boxers work on from the beginning."

"So, you were defending my mother's honor, right?"

"I didn't think of it that way at the time. It was just his overt racist insult about your mother to ME that triggered it. See, creeps like Lonny Shell don't think about what they're saying. Their lives are so limited and shallow that hurling racial slurs and insults seems perfectly natural to them. I doubt he will change even after they unwire his jaw. Guys like that usually just end up being more of what they've always been.

"Sorry for the sociology lecture, but I probably needed to speak those words out loud. I don't feel guilty for what I did. I just wish the racism from people living in their hateful worlds didn't have to be so destructive to our society."

"Man! You are a heavy thinker. Yeah. Some of the people at school and in town are racist toward white people. Being that white people invented slavery in this country and still want to make life hard for black people, who can blame them?"

"Thanks for sharing your thoughts, Benny. I'm very happy that you started talking to me. Too bad it has to be under such circumstances, but I guess it's whatever it takes sometimes. By the way, slavery, in some form or other, has been around ever since humans learned how to write things down. It probably occurred before that too, but there's no evidence. It makes sense when it comes to profits for commodities. So, extrapolating, slavery probably started after humans learned about agriculture and could create a surplus of goods to sell. Profits from free labor."

"Yeah. Mom says you aren't like the other people she's known." He smiled a handsome smile and said, "You're looking less white every day. Nice car, by the way."

That brought a chuckle from around the table. Gerry was fairly glowing as she cast *that* look Bill's way.

Bill drove everyone back to Gerry's house and she asked him in for a goodnight cup of decaf coffee."

Alice and Benny, taking an unseen cue from Mom, disappeared into their rooms leaving the adults alone on the couch. Gerry gave Bill that special look again and said, "We've been seeing each other fairly regularly for over a month now, Bill. Do you feel as if we're going steady?"

Before he could respond, she added, "I couldn't stop thinking about what you did for me at the insurance office. Black people are constantly getting screwed like that. You should hear what some of my colleagues say when they try to get a loan for a house or a car. Their interest rates cross over the line of usury, but there is nobody that we can afford to fight for us and for fairness. It's surely a race thing. Do you agree?"

"Well, I don't have any experience with how finances and such work for black or brown people, but from what I've seen recently, I would have to strongly suspect that you are right and that I've only seen the very tip of the iceberg."

"Indeed, you have. Even at Glennville, the white teachers earn more money than the black teachers who have the same seniority and teach the same subjects. It's a disgrace – if one believes in fairness.

"I noticed that you didn't flinch when that insurance kid

asked if you intended to marry me. Are you thinking of asking me to marry you someday, Bill Bannock?"

Chapter 15
Speaking Truth to Truth

"I don't know, Gerry. I wouldn't know how to go about doing that. We've only been seeing each other for a month, maybe five or six weeks. I always look forward to seeing you. Alice and I get along great and her golf game is leaping forward. Then, I look forward to bringing her home so I can see you. I love the affection we share. But as far as that level of commitment goes... I haven't a clue. I told you a little about what passed for my previous love life, so contemplating marriage with such a high-quality person as yourself is not a very well-formed subject in my head.

"Look, when I graduated from OU and got a good-paying job, I left the comfortable parent's nest and rented my first apartment—not too far from here, actually. I had maybe three girlfriends in high school, but between golf and my nerdy interests in science, those relationships went nowhere in a hurry. Hell, I didn't even go to my senior prom. College was mostly more of the same.

"Anyway, in a couple of years, I'd managed to save up and buy the condo on the lake shore. I got in on the ground floor – so to speak – as they were selling units not yet completed. I was able to afford the twelfth floor with a view for very little down payment."

"I'm looking forward to seeing that view someday, Bill," Gerry said with a warm smile.

"Yes. Of course. Sure. Where was I?'

"You were telling me about how you never contemplated marrying."

"Right. As I said earlier, Linda was the closest I came to grasping that concept, but her infidelity was a sharp kick in my psyche that I'm not sure I've fully recovered from. See, I figure that a job worth doing is a job worth doing well and completely. Back then, I thought getting married was that kind of a thing; something that was worth doing well.

"I've never liked going to singles bars, I don't care for churches and I don't meet very many unmarried women on the golf course. So, making the break from my itinerate bachelorhood into something like what we're doing is all new territory for me."

"Why? Do you trust me more than the others, such as they were?"

"I think so. Your story and the short time that we've been together have shown me a consistency and a sweetness I haven't ever known from a woman other than my mother. Even Linda wasn't as sweet as you. I found out the hard way what that kind of superficiality was like. In retrospect, I don't even remember how she and I got so far as to talk about getting married. Must have been a moment of passion.

"So, to be as honest as I can... I trust you as far as I know how to. Everything in my head says that you are very special and that I should continue to see you. I feel a special kind of connection I can't ever remember having with anyone other than my parents. My feelings for you have to mature, I guess. The physical part doesn't seem that urgent to me, though I enjoy the affection we share. And yes, you turn me on sexually. What I am concerned with is that lovemaking might interfere with the relationship we seem to be building. It would be a whole new level of involvement. I'm not afraid of that, mind you, it's just a sense of timing. I'm guessing that the timing will dictate itself."

"Well, my dear Bill... That was a very interesting dive into what makes you tick. First, let me say that I don't doubt your honesty and your fearlessness. Your time with Alice and what you have done with us speaks louder than any voice about who you are and what sort of character you possess. I very much like the way you touch me, hold me, stroke me and kiss me. I've never felt more physically comfortable with a man before. Lester was a good and gentle man, but I was so young when I met him that most of my reactions to our physical relationship were just basic instincts and did not have an intellectual component. Do you understand my meaning?"

"I do. That pretty much describes my entire love life." They laughed at that. Bill blushed.

"Come here into my arms, Bill. I think we need to not talk for a little while and just feel each other's closeness."

They embraced. Bill held her more tightly than he ever had before and she responded by squeezing him with surprising strength. They eventually leaned back a little, looked into each other's eyes without saying anything, and then kissed warmly, deeply and with commitment. The kiss was broken after what seemed like five minutes.

She said, huskily, "That's what I mean about the affection and tenderness part. I've never kissed anyone but Lester with that much, uh, intensity. This must also be part of the maturing process." Her following smile almost seemed shy, dimples on full display.

Bill felt himself falling, not wanting to let her go. He kissed her again. They heard the refrigerator door open and close. The moment was put on hold.

"I'd better be on my way. Oh, did I tell you that I start my first class on Monday?"

"No. Are they starting you with *Classroom Management*?"

"Yes. I look forward to sharing with you what I learn. You're an experienced teacher, after all."

"Yes. Well, don't underestimate your ability to teach. Now, say bye to the kids."

Bill called down the hallway to the children's rooms and heard "bye" back from Alice and Benny.

Gerry and Bill looked at each other and raised their eyebrows at Benny's cordial-sounding response. She walked him out to the side door, kissed him, stroked his face and pushed him out the door. It felt good to him to tell the truth tonight. He realized that he was far too old to be playing games of the heart. He knew he had to decide soon whether he was in or out with this woman.

God only knows I'm captivated by her physical beauty and her seemingly genuine sense of just plain goodness.

Chapter 16

Learning and Teaching

Bill walked into his first class as a student in almost twenty years to discover that he felt like the chaperone at a school dance. All his fellow students in Dr. Celia Arthur's *Classroom Management for Secondary Teachers* looked like they were just out of high school themselves. It amazed him to see the big difference in appearances eighteen to twenty years can make. Dr. Arthur didn't blink when she called the roll and he answered "here" as a student. He did receive a few sidelong looks from some of the young people in the class.

The whirlwind opening lecture involved some segments that, at first, surprised Bill, but soon provided the first of many "holy crap" moments. The most important parts revolved around the teacher's role in the life of so many young people.

"You will be their best alternative model of what an adult should be like. You won't, of course, have the filial connection of being their parent. In fact, with one exception in this class, you won't be more than ten to fifteen years older than your students. If you're going to teach high school, you'll be *less* than ten years older. Sorry, Mister Bannock."

The class turned toward him and chuckled a little.

"Don't worry," he said. "You've been around more young people, er, younger people, than I have. I look forward to you teaching me what young people are like."

That brought more laughs and a chuckle from Dr. Arthur. "Okay. Now that we've thoroughly embarrassed Mr. Bannock, the other major point I wanted to make today was that you teachers will often be the only source of caring the tougher kids see in their entire day. You'll know who they are right away. They will be the reluctant learners who will act out or resist any attempts you make to teach them something. Be patient. It's not personal for you.

"But in spite of the curled lips, the interruptions, the projected hostile attitudes and the poor study skills, these kids will keep looking for a crack in your armor as a person. You, on the other hand, must impart upon every one of your students the fact that you do care about their welfare and their futures as citizens. You must project caring at all times. You must *never* run out of patience even with the most resistant students. And, oh, by the way, you must also keep in mind that you will NOT reach all of the kids. Some cases are so hard that no teacher trying to present an academic curriculum will cause those unfortunate kids to change. That's why we have counselors. You cannot allow disruptions from these hard cases. Always remember that you have twenty-five to thirty other kids who are eager and willing to learn and succeed in your class.

"As a major component of classroom management, I've always promoted combining the Socratic method—letting the students participate openly in each class—with humor. Lots of humor. Even if it means self-deprecation, get the kids to laugh. Laughter heals most souls. A most important part of that management structure involves high-quality lesson plans that use as many modalities of instruction as you can muster in any class. Those of you who will work in ninety-minute block classes can use more modalities in a day than those working hour-long classes."

"What are the modalities of which you speak, Doctor Arthur?" Bill asked.

"Thank you for not ending the sentence with a preposition, Mister Bannock."

My lady friend is an English teacher."

The class laughed.

"See. That's getting humor into the lesson." More laughter.

"To your question: the modalities include but are not limited to lecture, expert groups, student-lead instruction, audio-visual, worksheets, puzzles, laboratories in science, in-class reading by you or the students and any other ways you can discover to keep your lessons rolling along. Student boredom is a lesson killer and a classroom management disaster."

Bill left Dr. Arthur's class with an entirely new perspective of being a teacher. He tried recalling how his high school teachers managed their classes and what kind of lessons they produced. His "best" teachers, he recalled, offered varying lessons using the modalities mentioned today. There wasn't all that much audio-visual stuff then, only the occasional 16 mm movie. He also recalled that his favorite classes involved student participation, aka *The Socratic Method*. He began thinking about using some of that with Alice while she was perfecting her golf game. They had a tee time at Sleepy Hollow today, so he thought he'd give it a try.

After almost two months of practice and instruction, Alice and Bill had only played two rounds together at Highland Park. When she struggled with bringing her practice range quality to every shot on the course during their first round together, she told him she didn't understand why she couldn't bring those skills to the course when she played.

"My dear Alice. Welcome to the reality of golf. Instead of just pounding balls, you are now *playing* the game. You're gonna have to shift from just grooving a swing to actually playing each shot."

She did much better the second time out, shooting a ninety from the middle tees. The girl could flat-out putt, and Bill knew he couldn't say a word about that. That ninety at Highland Park included a mere thirty putts.

At Sleepy Hollow, Bill started asking her why she chose the club she did and why she hit it in the direction she did. "Why did you chip that seventy-footer with a six iron instead of something with more loft?"

"Well, I read the break and the grain – which was coming toward me - and wanted to get the ball on the ground and running right away."

"Why?"

"If I'd have used a more lofted club, the grain might have grabbed the ball too soon. It was an easier read for my eye and how I read the green."

"Correct answer."

They played a couple more holes.

"Why didn't you hit driver off that short par four? You could have ended up hitting a punch wedge if you had."

"I didn't feel confident with a punch wedge. I wanted to hit a full shot, so I used the three wood. You saw that the full nine iron I hit ended up pretty close. Made the putt too."

It was time for Bill to shut up and let this very bright and talented girl figure out her own game. All it took were a couple of inputs and her brain clicked INTO the game. He hoped that he would have students like Alice in his classroom. He knew that was a fantasy, but the lessons with Dr. Arthur and his best-ever golfing student convinced him that letting the student figure out how best they could learn and improve would be his path to success as a teacher.

Bill took Alice home after that round at Sleepy Hollow and chatted with Gerry about it over a glass of iced tea.

"So, you think my daughter has some potential as a golfer? She has always been very precocious. She was walking at nine months and fighting to get her first words formed. Alice has told me how much she likes you and can't wait until you're together playing golf. I'm starting to get jealous." She gave him a mocking smile. "You should see her when she's expecting you. She makes sure every hair is in place and that her outfit is clean and pressed. When you're going out to play a round, she wears her best golfing togs. She loves the golf shirts you bought for her. When do I get to see Alice, the prodigal daughter, play golf?"

"Good question. I think I want to sneak you into seeing her a little at a time. Right now, she's learning to grasp the mental aspects of the game on the course, so knowing you're there would make it harder, I think. Mind you, she's rapidly developing the playing mentality; caddying and listening over the years has laid the groundwork for her quick development.

"By the way, I bought you something from the golf shop."

He handed Gerry the shopping bag with the Sleepy Hollow logo. In it was a short-sleeved polo shirt worn by women golfers. 'I hope it fits."

"Let's see." She stood up, unbuttoned her blouse and took it off. Seeing so much of her toned and beautiful skin was a jolt to Bill's libido. Without looking the least bit perturbed, she slipped the golf shirt over her torso and tucked it into her summer shorts.

"What do you think? It feels like the right size. You guessed right," she said.

He'd bought her a pale rose-colored shirt with thin, dark red horizontal stripes. He thought she looked marvelous in it, but then he was biased. "Go look in the mirror and see if I got the right color. I don't think I've ever bought an article of clothing for a woman before."

Gerry disappeared into her room for a few minutes and returned with a big smile. "Perfect!" she said. She then wrapped her loving arms around him and kissed him for a long time. "It's been a very long time since any gentleman has bought me anything at all. Thank you, Bill. I can see why Alice is taken with you."

"Well, being with Alice on the golf course seems as natural to me as any time I've been with a student or a friend. You're right about her maturity. I feel like we're really good friends and share just about everything. She's asked me what my feelings are toward you and I've told her the truth ... as best I can."

"Yes. She's told me that you've never met anyone like me before. She says I make you want to be around more often. Is that true?"

"It is. I've enjoyed every minute with you. Maybe it's just being forty, but there has been a kind of instant maturity about us. Do you feel that?"

"I think it's time I saw your apartment on the lake."

Chapter 17

Alice Breaks 80

As Bill turned into the driveway at Alice's house, there she was sitting on the porch steps with her bag of clubs. Bill popped the lid on the Cadillac and she carefully put her clubs in next to his. As they drove, Alice talked non-stop.

"I caddied a couple of times at Sleepy Hollow before we met. Once, there were some boys there that gave me a pretty bad time. It wasn't until this nice lady asked me to caddy for her that they finally got off my back. She scolded them and told them that they could make better money working rather than bad-mouthing some girl. I guess they worked at the course in maintenance or something because when we got back from our round, the lady made a point of handing me two twenty-dollar bills in front of the boys. She said, 'Do summer jobs pay this well, guys?' She became my immediate hero.

"I was so excited, I called mom to come pick me up. Turns out that forty bucks covered our grocery shopping for the week. Mom being mom, bought us ice cream. That was the last time I had any until you bought us some at Jackie's. A kid doesn't forget ice cream days when they are so irregular."

Bill never knew any teenage girls who used words like "irregular". He just smiled at Alice when he could and let her cook off the adrenaline before getting to the course. He wanted this particular golfing experience to be a good one. When they arrived at the course, Bill reached behind him to retrieve a shopping bag from the back seat. "Here, Alice. I brought you something that you might find useful today."

She opened the bag to find a shoe box. It had a famous shoe brand's name written across the top lid and the sides. "These for me?"

"Try 'em on. They should fit. I asked your mom what size shoes you wore. There should be a couple pairs of ankle-length golf socks in there too."

Alice sat on the edge of the open trunk and put on the socks. Bill showed her how to lace the shoes properly to prevent lace sores. The smile on her face when she stood up was like the sun breaking through cloud cover.

"Walk around a little. Feel any hot spots?"

"No. They fit perfectly. Oh, Bill, thank you SO much! They're beautiful. I love the saddle shoe design. How am I gonna keep my eye on the ball when I'm looking at these beautiful shoes?"

"Yes. Well, it'll be another test of your focus and concentration. Let's go warm up. It'll be good for you to get your footwork right with your new shoes too."

As he reached for his own shoes, Alice nearly strangled him with an embrace and a blubbering, "Thank you, oh thank you" in his ear.

They walked over to the range and started warming up. Alice couldn't get anything off the ground for about ten swings. She finally settled down and started drilling the ball as she'd done so often on the range. The caddy shack had five kids waiting for a job. Bill found a young boy to caddy for him and asked another to loop for Alice. Then things got a little tense. The boy Bill asked to caddy for Alice looked to be about fifteen. When he finally realized that he would be Alice's caddy, he said, "No thanks."

"Why not?" Bill asked. "I'm paying top dollar. What's the problem?"

"I ain't caddying for ... somebody like her."

"No? Okay. Tell me, who *would* you caddy for? Me? My guy here that I just hired can caddy for Alice and you can loop for me? How's that?" Bill's caddy's name was Pat. '

'So, Pat, will you be Alice's caddy today?"

"Sure. The money's the same color. C'mon Norm. Caddy for Mr. Bannock here."

Norm just gave them all a steely, angry glare and walked back to the caddy shack.

"Stay here with our stuff, Pat," Bill said.

He walked past Norm into the caddy shack and asked the three remaining boys who wanted to earn fifty bucks caddying for him. He made sure Norm was within earshot.

All three hands shot up and Bill picked the youngest-looking of the group. "What's your name?"

"Colin. Colin Hunter."

"Okay, Colin. Let's go."

As Colin and Bill left, they could hear Norm being berated by his colleagues. The word "nigger" was heard in Norman's response to the needling.

JESUS CHRIST! Does everything have to be about skin color? I'll bet Alice could give these kids five strokes a side and whip them for their lunch money. Well, we have two kids who understand the value and dignity of work.

Alice proceeded to charm the ears off of Pat by swapping caddying stories and how Bill "discovered" her. As luck would have it, Pat Roseller was on his high school golf team and knew what he was doing around the game.

This was Colin's first year around golf and he told Bill he really liked being outdoors. He asked Bill if he'd teach him what to do and what he was doing with each shot. Bill said he wouldn't mind at all since he was going to be a science teacher and, hopefully, a golf coach too.

The partnership between Pat and Alice worked well. She showed none of the jitters she had in previous rounds Bill and she played. Instead, she became much more focused than he'd seen her. He could hear Pat giving her club selections, yardages, wind direction and an encouraging word. They acted as a real team when it came to reading the greens, and they had few disagreements.

Bill asked Alice how the shoes felt and she just smiled and said, "Very comfortable."

Both Alice and Bill played well and Colin seemed impressed with some of the better shots and putts they both made. Bill talked his way around for Colin's benefit, and gave him tips about what a caddy could do to improve his tip potential from customers.

But the Alice and Pat Show was something to behold. They were not flirting, but were totally involved with the game. When Alice rolled in a curving thirty-footer for a birdie, Pat whooped and patted her on the back.

"You really have some game, Alice. You could whip half the guys on my school golf team. I'd even ask for strokes."

When they finally holed out at eighteen, Alice was beaming. She'd just carded her first sub-80 round by making a sidehill six-footer for par and a seventy-nine. Bill paid Pat and Colin the fifty he promised them. They were very thankful and happy.

Pat said, "Man, you two are the best pair I've seen around here. Are you going to enter the Cleveland amateur?

"I've played in the boy's division a couple of times, but I think maybe Alice would enjoy the experience in the girl's division."

Pat turned to Alice. "Alice, if you get into the women's tournament, can I caddy for you? It's gonna be right here at Sleepy Hollow on Labor Day weekend. Here's my phone number. Thanks, Mister Bannock. You guys were great."

It was doubtful Alice heard her spikes clicking as they walked across the parking lot. She was most certainly walking on air.

"So, how're the shoes feeling after walking eighteen?" asked Bill.

"Well, it took just a little while to feel the extra strength and confidence of my feet not slipping when I swung. I think I swung harder today than ever before. SEVENTY-NINE, Bill!!! Everything was clicking today."

"I think you and your caddy had some serious chemistry going. I just tried to stay out of your way."

"Oh yes. Pat was great. He spoke a lot like you do about the game—the shots and the course management stuff. He's a really smart guy and knew how to caddy. All I had to do was put out my hand and the right club landed in it. He's cute too."

"Why Alice Morgan... I do believe you're blushing."

"How can you tell? Brown people don't blush... Not so you can tell," she said jokingly.

"Well, I know you blush. Now, let's get you home to Momma and celebrate your first seventy-nine."

"Momma", of course, was thrilled to hear the news. Alice was fairly jumping up and down, and when she finally left to clean up, Gerry looked at Bill with eyes full of tears that gently cascaded down her smooth, brown cheeks.

Chapter 18

The Apartment on the Lake

"Bill, I've never seen Alice this happy and excited. She's a brave girl and has not had much of a childhood, never mind an adolescence. Buying her those golf shoes was a brilliant move on your part. I am ever so thankful that you have entered her life ... and mine.

"I'm sure you've noticed that Alice is a very special young lady. Her intuitions are almost always on the money. I know she thinks the world of you and the best way into a mother's heart is through her children. But you probably know that."

"No, I don't know that. It sounds manipulative, and that's not how I work. I try to be a straight shooter and not a con man."

"Oh, I'm so sorry. Please forgive my awkward comment. I was trying to tell you that you hold a special place in my heart. The fact that my daughter likes you so much has made me pay closer attention to you and me. I apologize again if I've offended you."

Before he could say anything clever, Gerry was in his arms, kissing and hugging him with a kind of ferocity she'd never shown before. Bill was a little taken aback, but soon felt the passion and the power of the moment.

"Now, I want you to go home, clean up and create a special dinner for the two of us. I'll make arrangements here for the kids. Write down your address again. I prefer red wine, so I'll bring that. To me, it doesn't matter what the entree is. Will six-thirty be okay for me to arrive? Will you have everything ready by then?

"Sorry for the boldness, but I think you know that with children in hand, I have to take more of the initiative here. Anyway, I'm looking forward to watching the sunset with you on your balcony."

"Uh, yes, six-thirty will be fine. How about I grill a couple of steaks with a baked potato? I'll make a salad from fresh stuff I get on the way home. What kind of dressing do you like?"

"Hmm. Just Italian, I think. I don't want to overpower the taste of the steak or potato. Don't forget the sour cream. Baked potato without sour cream is not acceptable."

She then nailed Bill to the wall with that impossibly fetching, dimple-framed smile, patted him on the head and sent him out the door.

Bill suddenly realized as he was pulling into the grocery store on Lakeshore Boulevard that he'd never cooked dinner for a woman at the condo before. He had cooked for himself almost every day, so he knew his way around the kitchen. He hated going to restaurants by himself, and going out with the guys was just not that much of a rewarding experience.

There were two lovely sirloin steaks sitting in the butcher's glass cooler that spoke to him. Steaks had to be thick, so they could be cooked rare with a crisp outer layer.

Gosh, I wonder how Gerry likes her steak cooked?

A bag of charcoal, lighter fluid, two nice potatoes and sour cream. Salad makings for a nice spinach salad included tomatoes, sweet onion, croutons and the dressing filled the basket. He selected a sweet apple at the last minute to chop and add flavor variety to the salad. Bill then stopped by the housewares section and bought two long candles. Those silver candlesticks from the collection of his parents' wedding gifts had never been used. *Better buy some silver polish too.*

It was a warm evening in this last week of July, so after making the salad to chill, Bill showered and put on comfortable shorts and a colorful Hawaiian shirt that should absolutely not be tucked in. His belly was still quite flat, so he wouldn't be looking like he was trying to hide a beer gut.

At six-thirty sharp, the intercom announced Gerry's arrival. Bill buzzed her in and opened the door to her knock. What greeted him was a vision in muted tangerine, leather strap sandals and a beautiful, smiling face offset with two gold hoop earrings that could have allowed passage of a handball. She had a cream-colored wrap around her shoulders.

The look on Bill's face must have reflected his appreciation, because Gerry just grinned and said, "Well, I've brought wine. Aren't you going to ask me in?"

He laughed that kind of hollow laugh only stupid people make. "Sorry. You look astonishing."

It became clear, watching her move across the floor, that there was very little—if anything—under the loosely fitting, ankle-length dress. It had shoulder straps attached to a modestly plunging neckline and the entire dress clung to her moving parts perfectly.

"So, would you like a cocktail while I put the coals on? I waited until you got here before I lit the fire. I haven't made dinner for anyone in a very long time, but I remembered that timing was important. Cleverly, I've had the baked potatoes in the oven for almost a half-hour now, so we've got that to measure against."

It was clear to Gerry that he was nervous and, sensing that, she put the wine in the refrigerator and gave him a sweet kiss. She hadn't worn any makeup or lipstick, and she smelled like he'd imagined the Garden of Eden would smell on a summer day.

"I'll have what you drink in the evening," she said. "Oh, look at the view!"

She opened the sliding screen and went out onto the small balcony. Bill brought her two fingers of good scotch, neat. He always felt that if you're going to drink good spirits, you must learn to drink them without ice so that you'll sip and get all the flavor for the entire drink. Ice lent itself to guzzling, and guzzling lent itself to getting drunk. That was a waste of good whiskey. If somebody wanted to get drunk, he felt, they should do so with the cheap stuff. Then, you *needed* the ice to soften the sharp edges of the liquor.

The sun was lowering, but still had a couple of hours to go before kissing the edge of the world. Over in the downwind corner of the balcony was the small, covered charcoal grill. Bill had loaded the briquets earlier, but now added the fluid, let it soak in and lit the fire.

"The coals should be ready by the time the potatoes come out, and it only takes a few minutes for the steaks. Oh. How do you like your steaks cooked?"

"Just a little more done than rare. Do you know how to do that?"

"I do. I've been feeding myself steaks for some time. I think I've got this down."

When the flames died, he put the lid on with all vents open to allow the natural flow of air to get the coals going. They went back inside.

"This is really good scotch, Bill. Is this what you usually

drink?"

"Not this particular brand of single malt. I only bring out the twelve-year-old whiskey for special occasions. I can afford it, and it makes no sense to me to guzzle cheap scotch. Sipping good scotch, paradoxically, keeps one from drinking too much."

"Good thinking. So, show me around your apartment."

"Oh. Right. Follow me."

There were two bedrooms and one bathroom, the kitchen, a nice-sized dining area, the living area with couch, chairs and TV/stereo and, of course, the balcony. One bedroom he used as an office and library. There were a few paintings he'd bought over the years and some posters of Arnold Palmer hanging in the office.

"Is he your hero?" she asked.

"I don't know. I just admire what Palmer does for the game. If I had a hero, though, it would have to be my father. He was the great provider of wisdom and information for me. I sometimes still hear his voice when I'm thinking of certain things."

"Where did you get that nice painting of dolphins in the surf?"

"On one of my winter trips to Florida. I picked it up at a little shop along the beach near Ft. Lauderdale. You like it?"

"I do. It gives one a sense of exquisite life surrounded by the eternity of the sea."

"Nice. I did some biology research involving dolphins, so I share your view there. There's the buzzer. Time to cook the steaks."

Bill put the steaks on without stoking the coals so they would get a little crispy on the outside. He'd put a nice sea salt and black pepper rub on the meat earlier, and wanted to be sure to keep it as part of the flavor package. He lit the candles, then brought the salad bowl out along with the dressing, sour cream and his parents' silver salt and pepper shaker service.

"While I'm turning the steaks, please serve up the salads." He'd unwrapped the potatoes from their foil jackets and put the butter on the table next to the sour cream.

"Those wine glasses with the silver lips are from my parents' wedding present collection. When they died, I inherited these keepsakes."

"They're beautiful and elegant, Bill. I've always liked thirties-style silver and glassware. I'll go open the wine. Where do you keep the corkscrew?"

As they ate dinner, the conversation turned to Alice's excitement over her golf game. Her wide-eyed happiness truly delighted Bill and Gerry too.

"Benny had been out playing baseball that day, and when he got home Alice couldn't stop telling him of her day when she broke eighty. He finally had heard enough. He told her that he had three hits himself and just wanted to clean up.

"I think Benny is getting closer to liking you. He was impressed that you bought Alice the golf shoes and handled the caddy situation the way you did. You may be making a believer of Benny that not all white men are evil."

"I am not evil. And I'm very much liking his mother. What could possibly go wrong?"

Gerry laughed. They bussed their dishes to the kitchen and filled the dishwasher.

"Does it get chilly at night?"

"Not now. Hell, it was over ninety today, so it should be just pleasant on the balcony." He had closed off the vents and the charcoal grill obediently and slowly went out.

They grabbed their wine glasses and what was left of the very tasty cabernet and sat in the two comfortable folding chairs to watch the sunset. Gerry sat upwind and what little breeze there was that evening kept sending Bill the delicious smell of her body. The sun did indeed do its daily duty and provided them with the explosion of colors on the water and the wispy cirrus clouds in the sky.

Without any dialogue, they just got up and took their empty glasses into the kitchen. The candles were the only light generators but Bill knew how to operate the turntable in the dark. He put on some good jazz by the Dave Brubeck Quartet. It wasn't the romantic mood music that one might get from Johnny Mathis, but it just seemed to be the right thing for the moment. Paul Desmond's sax just sang its songs to them as they sat close together on the couch.

Gerry laid her head on Bill's shoulder and draped her other arm across his chest. She looked up with a kind of dreamy look in her eyes. They kissed. They kissed longer and deeper than ever before. Bill's hands discovered that she was indeed not wearing anything under her dress. She allowed those hands to wander wherever they wanted to go, moving her legs to accommodate his explorations. Her hands found his very firm arousal and gently stroked it.

She broke free and stood up. She reached for Bill's hand. He gave it. Gerry led him to the bedroom and started unbuttoning his shirt. He let the shirt fall to the floor. She stood away and with one sweeping motion had the dress off over her head and tossed in a heap next to his shirt. What stood before Bill Bannock was the bronze beauty he had only previously imagined. Her breasts were somewhat pear-shaped with hard, brown nipples that stood out proudly. Her skin was flawless. Her torso was firm and lean. It tapered to form her waist and eventually met the flare of a most inviting set of hips and all that lay in view. The thighs retained their shape and tone from her days as a volleyball player, showing muscle definition. She let him just look at her nakedness, standing motionless. It was all very erotic for him at this moment, and he let his basic male instincts rule his actions.

It took Bill only a second or two to be out of his shorts. He encompassed her waist with his arms and lowered both of them onto the bed. Their bodies merged automatically. The foreplay had been going on for the last hour, so there was absolutely no question that they were compatible lovers. Their movements were coordinated from the start. The rhythm of their lovemaking emulated that of two mature people who were relishing every second and not rushing to the finish. Bill's climax happened before hers, but he was so involved with the moment that he managed to stay with her until she shook with similar pleasure.

They lay in each other's arms, still breathing somewhat heavily. There was a light sheen of perspiration on their skins.

"Gerry, this has been building for some time. I'm glad it came about this way. I hope you don't think this is just a one-night stand," he said teasingly.

"Not on your life, pal. This lovemaking is exactly how I thought it would be... With a couple of surprises, of course."

They chuckled.

Gerry said, "I want some more of this with you. It's been a very long time since I've felt these parts of my body responding so wonderfully. Where are you in all this?"

"I knew that the timing for this moment had to be right if we were going anywhere. I have wanted to make love with you since the first time we kissed. It was like an electric current going straight to my, uh, male parts."

"It's okay to say 'dick' or whatever you want to call it," she retorted.

Bill grunted.

"Yeah. Sure. Seeing you just standing there naked tonight was incredible. Speaking of which... My 'dick' feels like visiting your pleasant place once again."

"M-m-m. That sounds good to me. More talking later."

Chapter 19

Necessary Details

"What time is it? Oh, I have to get back to the kids. They'll think you've kidnapped me."

"Not a bad idea. Do I need to?"

"Not now. Maybe another time. Right now, I need to take a shower. Care to join me? Do you have clean towels?"

The shower together was more than a little erotic, as mutual soaping and 'scrubbing' just made those special nerve endings leap to alertness. After some careful maneuvering and rinsing, Gerry reached for the shower knob and turned it off.

"I really have to go. Mrs. Haley will be worried. I asked her to watch the kids while I was out. She gave me this knowing, leering look without saying anything, but it made me feel a little like I was a schoolgirl stealing a cookie. Nice cookie, by the way."

They toweled off and Gerry slipped back into her garment, slid into the sandals and guided Bill to the door. In the meantime, he'd put his shorts back on.

"Call me tomorrow, my dear," she said. "We have things to discuss. Don't you agree?"

"Yes, we do."

Gerry kissed him one last time, looked into his eyes with that riveting look, smiled a little bit, then turned and was out the door. Bill stood there for what seemed like a minute, turned and passed a mirror that showed a rumpled head of hair above a face that had an other-worldly, almost giddy smile on it. He hadn't seen that face before.

I have to snap out of it and start thinking clearly. Okay. Not necessarily clearly, but maybe happily.

He then put on a long-sleeved polo shirt, poured three fingers of the good scotch they drank before dinner, and went out and sat on the balcony. The stars were out; the cool night air contained low humidity and felt comfortable. A half-moon had risen high enough to start reflecting off of the ripples of Lake Erie. He sipped his scotch.

For a time, he just blanked out and watched the lake answer the rhythmic rules of nature. He recognized that his own natural rules were more complex than those of the lake, but they still had rhythm and purpose. At this point, he stopped being analytical and just drank his 12-year-old whiskey.

After about a half-hour more of this reverie, some things started to pop up in his consciousness—or at least what passed for consciousness at this hour.

What about birth control? Is she taking anything? Did she time this correctly? How are we going to introduce her kids to this new level of intensity in our relationship? Will going out in public together be okay? The baseball game went without a hitch and the kids nearly emptied my wallet by buying hotdogs and ice cream. Nobody really gave us a second look. How will I blend in with Gerry's friends? Well, these questions will need time to answer. I will ask them tomorrow when I call.

The ringing telephone woke him from a mildly interesting

dream that had him climbing a snow-covered mountain somewhere.

"Good morning, sleepy-head. I couldn't wait for you to call me."

"What time is it?"

"Just after ten. Did you stay up watching the moon after I left?"

"How did you know?"

"Well, after the kids were in bed, I went out and sat on the front porch and listened to neighborhood dramas being played out, one family disturbance at a time. Then, I went to the back and sat on the glider where it was quieter. I guessed that you would be doing something similar. Am I right?"

"Yes. Let me get a drink of juice and put the coffee on. Be right back."

They paused the conversation momentarily, then he returned.

"So, yes, I thought about a few things," he said. "Do I need to buy protection for our more intimate moments? You never know when the mood will hit us, right?"

"Not to worry. After Benny was born, I had my tubes tied. Lester and I decided that two were enough because he didn't want to deprive his children of anything by having too many of them. Practical man, Lester. So, we're good to go with the non-pregnancy part. I'm guessing you don't mind that situation right now."

"Correct. Easy answer. Okay."

As if she was reading from his to-do list, she said, "I've been trying to figure a way to introduce the kids to our new status. We *have* changed our status, haven't we?"

"Oh, most definitely. We should now be considered a loving couple," he said, barely comprehending the words coming from his own mouth.

"So, do we sit them down and tell them what's happening? They probably know from looking at how we look and talk to each other that something's up."

"They do. They've asked me pointed questions a few times. I've given them straight answers, so it won't be a thunderbolt to them when they see you walk out of my bedroom some morning."

"I'll remember to wear shorts."

That brought a laugh.

"Yes, you will!"

"Do you have concerns about us being a mixed-race couple in public?" he asked.

"I honestly don't know. I've never been out in public as the consort of a white man before – at least not outside this neighborhood? What do you think will happen?"

"Well, I expect a lot of stares. If my ex-golfing buddies were any indicator, it will be something like thirty percent who won't care or will admire our courage, fifty percent who will disapprove but not say anything, and twenty percent who will go out of their way to be absolute jerks. Sorry. That's the engineer/scientist speaking. It's always the twenty percent that tend to screw everything up."

"Are you concerned about those twenty percent?"

"No, Gerry. I'm not. It's *their* problem, not mine. They wouldn't be worth our time irrespective of our comparative skin color. That guy I decked—Lonny—was one of those twenty percent. We won't have anything to do with them, no matter what.

"Did I mention that my couch opens up into a single bed? The other chair tilts back all the way and is very comfortable. I've fallen asleep in it more than once. Perhaps the kids would like to visit my place sometime too."

"Perhaps. But let's not get too far ahead of ourselves.

Understand, Bill, that I have feelings for you that I've really never had before. I was so young when I married Lester. This is different in just about every way. You've shown me only that you have a true heart and are not a player – somebody who works the clubs and the women. You are a gentle soul, but you have a fire too. That episode in the insurance office sold me on your dedication to doing the right thing. I feel I can trust you. I have children yet to raise and I simply can't afford to screw up with bad relationships. That's one of the reasons I've stayed out of any social scene. The children are critically important to my happiness. That said, Alice's attachment to you and Benny's grudging acceptance means almost as much to what I expect in our relationship as the time you and I spend together.

"Sorry for the speech, but I felt it was the right time for it."

"No worries. It was a good speech. To be even more honest, I've never had anyone analyze so much with me since my mother started coaching me about how to act around girls. Of course, my golf teachers were pretty analytical too, but that was different."

That brought a laugh.

"I hope so. So, what did your mother tell you about girls?"

"Well, the first thing she told me was to always be honest. Girls know when a guy is bullshitting them. She used a different word. She said that pretty girls were especially sensitive, because guys would say and do anything to gain favor. So, sincerity was job number one. What I found out, though, was that all too often girls didn't believe the sincerity because so many guys faked it. I decided that faking it was harder than just being honest the first time around. Maybe I was just too lazy to try remembering all the lies. If the girls didn't like that, too bad. I had golf balls to hit or weights to lift. Of course, I was a teenager, so..."

"Yes, my dear Bill. Your sincerity is your most endearing quality. I also think you're funny and when you make me laugh, it's very disarming.

"Did your sincerity help you when you went to college? Did you make friends there easily?"

"Well, not really. I had little spending money and I hung around the gym and golf course a lot. The girls were beautiful but didn't seem to be too interested in me for whatever reasons. I had a few dates, but the girls I was interested in were too popular and seemed to be looking for the best husband material. That often translates into how much money they thought the boys had. Add to that, I studied a lot. I'm not brilliant, so I had to grind out my grades all the time.

"So, speaking honestly, I now look at myself—in this moment—and say, 'Well, pal, here you are, forty years old, falling in love for perhaps the first time, and the woman is NOTHING like any other you'd ever known, dated or just chatted up. What are you gonna do with that?'"

Gerry laughed. "I laughed because I have had my version of that self-talk too. So, yes, Bill. I think I'm falling in love with you too. The sex was inevitable, but it's way more than that. We must take the necessary time together we need. We will have to incorporate the children. I insist. If you're going to be a big part of my life, they have to be involved too. Do you have any problem with that?"

"Not at all. I love Alice already. Her intelligence, drive and sweetness won my heart even before I got to know you. Benny is still a work in progress, but we both love baseball. I'll take him to some Indians' games before the season ends, and we'll see what comes from that.

"Gosh, Gerry. This all sounds so reasonable and calculated."

"Indeed. And, my dear, at our ages and stages of life, we

should be compelled to do the calculations. There is so much more at stake, and time is not on our side."

Chapter 20

The Foursome

After that 'sort of' commitment conversation, Bill's life became very busy. During most days he was helping Alice groom her game for the Labor Day city amateur tournament at Sleepy Hollow. They played there every chance they could and built a pretty good 'book' on the course and how the greens rolled. Alice registered her scores, of course, so she could obtain a handicap. She soon zipped past double digits and was carrying a "6" handicap when they stopped playing together and worked solely on her short game. That's where the scoring happened, and Alice was diligent and often chipped and putted until dark.

It was too bad that Glennville High School didn't have any sort of golf team. Her taste for competition would have to come in the summer and fall leagues Bill could get her into. They decided that the goal was to build her reputation and lower her handicap so that some college or university would take her on either as a scholarship athlete or at least because she was good enough to make the team. But that was a year away, so there was time for her to get stronger. There was nothing Bill didn't like about her swing, her attitude and her work ethic. The tricky part was seeing how well she held up under pressure from competition.

Because she would be the only non-white girl in the tournament, Alice would get more scrutiny than most and would have to deal with the snide remarks, the rude distractions, the shunning in the clubhouses, and all the rest of the racist bullshit.

Bill tried to prepare her for the coming storms by playacting with her, having heard everything she was about to hear. He created non-verbal distractions just as she was about to take her swing, or stroke a putt. He kept poking until she would get really pissed off, start to cry, or both.

He would then hold her and soothe her until the pain and the anger passed. He did this routine once in front of her mother and brother, who came out to watch her practice one evening. As Bill held Alice and rocked her back and forth, Gerry, hands to her mouth, with tears streaming down her face, choked back sobs of her own. Benny just couldn't believe the scene.

"Bill, is she really gonna hear that shit?"

"Yes. Sorry to say... But you know what? Your sister is one very strong and willful young woman. She's going to be just fine. Do you understand what I'm doing here?"

"Yeah. But, man! When she goes and plays in tournaments and stuff, are you gonna caddy for her?

"Yes. For the first few times, I will caddy and be her go-to guy. My presence, I think, will keep the bad stuff to a minimum. There will be times when I can't be there for her. She's going to have to learn to be like Jackie Robinson was. She's going to have to take it, while not letting it affect her game. She's going to whip a lot of the white kids and adults, I expect, and they're not going to be happy about it. Just look at how she focuses. She just bawled her eyes out five minutes ago and there she is, back to running in putts. I will tell her later, but I'll tell you two now, I really love this girl. She's gonna be a star at everything. Golf is just going to be her ladder to greatness."

Benny just nodded and said he thought so too. Gerry fell into Bill's arms and thanked him for helping her pride and joy become a woman.

"My heart aches with love for what you do with and for us."

While they clung to each other, Bill said into her ear, "I love you too. For me, it's bonus time. I get to love three of you instead of just one of you. But the one I'm now holding is a pretty good thing." He squeezed her even closer. Benny turned and looked at Alice so they wouldn't see his emotions.

The dreaded New York Yankees were in town for a weekend series, so Bill took Benny to both the Friday night and Saturday night games. The teams split the two games, and they cheered, ate bad food, and cheered some more. Benny was clearly having a good time at the ballpark.

"Man, I never had seats this good before. Are they expensive? Do they cost more than the ones we sat in last time?"

"Well, I know people here, Benny. I've been a season ticket holder for over five years. To your question, yes, these seats are more expensive, but not by much. I get a season ticket holder rate. Besides. I don't care about that. I'm just happy to be bringing you to the games. Seeing it in person sure beats the hell out of TV, don't you think?"

"Oh yeah. I think it's the sounds that don't come through on TV. We're so close I can hear the players talking to each other. That's really cool. The best part was when you took us all to a game that first time, and I walked up and out of the tunnel to see the whole green field in front of me and the grandstands surrounding the field. Man, it was like going to church. *The Church of Baseball*."

"Benny, I think you've said it all. The *Church of Baseball*... I'm going to remember that. It might be something to use in a book or a movie someday."

It seemed like a most natural occurrence when Bill spent his first night at Gerry's house. He and Gerry had a little conference where they informed the kids that they were getting serious about each other and that their love was growing every day. They felt they had to tell them that the relationship couldn't be complete without the children being part of it. Bill made the point about his feelings for the kids. When he told them that he loved them, Alice leaped into his arms, nearly knocking the couch over.

Benny was more reserved, but he hugged Bill too.

"Bill," Benny said, "I don't see you as a white guy anymore. It's really hard for me to say it, but I trust you. Momma seems to trust you too. After watching what you're doing with Alice, I'm convinced that you do love us. I'm glad beyond words that you're treating Momma so well. I can say these things in proper English because she's my English teacher all day, every day."

That brought a faux scowl from Gerry and a laugh from Alice and Bill.

"Well, Benny, I'm glad you've come to that conclusion about me. I don't think I could have made a commitment to your mother if you had not allowed me in. What none of us need, it seems, is friction. If everything proceeds as I expect it will, we will have a lot of years to enjoy many, many things. You just never know what's around the next dogleg."

"Very funny, Bill," Alice said. Then she changed the subject. "Look at the callouses I'm getting from hitting all those golf balls." That caused everyone to crack up.

"Don't worry, my dear Alice," Bill said. "Nobody will mistake you for a lumberjack. By the way, how much weight are you bench-pressing these days?"

That statement was greeted with blank stares. "Oh, didn't I tell you? Let's go see what surprises there are in the garage."

Bill had bought a full set of weights complete with a bench and bar rack. He'd set it up with Gerry's help and they giggled like kids themselves while guessing what Alice and Benny would say when they first saw the set.

Alice was, for once, at a loss for words. Benny, however, jumped on the bench and started pressing up the hundred pounds that were on the bar.

"Bill, what do I do with this?" Alice asked in a shocked tone.

"Well, do you see the instruction chart on the wall? I think we're all going to benefit from staying strong and in shape. But you, young lady, are going to put on some muscle so you can hit your golf shots with more authority than ever before. You want to feel as strong on eighteen as you did on one. You have natural strength, of course, but more power in your legs, especially, will enhance every shot you make. Don't worry. You will still look very much like a girl. We won't be training for any body-builder competitions, just golf championships. Are you willing?"

"Oh, sure. But how do I do that?"

"Well, I drew up this training schedule beginning with weights I think you can handle. Then, we'll add weights and exercises as you get stronger."

Gerry went back into the house to make them all a nice dinner while Bill demonstrated to Alice and Benny the different exercises, how to change the weights, how to warm up first and what muscle groups each regimen strengthened.

After an hour of this, they were all pretty sweaty.

"We'd better go get cleaned up. I'm sure your mom doesn't want any smelly body-builders at her table."

The kids thanked Bill and ran inside. As per the house rules, Alice showered first, then Benny, then Bill. There was just enough hot water left for him to hurry through a three-minute cleansing.

It was pasta and marinara sauce tonight, and everyone ate heartily. Gerry kept catching Bill's eye and smiling. The feeling of love around the table made him tremble. He knew there would be rocky times ahead, but he was now determined to overcome them all. He accepted that he was absolutely in love with this dark beauty and her wonderful children. These three people were now embedded in his heart, and he yearned to be with them all the time.

Chapter 21
Alice's First Test

Alice had lifted weights for almost three weeks before the junior women's championship was to be played at Sleepy Hollow. Bill was careful to make sure she stretched before and after her weight training and golf practices. Flexibility and suppleness were as important as strength for playing good and consistent golf. In just this short time, her driving distance increased by almost ten yards, so she had to re-calibrate the 'book' for her approach shot distances, as those distances changed too. They also spent more quality time with the short game to supplement her increased strength. Bill surmised that she was as ready for the Labor Day two-round championship as she could be.

Alice was up and about at the crack of dawn that Saturday morning. She emulated a drop of water zipping around a hot skillet. Bill rose and dressed. He and Alice took a short walk to burn off the nervous energy.

"It's good to see you keyed up, Alice, but we've got to burn off some of your nervousness. Butterflies are good, but you have to fly them in formation so they don't jangle your nerves.

We'll warm up as always. I will be with you all the way. The first tee will be the hardest. I've seen guys not able to take the club back, they were so nervous. You'll not have that problem, will you?"

"No, Bill. I wish I could tee off right now."

"I'll bet you could, but our tee time isn't until 11:30. It's just 7:30 now, so let's not get worn out. Let's go in and I'll cook you a nice breakfast. We'll take some snack bars and a banana along for when you need something in your stomach. When you're hungry on the golf course, you can lose your rhythm."

"Yeah, I remember that from practice. How about eggs and pancakes?"

They headed back indoors and Bill proceeded to prepare breakfast for everyone. Gerry and Benny were up, dressed and looked almost as excited as Alice.

"Take it easy, folks. Relax. Eat slowly. We'll even take a rest after eating to let the breakfast digest a little. None of us, least of all our champion-in-waiting, can afford to have a lump in their stomachs."

Gerry and Bill cleaned up and did the dishes. They packed snacks and lunches for everyone and put them in a rucksack that Benny would carry around for them. Alice gathered her snacks and juice bottle to put in her golf bag.

"Alice, bring your sticks out to the garage. Let's make sure they're clean. We probably should clean the skin oil off the grips from practice."

Bill, often fancying himself as the king of surprises, opened the garage door and let the sun shine on a brand new, all-leather golf bag with a wide, comfortable carrying strap. Alice's eyes almost exploded out of her head.

"Wow! This for me?"

"Yes. I thought a new golf bag would be appropriate for you and me, now that I'm your caddy."

"It's beautiful. The colors match my shoes too. Has Mom seen it?"

"Yes. She helped me pick it out. She chose the color scheme. Your mother is one creative lady."

"I gotta transfer all my stuff into the new bag. You have to watch so you know where everything goes. Oh, I see you already loaded a dozen new Titleists."

"Of course. A new bag should always come with golf balls."

After Alice finished loading the new bag, Bill went inside to hug Gerry. "She loves it. The color scheme is perfect."

When Alice came back inside, Bill told her to lie down for the half hour they had left before they had to leave for the golf course. Gerry and Bill snuggled on the couch, not talking or watching anything on TV. Benny went to his room.

"Well, my dear, it's about time to launch our girl into her first competition. Be sure to bring your sun hat. It looks like it's going to be a warm one, Bill said."

The drive to the course was silent. No radio. No chatter. Bill glanced at Alice in the mirror and saw that she was just looking out of the side window. Benny was looking out the other side. Gerry, sensing the moment, kept quiet too. They arrived at the golf course and Alice went right to the trunk. Gerry and Benny went off to sit on the clubhouse patio. They would wait until Alice's threesome was called to the tee before joining her group outside the ropes on the first hole.

Alice put on her new ankle socks, snugged them up and slipped her feet into her now well broken in shoes. She'd replaced the cleats she'd worn down, so she was now walking on a new set of "nails".

"You have to check in first, then we go to the range. I'll stand to the side to make sure there are no glitches with you signing in."

The nice lady at the sign-in desk smiled at Alice, found her name on the tee time roster, and handed her a scorecard with her name and her two playing partners' names.

"Your tee time is 11:30, honey. Get to the tee a few minutes early and tell the starter you're there. Show him the scorecard. Good luck."

Bill hefted the bag and headed for the practice range. Alice caught up with him. The range balls were free today. She stretched and started hitting some smooth wedges to get into rhythm. She hit everything on the nose. At 11:10, she hit a few chips on the practice area, then went to the putting green. They'd mowed everything that morning and the green was faster than the last time she played.

"I think you should shorten your backstroke on the putter until you get a feel for the green speed today."

"Okay." That was the first word she'd spoken to him since they left the house. It looked like she was finding her focus. Bill said no more.

The two girls with whom Alice was paired greeted her with curious stares. At 5′10″ or so, Alice was a good head taller than either of them. To Bill's eyes, her playing partners looked ever so much like country club kids. He could see bejeweled people outside the ropes alongside the first tee.

Gerry and Benny eased up into the small gallery as the starter announced the players. Alice drew the third honor. The first girl hit her opening drive right down the middle of the 370-yard opening hole. The second girl hit her drive to the right, where it ended up in deep rough. Alice went through her pre-shot routine.

One practice swing. Line up the shot. Take the stance. Waggle. Swing.

She laced her drive right down the middle. It landed about even with the first girl's ball and kept rolling for another twenty or thirty yards. Gerry and Benny applauded. The other members of the gallery just turned and looked at them. Alice handed Bill her driver, and he followed her down the fairway.

That's a great start, he thought. *Let's see if she can hold her focus.*

The girl whose drive was in the rough managed to gouge her ball back onto the fairway, but she was still a full wedge away from the green. The other girl hit a nice, crisp, 4-wood that rolled up onto the green. Good shot! Alice only had a seven iron to the middle of the green. Bill handed her the eight. She looked at him with a question on her face.

"You're a little pumped up right now. Just flush the eight. You'll be fine."

She did flush the 8-iron and it stopped four feet from the hole. She turned and smiled at Bill for the first time since breakfast. "Good choice, caddy."

That broke the ice and landed all the butterflies. She rolled in the 4-footer for birdie, but that was the last one of the day until the last hole. The putts just wouldn't fall. She was hitting every shot solidly, and hit thirteen of the first seventeen greens in regulation, but couldn't make any putts longer than five feet. The two girls in her group also struggled with their putters. That finally affected their games on the back nine.

As the group approached the 18th tee, a finishing par five, Alice still had the teeing honors. She was five over par at this point. She looked at Bill as he handed her the driver. She smiled a small smile, sighed and teed it up. She pounded her longest drive of the day, maybe 260 yards down the center line. The other two girls were in bad shape, mentally. For almost the entire back nine holes, their cheeks were flushed. They threw clubs. They cursed. Their caddies had the good sense to stay out of the way. The two boys would look at Bill after an outburst and just roll their eyes. One girl hit a respectable drive on this last hole and just shook her head and shrugged. The other girl topped her drive which barely made it to the fairway.

When they finally got to Alice's ball, Bill handed her the 3-wood. "Smooth swing. Don't try to overpower it. Aim between the two bunkers in front of the green."

Her "smooth" swing caused the very center of the club face to make contact with the center point of the golf ball and sent it flying toward the spot she'd aimed for. The ball bounced once, twice and rolled up onto the green. Bill could see Gerry out of the corner of his eye, clapping and jumping up and down.

Alice handed him back the 3-wood and winked. She *winked*!! No, no. No winking. He handed her the putter and said, "You winked at me. Wink at me when you roll the putt in for eagle. You aren't done yet. We still get to do this again tomorrow."

She missed the putt, but made the birdie for a very nice 76. They shook hands with the other girls, who had the courtesy to follow protocol and shake Bill's hand too.

One girl said to Alice loud enough for everyone to hear, "You played great, Alice. We don't see any colored girls playing golf. Where'd you learn to hit it like that?"

Alice thanked her and shot her thumb at Bill. "He's my mother's boyfriend and a really good golfer. He taught me how to play. He's a good coach too."

The girl was at a loss for words. She looked at Bill, then over to the side of the green, then back at Bill. She smiled at Alice and said, "Your mom is very pretty. I can see where you get your looks. Good luck tomorrow." And she was gone into the arms of the bejeweled escorts.

"Well, my girl, that was a pretty good first day. How do you feel?" Bill asked as they walked toward her mother.

"I'm exhausted. I gotta turn in the card. Hey Mary! You gotta sign the card."

"Yeah. I'll meet you at the scoring table."

With the scorecard signed, the four happy souls walked back to the Cadillac.

Along the way, one of the men who was in the gallery following Alice's group stopped Bill. "You know we can't let nigger girls win these tournaments, don't you? Next thing you know, their fathers and brothers'll all be out here hustling our women. What the fuck is wrong with you? I see you here tomorrow, there's gonna be trouble."

"I don't know who you are, but the trouble is going to be on you," Bill responded while grabbing the guy by the shirt and standing him up on his toes. "You fuck with me or mine, hotshot, and I will beat you purple from head to toe. You got that?! Then you can tell all your country club people about the bus that hit you."

Bill pushed him away. He just glared at Bill and walked away, straightening his shirt. Bill picked up the golf bag and they continued their walk to the car.

Benny said, "Bill, I thought you were gonna break his face."

"It took a lot of energy not to, Benny. Gerry, why don't you drive us home, I'm going to be cooking off some adrenaline for a while."

Alice wrapped her arms around Bill's waist. "You were right, Bill, those kinds of people just don't like us. He's probably mad because I whipped his little girl."

"Yeah. Probably. I'm guessing that he's a country club sort, and it's whites only in those places. That kind of snobbery is the main reason I never wanted to join a private club. I've been to a few and the only brown faces I saw were waiters and janitors. They just fear that their white—maybe privilege is the word I'm after—will be usurped. Well, forgive my language, but fuck them and their 'whites only' backwardness." Alice squeezed him tighter. Gerry raised an eyebrow. They drove home in silence.

"I'm sorry I used bad words around your daughter, my love. I was pretty worked up. If that asshole would have said another word, I would have decked him."

"I understand. But you've been such a gentleman around us. Hearing you curse was a shock. Benny said he just got more respect for you. That guy's ridiculous confrontation is why we should always try to make lemonade out of the lemons."

"Maybe, but lemonade will never taste the same. Pour me a stiff scotch when we get home, will you?" Gerry laughed.

On the second day, Alice started making putts. Her ball striking was a little off, but she saved par several times by making good, tough putts. She carded another 76. With her six handicap, that put her at four under par, net. The winning girl, a seventeen-year-old beauty from Shaker Heights Country Club, won the net trophy with a six-under. Another athletic young lady from Canterbury Country Club won the gross trophy with one over par. Alice received a certificate at the awards ceremony for finishing third in net and fifth in gross.

The "gentleman" they'd met yesterday was nowhere to be seen. Neither was his daughter. Bill could only imagine the joyride and fun evening they had. Even though Alice's second-day playing partners didn't play as well as Alice, they soon got into the proper golf etiquette mode and showed Alice the respect they would any other player. Maybe there was hope for the younger generations in dumping their parents' closet of prejudices and bigotry. Time would tell.

Bill treated Alice, Gerry and Benny to a nice dinner at a

restaurant that used cloth napkins. Alice ordered the biggest banana split Bill had ever seen. There were lots of laughs in the group that night. Sweet Alice was the toast of the very happy little group of four.

Chapter 22

Back to School

Gerry and Bill began splitting time between residences. She brought Alice and Benny along to the 12th-floor apartment a couple times and the kids said how much they enjoyed the view. School started for them, Gerry and Bill on the Tuesday after the tournament. Bill had completed his classroom management class, earning his first 'A' in almost twenty years.

For Alice, school was sort of an anti-climax after all the excitement surrounding her first excursion into competitive golf.

Bill came to feel that it was his job to keep things in perspective for her. She didn't win the golf tournament, but she played through some nervousness and learned more about herself and her ability to cope with stress. He reminded her that for her first time in a competition, she did spectacularly well. She did what few could do: block out distractions and keep one's head in the game.

After the first week of school, she told Bill that the focus and concentration she was learning from golf helped her with her trigonometry and physics classes. Of course, he was there to help her with all the math and science, much to the infinite gratitude of her mother. With each passing day, the four of them seemed to be growing together as a family.

Bill's classes at CSU went well, but compared to hard science, they were pretty soft things with lots of opinions distilled from class discussions. Learning about the so-called disadvantaged kids they would see as teachers was all new to him, and he took it to heart that he would work with those kids as best he could. The trips to observe real classes taught by real teachers were eye-openers too. He saw various classroom management techniques and took copious notes from each of them. When he got home from school every day, he'd type up his class notes while they were still fresh. His old typewriter got a good workout for the first time in a decade. Erasable bond typewriter paper became his newest best friend. Gerry teased him about wanting to buy him correction fluid in a 55-gallon drum.

"Very funny. I'm getting better all the time. You'd have loved my typing teacher in high school. She made wise-guy comments like that all the time."

Gerry had her usual collection of English classes, and coached the mock trial team at her school. She told Bill that the students' language skills were considerably below grade level.

"It is very challenging for me to improve those skills in preparation for the rest of their lives. Most of their home environments simply don't lend themselves to quiet time for study or anything else. Their working vocabulary is probably not much more than twenty-five hundred words. By comparison, you and I, with college degrees, have working vocabularies of around ten thousand words. If we had advanced degrees, the gap would be wider. You see my point?

"The other thing I would suggest when you start teaching science, is to incorporate vocabulary and language components into each lesson. So many of these inner-city kids—and, I expect, to a lesser degree, the suburban kids—don't even know that they're smart. Everything they hear and see on TV that isn't trying to sell them sugar-laced food is presented at around an eighth-grade level. The programs that go beyond that exceed their awareness and skills of understanding.

"How can a Glennville kid think about law school if he can't read a tenth-grade textbook when he or she is a senior? I would never tell them that, of course. I just push them to read more and improve their skills. Writing perfect grammar may be tedious for those kids who'd rather be bouncing a ball, but if they don't get it here and now, when will they get it?

"Sorry for bending your ear, but you should be aware of what is coming down your road. You'll probably end up in a school that has predominantly white kids, but if you're not teaching in the heights, you're going to see kids from blue-collar households similar to the one you grew up in. Not all of them are going to have parents who would have a conversation like this with them. My kids hear this from me all the time."

"This is the best lesson I've received in teacher education, my dear. I'm lucky to have you filling my head with this realism and my heart with your love."

She rolled her big, brown eyes and groaned at the corniness of his comment. "Boy, you sure know how to make a girl feel romanced. Please try to upgrade your phraseology to make me feel like I'm living in the twentieth century, or at least in the second half of it."

"I'm working on it. When I sit on the balcony, I take stock of what's going on, and you have been directly or indirectly responsible for the most significant changes in my life. Going back to school to get a teaching license... Teaching your daughter to be a champion golfer... Falling in love... It's been quite a ride.

"Now, I have to get back to my typewriter while I'm still somewhat fresh. Thank you for a lovely dinner. It's my turn to cook next time. Let me say goodbye to the kids."

The kids bade him farewell from their respective rooms. Bill kissed Gerry, hugged her, and drove home with the usual feelings of joy that he always felt when being with her. He had come such a long, long way in such a short time. He felt his head spin when he thought about it.

Oh, Right. I have to start querying colleges about women's golf teams. I'll go to the big library downtown tomorrow after my audio-visual class and look at college catalogs. That should get me started on that task.

Bill discovered that Ohio State had a women's team, as did the mostly black-student college, Wilberforce in Xenia, Ohio, near Dayton. By perusing different colleges and universities, he also discovered that San Diego State University had an excellent reputation for women's golf. The city also had youth golf programs that provided abundant learning and playing opportunities for boys and girls. Part of the city's promotion included mentioning that it was the golf mecca of the western United States, with more golf courses per capita than any other city its size.

Many of the kids who participated in San Diego Junior Golf went to college teams, and a few even made it to the pro tours. The famous LPGA golfer, Micky Wright, was from San Diego. As were Billy Casper and Gene Littler, two PGA champion golfers. From this information, Bill took it upon himself to solicit application packages for these three schools as well as potential scholarship information.

There was also the women's club championship at Highland Park during the first week of October, and he wanted to get Alice entered in that. He stopped at that golf course after visiting the library, and got the particulars for the women's club there and how to apply and register for the championship. Alice would turn 17 the week before the championship. He didn't know if there was an age requirement, but one phone call to the club membership chairwoman solved that problem:

"No. We only have twenty-six members, and three of them will be out of town for the championship. What's your girl's handicap?"

Bill told the very nice lady that Alice had a "6" before shooting 152 at Sleepy Hollow.

"Oh, well, she'll be in the top flight with that handicap. Please send in a copy of her handicap records along with the membership check, and we'll get a package to her right away. Thank you, Mr. Bannock. Say, haven't I heard of you?"

"Maybe. Alice and I play together at Highland Park quite a bit these days. I used to play there all the time in high school."

"Oh, sure. Well, I've been around here for a long time, so I probably know half the golfers who play here by their first names. We look forward to meeting Alice. Talk with you soon."

It started to feel like Bill was learning to be a parent. His first thoughts on anything always seemed to include something about Gerry, Alice or Benny. He'd been reluctant to have any serious talks with Benny but could feel that day approaching. The baseball games were just guy stuff, but afterward, when he thought about their interactions, it had echoes of times he'd spent with his own dad.

But before he could make plans for a future with his "family", he had to get a teaching license and job goals achieved so he could become a golf coach and science teacher – not necessarily in that order.

Chapter 23

Love All Day Long

"Bill, I really love playing golf with you. I learn so much and it's really cool to see the wildlife and the birds too. You're gonna be a great science teacher... And not a bad golf coach either."

Alice Morgan smiled that certain smile that defined real joy and happiness. It became increasingly impossible for Bill Bannock to not fall over the cliff for the things he loved: golf, Gerry, and Alice herself. The order didn't matter. Benny was still a work in progress, but they WERE making progress. Bill's everyday routine after he woke up, began with going to class. He met Alice for golf practice when the weather cooperated, returned home, or stayed at Gerry's and helped make dinner.

Now that school was in full swing, it was harder for Gerry to give as much attention to Bill and the kids. She had lessons to write, papers to grade and parent contacts to conduct. The ten or fifteen minutes she and Bill talked on the phone, or after dinner, give them both a break from the chores and job duties.

Bill asked to start student teaching in January. He would thus become as busy as Gerry after the new year turned, so he relished each time they were together.

They spent weekends together, of course. The lovemaking was sweet and often languid as they both hated rushing those exquisite moments of bliss. They often lay in each other's arms afterward with a sheen of perspiration that helped them decide to save water by showering together. Bill appreciated Gerry's true beauty and sweetness more each day. His heart ached for her all day long.

As he thought more about this newest chapter in his life, Bill compared it to the previous ones.

If destiny is a thing, I was destined to not have close friends from the "bubble" of absolute whiteness. After meeting Alice and getting to know her and her mother, much of that stuff that is exclusive to white society no longer fits with my personal likes. It's not that I hate white people. That would make me a bigot too. It's just having a clearer vision of how society has fractured into racial camps. Gerry and I talked about white guilt, and I told her that I had to fight it off often. She just patted me, kissed my anxiety away, and told me that I have become race-neutral.

This comment kicked off a necessary pillow-talk episode.

"What? I'm still white. How can I be race-neutral?"

"Now, don't take it so literally. Of course, your skin is white, but your mind and heart are neutral. You don't see us as black anymore, do you? You don't see yourself as black either, right?"

"No. I told you that before. You are Gerry, and I love you all day long. The superficial stuff just doesn't make it into my frontal lobes anymore. That day I decked Lonny was the major turning point, I think."

"It was for me too. It was then I knew you would fight for me... And for us: you, me AND the kids. That's when I knew I would pursue this relationship for what it was worth. So far, it's turned out pretty well, don't you think? Don't we say 'I love you' at least once a day? That's a good sign ... unless you don't mean it."

"Don't be silly. Of course, I mean it. I think I only told Linda that once, when I asked her to marry me. We know how that turned out.

"Anyway, here I am, in your arms, feeling your body next to mine, enjoying the closeness, the smell of you – all of you."

"Have you ever felt discriminated against for just being white or something?"

"Yes. There was this one time after my freshman year at OU. My mother always accompanied dad to the junior league baseball games, where he coached a team. Anyway, the sponsor for my dad's team was a clothier in our end of the county. His wife also came to some of the games. She and my mom got to be friends from these little encounters.

"Well, one day they plotted to be matchmakers for their daughter and me. Their family name was Goldman. So, they had us kids talk to each other on the telephone as a favor to our mothers, and we got along wonderfully. Naomi was smart, witty, sweet and, as I soon discovered, drop-dead beautiful. Of course, me being the handsome stud that I was, she was attracted to me also. We had a couple of dates and it was infatuation of the first degree.

"Then, shortly before I was due to back to OU – she was attending Denison College – I received this tearful phone call from Naomi. Through her tears and sobs, she told me that her traditionally Jewish father had heard about our dating and infatuation and told her, in no uncertain terms, to break it off.

"I asked why. She said that it was against the Jewish tradition for her to marry a non-Jew. End of story. Dad's word was the final decision. Silly me... I suggested we run away and elope. In the end, neither of us had the courage to actually do that, so that was the end of Naomi Goldman and me. I was a 'victim' of religious bigotry, I guess. That little hurtful episode stuck with me.

"A few years later I learned that Naomi had married a man who abused her terribly, beating her and running around with other women. It broke my heart all over again. So much for arranged marriages."

"That's just awful. Racial, religious or ethnic taboos are so primitive. It's like there are still tribes out there run by shamans and witch doctors. I'm so glad we—you and I—have passed by that nonsense."

"Me too. I've never been so comfortable with someone, man or woman, as I am with you. I couldn't imagine it being any better. I just enjoy being around you, chatting about things. I guess this is what my idealism was always meant to be.

"Now, we have my career to get rolling and Alice's game to shape up for the club tournament in two weeks. I've also discovered some women's golf teams in a few colleges. Ohio State's, of course, but also the predominantly black college, Wilberforce, down in Xenia near Cincinnati. From what I could glean, San Diego State's women's golf team has a tradition of having nationally competitive teams. Nice weather too."

"Wow. You've indeed been doing some due diligence! I'll ask around and see if anybody at school knows more about Wilberforce and its academic quality. Now, let's take a shower and get some sleep."

Chapter 24

Winning is Fun

October first dawned clear and cool. It was a Wednesday and Highland Park had reserved eight tee times for the women's club championship for both Wednesday and Thursday. The first group off was scheduled at eight o'clock. Alice would be in the second-to-last threesome, teeing off at nine o'clock. For some reason, Alice seemed very calm, without the usual chatter at breakfast. Gerry and Benny talked with Bill while Alice kept her head down and ate her scrambled eggs and slice of ham.

Bill and Alice were on the road at seven-thirty and, enduring morning traffic, got to the golf course just before eight. They hustled over to the range. Gerry and Benny had to go to school, so it was just the two of them today. After a few swings with the wedge and some well-struck 6-irons, Alice looked up and smiled for the first time.

"I feel really good, Bill. Let me hit a few more balls then chip and putt. How does the swing look?"

"You look very much in the groove and your ball flight says your pinching it against the ground perfectly. Hit a couple drives and let's chip and putt."

Her drives were a thing of beauty. Those old Staffs still had a few good shots left in them, and Alice was wringing out their last, best performance. Those vintage clubs were top of the line in their day, but newer materials and designs were helping everyday golfers play better. Bill smiled at his covert plans to buy his young charge a brand-new set of more modern designs of woods and irons - designs used by the professionals - for her belated birthday present. Gerry was, of course, sworn to secrecy. But this was now, and they had some serious golf to play. The Staffs would get one more shot at glory.

The players were scheduled to play from the men's gold tees which gave them a 5,420-yard venture through hill and dale. The first autumn colors were kissing the tops of the trees with their splendor. For a public course that received more playing rounds than any other in the city, it was in pretty good shape this late in the season. From what Bill could tell, the fairways were patchy but playable. The bent grass greens looked to be in very good shape. He left Alice to stroke some putts and carried her bag over to the first tee.

Number one was that 353-yard beauty that required a positioned drive. Just as he did when Alice was caddying for him, she hit her 4-wood into the correct position. This allowed the two other women in the group to comment, "Good shot."

Mabel Grossman and Harriet Foss were Alice's playing partners. They both had single-digit handicaps, looked to be in their early 40s or late 30s, and carried their own bags. All three women hit the first green and two-putted for pars. Then, it got interesting.

The next three holes were short par 4s, and Alice needed only wedges to the greens. On the fourth hole, her approach shot bounced once, hit the flagstick and dropped right next to the hole for a tap-in birdie. Then, she birdied the 432-yard par

5 fifth hole by rolling in a 20-footer. Mabel and Harriet started exchanging looks. Alice remained focused and seldom looked at Bill. She just held out her hand and he placed the correct club in it. Bill saw that she was on fire. The trick was to make it last through tomorrow.

A bad-bounce bogey on the long par-3 seventh hole set her back a little, but she recovered on number eight with a great second shot out of a fairway bunker. Her two-putt par had her playing partners openly complimenting Alice's game and poise. The five she took at nine was disappointing as her 8-iron took a big bounce to the back of the green. Alice missed the 4-footer coming back for a 3-putt bogey. Even par for the first nine seemed like a winning score to Bill.

The back nine was par 35 with only one par five and two par threes. Alice's putter cooled off some with another three-putt bogey on the massive green at 16. She finished the first round with a very strong, two-over-par 73, putting her into first place, gross. They didn't stay for lunch but went straight to Jackie's for her burger special. Finally, Alice came down to earth and started reviewing her round with Bill.

"That's my lowest score ever, Bill, and it felt like I left something out there."

"I agree. If you hadn't jerked those two putts, you'd be sitting at even for the round. Are you gonna be able to keep it going tomorrow?"

"I don't know, but I'm gonna go home, shower, do some homework and take a nap. You'll wake me for dinner, won't you? I want to tell Momma and Benny about our day. What's our tee time tomorrow, caddy?"

"We tee off in the last group. They reshuffled the groups as they do for TV golf tournaments, so you'll be playing with two different people. To be precise, we tee off at nine-fifteen."

Jackie stopped by their table to ask what all the excitement was about. "Shouldn't you be in school, Alice?"

"I'm playing in a golf championship at Highland Park. I'm in first place after the first round. My caddy here is doing a good job too."

They all chuckled at that.

"I'd better be, or she would fire me. How would that look to her mother?"

More laughs.

"Well, Alice, I wish you the best tomorrow," Jackie said. "I know luck isn't supposed to be in the conversation, so just hit 'em straight."

"Thanks, Jackie, I will do my best. If I win, the whole family will come here to celebrate, right Bill?"

"Absolutely. Now, let's get you home and off your feet."

They followed the same routine for Thursday and Alice once again seemed focused, but more relaxed. She actually spoke to Bill on the drive to the golf course. He watched her warm up, then head over to the pitching area. She was hitting everything pure. Alice seemed to have the green speed locked in, so if she was hitting it close on her approach shots, putts would fall.

And fall they did. Her new playing partners, Ruth Hammond and Esther Smith, stood and watched with more than a little awe as this tall, still somewhat lanky brown teenager drilled drives down the fairways, hit crisp approach shots and sank putts from everywhere. They tried to distract her with chatter, but Alice just smiled and teed it up again. Alice didn't have the honors on the first tee, but after her opening par to the other ladies' bogeys, she never relinquished teeing first for the rest of the way.

Bill worked hard at keeping his mouth shut and just focused on his job. He had to stifle cheers when she hit a great shot or made a tough putt. He also managed to somehow keep from jumping out of his shoes when she rattled a 5-iron off the flagstick on number seven. The ball bounced once before hitting the stick but had enough spin so that it just dropped down right next to the hole, nearly going in for her first ace.

To complete the *tour de force*, Alice birdied the short par-3 18th too. That gave her a spectacular 69, two under par. With her handicap, she ended up winning both gross and net championships. To say that the other women in the tournament were stunned would be an understatement. Her playing partners from the first day thumped her on the back and congratulated Alice on her spectacular play. That move broke the ice and the other players came by to shake her hand.

Ruth said, "You know, we had a teenage girl play in our club championship back in the 50s. She won too. That was me. That's my picture holding the trophy. Your on-course etiquette was perfect and your caddy is pretty cute too. I wish more colored kids would pick up the game. It is a healthy game that teaches so many other things than just hitting a golf ball. Whoever taught you the game should be proud beyond words."

"That would be my caddy, Bill Bannock. Bill, this lady thinks you're cute."

"Mr. Bannock, if you've been coaching and training this fine young lady, you've done a hell of a good job. It's a pleasure to meet you. I just thought you were a high school golf coach or something."

"Not yet Alice is my only student." She shook his hand and walked back to the chairs arrayed for the presentation ceremony.

"Well, my dear, go get your trophy and medal. You were just great both days. I'm so proud of you, I could bust. Well done. Well done." Bill hugged her tightly and she hugged him back. As he stepped back, he could see large globs of liquid streaking down her cheeks. Bill walked to the back of the room while the club president and her committee presented Alice with the trophy and the medal.

"You're the youngest champion our club has ever had in its forty-six years of being. You are four months younger than I was back in the day." That brought some chuckles and hoots. "Your scores are records for the championship too. Congratulations, Alice Morgan. You are our champion golfer of the year for the Highland Park Women's Club," said the club president, Carol Herbst.

Everyone stood and clapped while Alice produced a dazzling though lopsided smile while thanking the president and her playing partners.

"Say something to the club, Alice," president Herbst said.

"I don't know what to say. I've never done this before. I guess I should thank my friend, coach and caddy, Bill Bannock for teaching me so well. My playing partners were great to be with. Thank you for playing with me and for your grace during our rounds."

The women were somewhat non-plussed by this brown girl speaking so eloquently and with perfect diction. After she finished, they once again stood and gave her a nice round of applause. Bill was surprised to see a couple of the women ask Alice to sign their sun visors. He heard one of them say, "I know you're going to be famous someday, so this autograph will be a big deal in a few years, I'll bet. Thanks, Alice. Good luck. I'll be watching the papers for your name."

Alice had an armful of trophy as they walked to the parking lot. Bill put the bag in the trunk. Alice changed her shoes and put the trophy on the back seat. She then fell into his arms, sobbing.

Sorry, Bill. I held it together for as long as I could. It's like the pressure valve popped. Won't Momma be proud?"

"I have no doubt. So, champ... How's it feel? Isn't winning fun?"

Chapter 25

The Winter of Contentment

Alice jumped into the shower after they got home while Bill cleaned her clubs—for the last time—as just something to do. When she came out wearing her favorite pair of jeans and a Glennville sweatshirt, she was fizzing like a warm soda bottle with a loose cap.

"Sweetheart, I've gotta shower now," said Bill. "We'll talk you down when I get out."

He came out of the shower to find Alice looking for a place to put the trophy so that her mom would see it when she walked in. Since Gerry always came in the back door with Benny in tow, the trophy ended up on the breakfast table in the kitchen. Bill made some coffee and Alice drank a cola. They talked and talked about her two rounds.

"Alice, I've never seen anyone who's not in golf for a living that has your long-term focus. That takes a lot of energy and even more discipline. You are truly special. I want to point out, however, that golf can be a cruel game for those who expect to be great all the time. There WILL be days when you can't make a putt of any length or be able to get the ball off the ground. The trick is to learn to shrug those days off and keep your head into those things you do well."

"I know you're right, but I'm really having a hard time staying calm and, as you say, in the moment. Since I've never done anything like this before, I'm feeling a bit overwhelmed. I have no place in my mind to put this experience.

"Bill, I've never been so happy in my whole life. There hasn't been a lot of joy in our family since daddy was shot. You have been a godsend to us all. Momma loves you with all her heart. I don't think she was ever this happy with daddy — God rest his soul. He was a good man, and treated everyone with kindness, but he didn't talk with Momma — or us kids, for that matter — the way you do. It's like she's discovered her mind for the first time. You treat Benny and I like adults, kind of. It makes us feel grown up to the extent we can be. Thank you. From the bottom of my heart, thank you. Also, you should know that I love you too. It's the respect you show for me that does it. When you correct something I do wrong, it's not a scold, but more of another voice in my head that causes me to make the adjustment. You always tell me why you are offering corrective comments. When you're teaching in a school that should be how you treat all the kids in your classes. They'll love it."

"Wow, Alice. Thanks. I love you too, of course. Your intelligence is marvelous to be around. Your sense of joy is enthralling to all of us. Your mother has spoken similarly to me, saying she's never seen you so happy about everything. I also appreciate your advice about teaching kids and how to show them the respect that they've earned. Respect just given is worthless, but when it is earned, it is pure gold. You and I are cases in point. You earned my respect right away with your grasp of my second love in life, golf. Just seeing you working hard and still being the sweet young lady you are, earned my respect forever."

Gerry and Benny came through the back door into the kitchen at their usual time of about 4:30 P.M. Gerry let out a squeal of delight and grabbed Alice in a huge hug as she went in to greet their arrival. After swinging her around, Gerry put Alice back onto the earth and asked her to tell her everything about the day and the tournament. Benny also hugged and congratulated his sister for winning the trophy.

As promised, they all piled into the Cadillac and drove down to Jackie's restaurant for her specials and ice cream.

"So, here's our newest champ!" Jackie exclaimed. "Desserts on the house, Alice. Well done!"

The chatter around the table during dinner was joyous and upbeat. Then, as if to slap them in the head and remind them that not everyone in the world shared their enlightenment:

"Why don't you niggers keep quiet?! Good people are trying to eat a peaceful dinner here. Who the hell do you think you are, anyway? And what are you, pal, some kinda nigger lover?"

As this time of joy and celebration was being disrupted by a mindless fool, Bill lost control of his temper. He leapt out of the booth before Gerry could restrain him, and grabbed the loudmouth by the shirt, dragging him out of his booth. Jackie's bouncer, sensing trouble, was already on his way over to their area. He got there a little late. Holding onto the ugly man with his right hand, Bill placed several quick and straight left punches to his mouth and nose. Before he could get his hands up to fight back, Bill shoved him and he fell backward onto the floor. The bouncer, Ernie Halko, then grabbed the offender and quite literally carried him to the door and threw him bodily into the parking lot. The woman and the child who were with him grabbed their things and ran out after him, screaming epithets and threats.

Ernie, breathing heavily, came back to the offended group

and apologized for the interruption. "That jerk has had it coming for a long time. He always finds a way to abuse Jackie or the waitresses. He calls our cook all sorts of racist names. Maybe he won't come back."

Just then, Jackie came to their booth and apologized profusely. "Dinner is on the house, Bill. Nobody should have to sit there and take crap from white trash like that guy. He'll probably go back to his trailer park and tell everybody that they should see what he did to the other guy. I'm not going to allow him in here anymore."

"No, Jackie, I will pay for my dinner and the bill from the asshole who just left. I can afford it, you can't. Now, what's for dessert?"

Gerry looked at Bill with an expression that seemed to blend *Welcome to my world* with *I'm so thankful for your defense of us.*

It took a while for everything to settle down, but Bill was determined not to let the incident ruin Alice's celebratory dinner. Jackie delivered the monster banana splits to the four, as well as some ice wrapped in a towel for Bill's somewhat bruised left hand.

The bad jokes slowly started to come from Benny and Bill. Gerry eventually smiled at some of the worst of them. Alice, sitting next to him, just grabbed his free undamaged hand with both of hers and squeezed.

Her facial expression just broke his heart. It said: *How could anyone be so ugly and cruel? Why did he have to ruin my day with his hate and stupidity?* Yes, the words weren't spoken, but her message was clear. Bill had no answer, spoken or unspoken just then.

How does one explain abject bigotry and hate to a beautiful teenage girl who has known real success and personal accomplishment for the first time? Winning that trophy was not as abstract as getting good grades in school. It was real, and a direct result of her talent and hard work.

Bill left a hundred-dollar bill on the table as they got up and left. He also paid the tabs and drove everyone home. That event, however, was the last bit of ugliness they would have to endure for the remainder of the winter. Everyone had work to do, and love to share. They all used their respective focus and discipline to keep their heads down, and took care of that which was in front of them.

On the Saturday morning after Alice's seventeenth birthday, she woke to find her golf bag sitting in the middle of the living room filled with the new clubs Bill had bought for her. He'd also added another dozen Titleists to the ball pouch. Her shrieks of excitement woke Benny, who stumbled out wondering what new disaster had befallen them. Gerry, of course, knew what was coming and just beamed as Alice examined her gift and tested the grips.

"Oh, thank you! Thank you! These are beautiful. Can we go hit them today, Bill? Let me get dressed." And off she ran to put on her golf clothes.

He looked out the window and saw that the sun was out, but a stiff, north wind was blowing, portending the first snow of the season.

Benny went back to bed, so Gerry, Alice and Bill went to the practice range so she could try out her new clubs. At first, she was ground shy, not wanting to "injure" her new golf clubs.

"Just hit them like you hit the Staffs," Bill coached.

Finally, she hit some shots and felt the sweet-spot reaction.

"Oh, Bill. They feel SO-O-O good! Thank you so much. Thank you too, Momma."

"Hit some drives and fairway woods to see how you like those clubs."

The drives kept fading just a bit, because her body got a little ahead, her arms leaving the club face open a touch.

"Slow down your first hip move a little. Let your arms and hands catch up. It's a new club, so your body has to get used to the new feel and weight."

She did those things and played it more off her left toe instead of the heel of her lead foot. Her drives straightened right out and seemed to carry further than before. "Those new shafts have a little more pop in them than the old Staffs, so you're going to have to re-learn your yardages. Do you like them?"

"Oh, yes. Too bad winter is coming. I would want to come practice every day."

"I understand, baby. But we have to get you graduated and find you a college too. I have to finish my teacher education and my student teaching this coming January. Don't worry. The clubs will be there for you when we get good weather."

And work they all did. Gerry helped Bill write lessons in science using the basic teaching principles he'd been learning in class, but with the added benefits of her experience. He helped her grade papers and learned a lot more about grammar rules and sentence structure. Alice continued to get all "A's", and Benny had to work harder than ever to keep up with his sister. The result was that he was earning the best grades of his life.

They also laughed together a lot. As the winter progressed, they spent more time at Bill's place watching Lake Erie display its anger during the winter storms... Until it froze over in late January. He'd set up a kind of kid's area, with Benny able to sleep on the fold-out couch and Alice on the recliner that Bill moved into the bedroom/office.

Alice and Benny treated Bill more like a sibling than a would-be parent. He often admitted to himself that he didn't know a damned thing about parenting, but he did know how to be a friend and a coach. Gerry kept telling him how much she appreciated how well they blended together as a foursome.

"You know, one of these days we just might have to make honest people of one another and make all of us a legal entity. What do you say to that idea?" Bill said one day without any preamble.

"Why, Bill Bannock... If you're suggesting that we should get married, my answer would be 'YES'! Of course, I'll marry you. The timing, though, will have to be carefully thought out. Let's talk about that tonight. Pillow talk is always good for exploring ideas."

Chapter 26

The Plans of Spring

Bill's student teaching assignment was with a crusty veteran science teacher named Larry Fontero at one of Cleveland's more notable high schools, Collinwood. Both his mom and dad graduated from Collinwood, so it was almost as if he expected to see their ghosts. As it happened, his dad's photo WAS in the trophy case as part of the conference-winning baseball team.

Blue and Gray All the Way, read the banner along the top of the case.

Larry's specialty was chemistry, so those were the classes Bill would be teaching. After settling into the routine of writing daily lesson plans, creating, setting up and implementing labs, he asked to meet the golf coach. George Pulaski was a balding gentleman who taught government as well as working with the golfers at the school. Both Larry and George were a little surprised that someone Bill's age would be just entering into teaching in public schools.

"It just seemed to be the right thing to do with the rest of my life.' I want to teach science and coach golf somewhere beginning next year. I think I can do very well at both. Does age matter?"

Coach Pulaski and Bill worked together well, and he let Bill work with the novices to help build their swing mechanics and practice routines—when weather permitted. Somehow, Pulaski learned that he was on the bag when "that colored girl" won the women's club tournament up at Highland Park.

"How did you get yourself into that situation?" he asked one day.

"She caddied for me one day at Willow Creek and she was so good and knowledgeable that I had her hit a few balls. She was a natural, so just a little coaching and some practice refinement, and she just went from there."

"Don't see too many colored people playing good golf around here. They're mostly just hustling each other for beers at Highland Park, from what I hear."

"Have you ever had any colored golfers here at Collinwood?"

"Yeah. Just one. He ended up going to jail for mugging an old lady down on St. Clair. You just can't expect too much from those people. He wasn't very good anyway. Didn't like to practice. Seemed lazy and didn't pay attention to the rules or etiquette."

"I guess you can't judge all colored golfers just by their skin color. Alice is going to be a star."

"Yeah. Well, no offense, but don't be too disappointed when she gets herself knocked up and ends up like all the rest of them."

Bill's anger kettle started simmering excitedly at these words. He changed the subject. He needed to get good recommendations to land a job for next fall, and that wouldn't happen if he knocked this guy on his ass.

Bill's conversations with Larry Fontero centered around keeping the chemistry labs safe and watching the kids like a hawk so they didn't hurt themselves or others. He was an exacting but gentle and kind man, who the kids seemed to like and respect. It took a while for them to accept Bill for what he was doing. He kept telling them that he wanted to be like Larry. That helped.

As it always does, winter gave way to March weather. In northeastern Ohio, the old adage of March coming in like a lion and going out like a lamb was ever so true. As if by magic, it stopped snowing by the 15th and the sun became warmer every day. The early flowers started poking through the ground, the trees started budding out, and the grasses everywhere began to green up. Then, naturally, it snowed some more.

Bill's birthday celebration was conducted by Gerry and the kids with a homemade cake and his favorite pasta dish. Alice, of course, was ever so eager to get back to the practice ranges, but they had to wait for the new snow to melt and the ground to firm up. Bill bought some of the new plastic, slotted balls and they went to the corner field across from Mayfair School playground and at least got in some exercise and swings. By the first week of April, they were hitting real balls off the ground at a nearby range and even getting in a couple of rounds on weekends.

Alice filled out over the winter and now showed real muscle in her arms and legs. It would only be a matter of time before she started hitting her shots as far or farther than Bill's. Her natural timing and flexibility were astonishing. The weight work she put in clearly made her stronger. Bill had to tell Alice to update her membership with the Highland Park women's club, and maybe another somewhere else. Sleepy Hollow's women's club accepted her, knowing what she did last year. They both agreed that the competition was necessary to sharpen her focus and sense of purpose for college golf.

Gerry and Bill spent some time reviewing destinations for Alice's college pursuits. As always, they discussed the pros and cons.

"If she went to Wilberforce there wouldn't be the racial tensions she'd get at Ohio State, no matter how liberal they think they are there," he said.

"Well, when I played basketball and volleyball at OSU, there really wasn't much racial stuff going on, except that 'we' knew our place back then, and didn't socialize with the white kids. I'm sure it's improved since then, what with all the all-American football and basketball players coming out of that campus. We'd have to go for a visit and interview the golf coaches and team members if we could."

"Yeah. The other choice I found was San Diego State. San Diego is a golf-crazy town and the weather allows year-round play. I'm sure her game would be enhanced there too."

"The other factors would include how good her education would be. I know at Ohio State she would have access to any and all of the vast resources and academics," Gerry added.

"True. I know little about San Diego State's reputation in academics. Maybe we should arrange a visit."

Gerry just looked at him and a smile slowly crossed her face. "Sweetheart, I've never been out of Ohio in my life. That would be very exciting. Could we take Benny too? He'd love it, I'm sure."

"Sure. We missed going during spring break, so we'll have to take a few days off. Do you have some sick leave time?"

The kids fairly jumped out of their shoes when they were told that they were going to San Diego, California for a campus visit. Bill found out who coached the women's golf team and conveyed to her Alice's game, smarts, and attitude in a lengthy call. Beverly Mason told him she'd keep a day clear and have Alice spend time with one of her best players, someone she expected to be an all-American.

The views from the airplane were very different from anything Gerry and the kids had ever seen. The kids were glued to the windows as they flew over the Grand Canyon and the coastal ranges before landing right next to San Diego Bay. Bill had never been to San Diego either, so it was a little disconcerting to see people in buildings looking straight at him as they approached their landing at Lindbergh Field. The flight path took them right over the city and past tall buildings perched on hillsides. There was a curved bridge that connected the mainland to what they would learn was Coronado. The bay was filled with marinas and many navy ships – including huge aircraft carriers.

They took three days to tour San Diego, the campus of San Diego State University, and even had Alice get in a round of golf with the potential all-American. They dropped Alice off at Torrey Pines to play with Barbara Brewster. Barbara later informed Bill that Alice's game was as solid as any she'd seen in college competition. There was not a single flinch about Alice's race from her or the coach.

While Alice was playing golf at Torrey Pines, Gerry, Benny and Bill went to the famous San Diego Zoo next to Balboa Park. Gerry and Bill walked around the zoo holding hands and not a single cross-ways look did they see. They visited the SDSU admissions office for information about different curriculums that might interest Alice. They also learned that SDSU began as a teacher's college and maintained a very high rating for degrees in education. Across from the administration building was a spanking new library that had been built just four years prior to their visit. They toured its five stories and were very impressed with the quality of the books, audio-visual technology and study areas.

The four ate their last dinner in San Diego at the famous

Anthony's Fish Grotto, set on pilings over the water of San Diego Bay. Right next to the restaurant was an old sailing vessel, *The Star of India.* They took that tour before dinner.

"So, Alice... What do you think? How was Torrey Pines?" Bill asked.

"Oh, Bill. There were some holes along the cliffs that were spectacular. I had trouble concentrating because the views were so incredible. At one point, you could see down the coast and the beach. Barbara told me that sometimes from the fourth tee, you could see dolphins surfing in the waves. It was just *beautiful.* Barbara was really nice and helped me read those greens. She said the grass here was something called Poa Annua. They were a little bumpier later in the day than our bent greens, Barbara said, but once you got the feel, the ball rolled true. I shot an eighty-one, though. Barbara shot seventy-three. She's really good."

Gerry asked, "What did you think of the campus and the curriculums available?"

"I loved the Spanish architecture of some of the older buildings. Everybody was wearing shorts, tee shirts and flip-flops. Everyone was so brown and tanned. Lots of blonde hair everywhere."

That brought a laugh from them all.

Alice went on, "You can sure tell that this is a beach town. The atmosphere just seems so relaxed. The catalog had all the stuff that would interest me. I liked the biology department especially. Is there a chance I can go to college here?"

That comment made Gerry and Bill look at each other. Out-of-state tuition would be four times what California residents paid. Then there would be lodging, meals, books and allowance money. Gerry looked at him with that certain expression that told him much about her ability to pay for it all. That night, before going to sleep, they discussed that and did some math problems.

"I don't think she would be cheated out of a good education here. Did you see Desi Arnaz walking across campus? He is an adjunct lecturer in their drama department. Cool, huh?" Gerry said.

"But my teacher's salary just won't cover the cost to send her here for four years. Since she'd only be a temporary resident in California, I'd have to pay out-of-state tuition. What do you think?"

"Well, my dear, let's ask Alice where she wants to go to college. If she remained in San Diego, she could claim permanent residency and get a break on tuition after a year."

When they got back to Cleveland, they did ask her. Alice said, "San Diego State. Can I go there? Will I have to stay there all year long? Will you come visit me?" She started to cry and buried her face in her hands. An outsider could have heard the cracking of everyone's hearts as they broke. Gerry and Bill looked at each other again and the stricken look on Gerry's face was all the impetus Bill needed to make his next move.

As he saw the task before him, it was about getting Alice a golf scholarship. His conundrum centered around the fact that he could afford to pay for Alice's college, no matter where she went, but it might be seen as charity no matter how many times he told her and her mother how much he loved them.

Bill called the coach at Wilberforce and was told that they didn't offer golf scholarships. Their program was a varsity program, however, and they played all the good teams in the state, but their athletic scholarships were limited to revenue-generating sports like football and basketball. Ohio State said they did offer two women's golf scholarships per year, but that both of them had already been awarded to girls from Texas and Florida. San Diego State said basically the same thing, though they said that they'd give Alice a tryout to make the team on her own. Coach Mason said that Barbara was very impressed with Alice's swing, course management and knowledge of the game.

"Sure. Send her out here and let's see if she can make the freshman team."

It was now late April, so Bill told Alice to fill out and send in her application packages to the three colleges they had discussed. Bill and Gerry helped her fill out the paperwork and get copies of her high school transcripts, letters of recommendation, and the obligatory essay. By June first, she had been accepted at all three universities. Alice still favored San Diego State. Gerry was fraught.

Bill had finished his student teaching and took the certification tests for licensing in Ohio. Cleverly, he'd also inquired with the state of California to see if there was teaching credential reciprocity with Ohio. There was. He applied and filled out that paperwork too. He gladly thought that bureaucracies existed for moments like this. By the end of June, he received his California teaching license to go with Ohio's.

He began the arduous job of trying to locate a teaching job where he could be the golf coach too. He received an offer from Cleveland Heights High School, whose golf coach was retiring. They also had an opening (surprise) for a science teacher. It looked like the perfect set-up. But there was the other thing...

After receiving the job offer from Cleveland Heights, everyone celebrated. Gerry was happy to have her fiancé and daughter in such good shape for the coming year. But still... Alice didn't have the same enthusiasm she'd had from visiting the San Diego campus. Bill noticed all this and took Gerry for a walk during the last week in July.

"Sweetheart, I'd love to send Alice to San Diego State," she said, "but we just can't afford it the way we are right now."

"Perhaps it's better that she attend her freshman year at Wilberforce. It's a very good school, academically, and she'll be the star of the women's golf team, I'm sure. I can help out with room and board," Bill offered.

"Yes. I can just afford her tuition and books. That would be terribly sweet of you to help out with the other things. As a mother, I always want to provide what my children want. I feel a little deflated that I can't send her to San Diego. We'll just have to do what we can do."

Alice still favored attending San Diego State, but after discussing the practicalities with her mother and Bill, she reconciled that staying closer to home would be an easier adjustment to college life for her first year. It would be Wilberforce for her.

"Well, I've been cooking up a plan for next year. Basically, it centers around my desire to make us a family. I'll get a year in teaching here too. So, here's the plan: I think we should get married before the school year starts in September. We can both spend the entire year looking for teaching jobs in San Diego while we pad our resumes here. I'll sell my condo – it'll be pure profit since it's appreciated about two-hundred percent since I bought it. Alice transfers to San Diego State in a year and Benny will be graduated from high school so he can also go to SDSU and play baseball. How does that sound?"

Bill was sort of ready for Gerry's reaction, but he soon had his arms filled with a sobbing, squeezing-the-breath-out-of-him woman.

"I'd hoped you'd come up with something like that! What took you so long to figure this out?" she said. "Of course, I'll marry you. I told you that before. 'Okay. Let's tell the kids at dinner tonight. I think you're right about Wilberforce for this coming school year. It's only a four-hour drive from here to there."

At dinner, Bill started the conversation. "Alice, what would you say if I told you that I will marry your mother right away, and we will all move to San Diego as a family next year?"

The silence was deafening. Jaws remained slack. Eyes snapped back and forth between the four of them.

Finally, Alice found her voice. "Momma. Will you say 'yes'?"

"I already have, baby. It is just a matter of timing. Bill will work at Cleveland Heights this year to get experience on his résumé´. His teaching license will transfer to California; in fact, he already has his California credential. I will find a teaching job in San Diego somewhere. SDSU also has an excellent baseball program. Benny could attend college there and play some ball all year long if he wanted to.

Alice jumped from her chair, threw her arms around Bill's neck and told him she was so happy that he wanted to marry her mother. He said the same things back at her. After she turned Bill loose, Benny came over and hugged him too.

"You're a good guy, Bill, and I have come to trust you. Seeing Momma being so all about you makes me very happy too. Besides, I'd love to play ball all year in San Diego. Do you suppose I can learn to surf?"

That last comment broke everybody up.

That night, after Gerry and Bill made love, their pillow talk came down to practicalities. Or, as the street vernacular went, they had to start 'takin' care of business.'

Chapter 27

A Year in Limbo

The wedding was in August before school started. Gerry decided that she would take Bill's name and became Geraldine Ayenew Bannock. Alice and Benny retained their father's last name of Morgan. The civil ceremony was conducted by the clerk of courts for Cuyahoga County, with Benny and Alice serving as attendants. One of Alice's fellow English teachers served as her main witness and Harry Holcomb forgave Bill and stood as his witness. Gerry wore a simply cut suit of dark ivory cotton. Beneath the snug jacket, she wore a bright white blouse with a large collar that folded out over the jacket lapels. A simple strand of pearls around her neck and baby's breath flowers in her hair completed the elegant picture of a most statuesque and beautiful bride. Bill and Benny dressed in similar blue suits with silver neckties. Alice wore a tan, form-fitting, flowered dress that accentuated her athletic form and skin tone.

They held a small reception at Gerry's Sixth Avenue house and invited some teachers she was close to, plus the few neighbors who knew her and had gotten to know Bill over the course of the last year. Harry had hired a photographer and he eventually produced a very nice album of their wedding day. The solo shot of Gerry clutching her bridal bouquet against a background of green shrubs captured all of her stunning beauty and happiness from the day. Bill asked for an additional 8 x 10 for his personal desk – whenever he got one.

"I'm going to put the condo up for sale this week, and I want to move us out of East Cleveland to a safer neighborhood. I'm a little tired of hearing sirens and gunshots. What do think of that idea?"

"Man, the sooner we get to a nicer place the better," Benny said. "I don't have any ties to East Cleveland. I'll still be going to Glennville with mom every day, so it's no big deal. Just make sure whatever you rent has big bedrooms and a nice yard."

"My sentiments, exactly," Bill said. Gerry just rolled her eyes and smiled.

They found and rented a nice four-bedroom place up close to Bill's high school and the Highland Park golf course. It was one of those older, classic family homes built in the 1930s in the Cleveland Heights area. Benny and Bill acted as the heavy-lifting movers while Alice and Gerry packed boxes for them to load into the rented trailer. They filled it with their mattresses, book boxes and kitchenware from both places. It took two trips, and they were all dripping with sweat from muscling the many items into the house.

"I'm glad you developed some muscles, Benny. Thanks for your hard work."

"Not a problem. I was looking forward to getting the hell out of there anyway. This move today was very satisfying."

Gerry made a large batch of her famous spaghetti sauce with meatballs along with pitchers of iced tea. Bill managed to slurp a couple of cold beers before dinner while he was cleaning up in their new bathroom. There was even a separate bathroom for Benny.

"So, here we are in our first house as a family," Bill stated at dinner. "I'm so happy to have us all under one roof and for me to be married to this marvelous, beautiful woman. What do you think, Benny? Did I do good?'

He just laughed. "It's about time you took care of this business. I worried that you were gonna break Momma's heart. I'm glad you didn't."

On the weekend before school started, they drove Alice down to Wilberforce and got her settled in her dorm. Bill had snuck five hundred dollars into her luggage for 'takin' care of business' money. On the drive home, Benny and Bill chatted happily about the many changes taking place in their lives.

They got weekly letters and phone calls from Alice. She liked her classes and said there were some really nice golf courses around Dayton and Xenia. She was indeed the best player there, but Gerry admonished her to get top grades so her transfer to SDSU next year would go through without a hitch. They missed her, of course, and relished the time with her during parents' weekend in October. When she came home during the Thanksgiving break, she took charge of her new bedroom.

Alice's only newsflash was that she'd met a boy she enjoyed being with. He was a basketball player and a biology major. "He's taller than me, so that's cool. He's also very smart and very polite. And no, Bill, he hasn't laid a hand on me."

That brought hoots of laughter from everyone as Bill turned a variety of colors that weren't white.

His classes at "Heights" were not as difficult as he had worried they might be. He just treated the kids like young adults, didn't talk down to them, and kept them on the ball with "gee whiz" stuff from his repertoire of amazing facts. The boys' and girls' golf teams had two or three good players each, while the others struggled with learning the game. Bill employed the better players as part-time coaches to the beginners, thus building team chemistry. His teaching and coaching methods seemed to gain favor with the students and players.

The golf team spent most of its practice time with short game drills and technique, as Bill knew that was the best way to score. Their fall league record was 5-3 against teams in greater Cleveland. Then it got cold, wet and snowy. The teams were deactivated during the first week of November, just before the first major snowstorm of the year blanketed the area with twelve inches of the heaviest, wettest snow one could imagine. Tree limbs the size of Bill's arm snapped all over town. San Diego was sounding better and better.

He also kept in touch with the SDSU women's golf coach. She sent him newspaper articles that featured her golf team and potential contacts for teaching jobs for Gerry and himself. Bill also subscribed to the San Diego Union-Tribune for those same reasons. He told the coach of his plan to move there next year. She was very encouraging.

Gerry's teaching job was fairly routine and continued to frustrate her as more kids simply refused to learn, skipped classes and got themselves arrested. "It just breaks my heart, Bill. Kids with so much potential who simply glorify the street thugs because they have new sneakers and a gold chain, or something. The poverty down there is just stifling. The competition for personal recognition gets more violent every day. These kids have so few choices and their home lives are often just horrific. Few read anything. The majority of my kids don't have a father around or even know who he is. The mothers are worked to death trying to keep a roof over their heads and some food on the table. The inner-city, black single mother is the paragon of virtue and strength in that culture.

They are all too often the only thing standing between their children's well-being and total destitution. In the cafeteria, people tell me they turn their backs while kids stuff their pockets with extra food to take home. It makes one wonder what kind of country we have.

"We have politicians telling us that we are the greatest, richest country in the world and the land of opportunities. What I see is chronic poverty, lousy schools, poor nutrition and high unemployment. One of my colleagues told me that this has been the way it's always been, and she graduated from Glennville in '38. Is it anything like that up where you teach, Bill? I'll bet it isn't."

"You're right. It isn't. We have some black students, but they're in the distinct minority. Most of them come from professional homes with both parents present and working. Most of the white kids treat the black kids with respect. There have been a few outright racist incidents, but the class leaders defended the black students... mostly, I think, because they were good athletes on sports teams. I have no black golfers. I should bring Alice up for a demonstration. That would open some eyes.

"I've had very little trouble in class, and attendance is pretty good. I caught a couple kids cheating the other day and I made their after-school detention very boring. My dad taught me the hard way, that boring consequences are often the most effective. He was right."

"If I tried that here, the kids would just get up and walk out. If the principal intervened, they'd just stop coming altogether. It's a mess. The thing is, the good kids who are trying to learn have to endure the bad behavior of the poor learners. Their patience and endurance is awesome to see. Sometimes, they'll tell the bad kids to just 'shut the fuck up!' I cringe when they do that, but I'm really thinking the same thing. I know I'm reaching a few kids and that's what makes me come to work every day. There are some real sweethearts who are trying ever so hard to get out from behind the eight-ball of poverty. Sometimes, I just close my office door and cry. My colleagues tell me they do the same thing."

Her parents and Benny enjoyed having Alice home for the two-week winter break. She was a fountain of excitement while telling everyone about her classes and activities at Wilberforce. She told them how she set up a putting tournament in her dormitory for kids who didn't play golf. She just refereed. Some of the stories were hilarious. Her grades were, of course, excellent. She only received one "B" on an exam in government because she forgot to reference a supporting document for her explanations on the voting rights legislation of 1965.

The four of them talked about how important it was to get good grades and to have extra-curricular activities on their résumés so Alice could transfer to SDSU and Benny would be accepted there. Gerry told Bill that she'd never seen Benny work so hard at his studies. He also joined the chess team ("WHAT?!" from Alice and Bill.) and soon became the first board player. His government teacher was willing to write him a letter of reference for all his college applications.

Things were falling into place and everyone was trying very hard to do the right thing. With spring on the horizon, Gerry and Bill had to get their connections in San Diego going. They filled out applications for employment with every district in the San Diego area. Job announcements wouldn't happen until April or May, so they had to wait—impatiently—to see who was offering what to whom out there. The women's golf coach at SDSU, Beverly Mason, was very impressed with Gerry's resume´, as well as Bill's golfing credentials and experience. She said she would try her best to keep everyone informed of any scuttlebutt that came her way.

Meanwhile, the marriage rolled along with great comfort and love. Bill and Gerry were both very happy and went out of their respective ways to give each other a little joy every day. Benny would often tease them about how they acted like teenagers around each other.

"That's the idea, my boy," Bill told him. "When you keep each other smiling and giggling, bad stuff doesn't happen."

"Sure, Bill. I try that with the girls at school and they just think I'm a jerk."

"Yeah well, I'm not going to tell you how to act around girls. You gotta figure that one out all by yourself. But if you pay attention, they'll tell you—one way or another—what you have to do to get their favor. The playing is the hardest part of the hardest game in town. Then, you have to decide if it's worth it. And remember, if you're being a good guy, the girls who aren't interested are the ones you don't want in your life anyway."

"No kidding. I gotta go study for my math test."

Chapter 28

All the Right Moves

Gerry was the first to receive a request for an interview at a San Diego high school. Henry High School had just had their long-time, venerable English teacher retire which created an opening for someone new. It seemed that the California schools took the equal opportunity stuff seriously, and the Henry principal came right out and told Gerry that her African-American heritage and inner-city teaching experience were very important to the school. This was not only due to achieving a racial balance of their staff but also to give a different perspective to the school culture. On 1st May, Gerry flew out to San Diego for the interview.

By the time she got home from Cleveland-Hopkins Airport, the phone was ringing and Henry High School was on the line offering her the job to teach freshman English classes, and the advanced class in English Composition. After accepting the offer verbally, Bill and Gerry jumped around, laughing and hugging.

Two days later, a similar set of circumstances landed Bill a job at Grossmont High School as a physics teacher and assistant golf coach. He didn't have to fly to San Diego, because they were in such dire straits for someone to teach physics. He was hired based strictly on his education and industrial experience. The golf coach easily made an opening for an assistant, seeing how Bill's game and coaching experience fit in with his program. More jumping around was in order. Champagne was drunk. But Alice and Benny were still watching the mailbox every day. They had both sent in their paperwork to San Diego State University two months ago and continued waiting impatiently for some sort of notice.

Bill told both kids not to worry. California had a great junior college system and if SDSU didn't accept them this year, they could enroll in a J.C. Then they could get in next year as a California resident. Bill and Gerry were especially keen for Benny to get accepted so he could change his Selective Service status to 2-S instead of defaulting to 1-A when he turned eighteen. The long pole in the tent, however, was getting Gerry and Bill their jobs. That first part was completed. Everything else would follow as a cascade of events.

The school year in Wilberforce ended for Alice on the first Friday of June. Glennville's year ended on the Wednesday before that. Bill let Benny drive most of the way down to Wilberforce to get Alice in order to give him highway driving experience. Gerry stayed home and started the packing routine for the move to San Diego. When they were all back together, they sat and discussed the next move.

"Well, we have to find a place to live," Bill said, stating the obvious. "Should we all visit San Diego and pick a place to live as a family?"

Alice, quickly becoming the organization maven in the group, said, "Yes. We're each going to have something to say. In fact, why don't we all write down ten things we want the house to be and where in the San Diego area we want to live?

Bill, do you still have that city map?"

The four wrote criteria and location preferences. They reconvened and Gerry took over making the master list. The kids wanted their own rooms, of course, and Gerry and Bill said they needed a good-sized office for their books and papers. Three bathrooms would be great, if they could find such a place. Benny wanted a big yard, but when reminded about who would be tending it, he backed off from that request.

The four were down to deciding the location. The kids, of course, wanted to be near the beach. Gerry simply wanted a place where the sea breeze would keep them cool all summer. Bill's pick was to be near a golf course. Since San Diego County had more public golf courses than any other county in the United States, his desire was sort of moot. The final and deciding factor centered on proximity to the teaching assignments and to San Diego State University. There were a few very nice neighborhoods north of the SDSU campus, across the I–8 freeway. Everyone seemed to agree. After all, the beach was just a 15-minute ride from the campus itself.

Bill dug out some classified pages from the San Diego Union and looked for houses for sale in the area across from the college campus. Grossmont High School was just a few minutes' drive from that general area, and Henry was fairly central to it.

"Okay," he said. "Let's call the travel agency tomorrow and book the four of us for a few days in San Diego. Let's see what we shall see. I'll call a real estate office or two in the Del Cerro and San Carlos regions to see what looks good."

Gerry got them reservations at the Stardust Hotel in Mission Valley. There was even a golf course there, so Alice and Bill decided to take their clubs along. They flew into Lindbergh Field, rented a station wagon, and made themselves comfortable in this very nice hotel and resort. Bill called the real estate agents he'd previously contacted and arranged for house tours for the next two days. Alice and Bill booked a tee time for day number three. But they had business to attend to first.

After spending hours looking at very nice properties and burning up an entire tank of the agent's gas, they were down to the last two places on her list. Late in the afternoon of the second day, they found their dream house. It was a split-level beauty with a smallish backyard, but an elevated terrace above it and a deck for watching sunsets. The house had five bedrooms, three bathrooms and even a wood-burning fireplace. The kitchen was very large, with a 6-burner gas stove and a brand-new dishwasher. A spiral staircase led from the entrance foyer up to the bedrooms.

After touring the house carefully, they asked the real estate agent, Norma Faust, to give them a minute together. She went through the sliding glass door into the backyard. The four all just looked at each other and, as if someone made a signal, they suddenly broke into big grins.

Gerry was the first to speak: "This is what I'd like to have, darling. It's beautiful. I love everything about this house."

Alice and Benny were at a loss for words. They'd never been inside a beautiful house like this.

"Oh, my God, Bill! I want the bedroom in the back so I can see the sunsets," Alice gushed.

Benny was quiet but just nodded. "Yeah. This is a really nice place. I'm in for it. Mom, are we gonna buy this house?"

Gerry looked at Bill.

Bill looked at her and the kids. "Everyone seems to like this house. I think it will fit us perfectly. Any objections? No? Okay. We'll take it. I'll get Norma and we'll start signing papers and stuff." But before he could get Norma, Gerry grabbed him and squeezed him tightly.

"Oh, baby, this is a palace. I've never dreamed of a home of my own that was this nice. Oh. How much does it cost?"

"I think the sticker price is three hundred and fifty thousand. Let's see if they'll take less if I pay cash."

Norma Faust did a very professional job of keeping her emotions under control. "How much are you planning to put down, Mr. Bannock?"

"Three hundred twenty-five thousand dollars. That's my offer. Cash. Today."

"Oh, well, let me call the owners." She dialed a number from the phone in the house. After a brief conversation, Norma came back to the dining room table and said, "The owners will accept three-thirty-five."

"Done", Bill said. "Today is June 21st. We'd like to move in before school starts on September 3rd. Will that be a problem, being that this is a cash deal?"

"It shouldn't be. The seller is Navy, and he is a retiring captain intending to move back to his home town on the east coast. He and his family are familiar with packing up and moving. Congratulations! Let's go back to my office and we'll do the paperwork. It'll take a few days to get the current owners to sign and get everything notarized, stamped and approved. We should have the final contracts, deeds and whatnot in the mail to you no later than next week."

In anticipation of this opportunity, Bill had sold a good amount of stock and deposited the cash in his checking account. He was sure Norma Faust didn't get a check handed to her for six figures every day, but she handled it like a pro and guided them through the signing process. "Since I'm a notary, I can validate your signing and signatures right now. It will save the hassle of mailing paperwork back and forth. When you finalize your relocation plans, give me a call and I'll have the keys waiting for you upon your arrival. It's been a pleasure, Mr. and Mrs. Bannock. I hope you're planning on spending a few days enjoying our beautiful city."

The next day, they toured their schools. San Diego State still hadn't approved Alice's transfer, and Benny's application was waiting for one of the admissions supervisors to return from vacation. The principal at Henry High School was delighted to see Gerry again and showed her the classroom where she would be teaching. The retiring teacher had left her a marvelous collection of literature, lesson plans, videos, slides and a host of other materials that she'd accumulated over her forty-year career. Gerry was agog at what she'd just inherited.

Bill's visit to Grossmont High School was equally fruitful, as he met the science department chair and the golf coach. The science chairman was Orville Tibbets. He showed Bill his lab and classroom. The apparatus and materials for teaching physics at Grossmont astonished Bill with their quantity and variation. He suddenly saw all sorts of opportunities for lessons. The golf coach, Bob Rogers, looked like he'd been in the sun for most of his life and the age lines were deep and many, even though he was only Bill's age.

Alice and Bill did play golf the next day, while Gerry took Benny up I–15 to the new San Diego Wild Animal Park. Bill was pretty distracted by recent events and three-putted four greens. Alice didn't play much better, as they kept talking about what they would do with their new house. She still hadn't decided on what her major field of study would be in college. They talked about various topics and subjects while their concentration kept drifting. They both shot something in the low 80s and just pitched the scorecard in the trash.

"Nice course," Bill said.

"Yeah. Too bad we didn't honor it with good play."

"Well, my dear girl, we will soon be here permanently. You'll be playing golf on Christmas day if you want. How does that sound?"

"It sounds great. Now all we have to do is make the move. Will you let me drive some of the way out here?"

Chapter 29
The Caravan

On the day after Benny's 18th birthday, both acceptance letters from San Diego State showed up in the mailbox. Bill took him to the local draft board office with that letter and obtained Benny's student deferment.

Alice wanted to go shopping for her new California wardrobe, but Gerry told her that she'd have better choices once they got into their new home in San Diego. She kept practicing and, now being a capable driver, took one of the cars to the practice range and golf courses almost every day.

Alice was now nineteen and had grown into a young woman with significant physical attributes that combined her obvious femininity with her athleticism. She and Bill had been jogging and running together for a few months, and that had developed stronger thigh muscles for them both. At 5'11", she was something special to behold. Bill and Gerry didn't worry about her social life interfering with her studies or her game; she was dedicated to both. Besides, her size, intelligence and beauty would act as a filter for young men not self-secure enough to engage her in conversation, never mind a romantic relationship.

After Bill's condo sold, he had the moving company store his furniture and other household items until it was time to move into the temporary home in Cleveland Heights. He kept some of the money from the condo sale in his checking account and bought more stock with the rest. This investment would serve to help pay for the new home in San Diego.

As anyone who has conducted a major relocation could predict, moving day was rainy and muggy. The movers knew what to do, but it was still an extra burden for them to keep everything dry while getting it on the truck.

They packed the Olds and the Cadillac to the gills with their personal stuff plus a few plants that the movers wouldn't take. Benny and Bill drove the Cadillac; Gerry and Alice drove the Olds. They left the Cleveland Heights house at three o'clock in the afternoon of August 20th, and never looked back.

They stopped for the evening just past Columbus at a motor inn on U.S. 40 west, just off I-70. Everyone was very tired after the long and exciting day, so they turned in early. Benny and Bill shared one room while Gerry and Alice shared another. Bill kissed Gerry and Alice goodnight and everyone went to sleep like they'd discovered the concept. Since they had long travel days ahead of them, they were up at six the next morning, ate breakfast, and were on the road with full bellies and gas tanks by seven. Next stop, Springfield, Missouri.

Outside St. Louis, they picked up U.S. 66, which joined Interstate 44 heading southwest. It was a long day through mostly farm country, but the kids and Gerry were very impressed with the size of the Mississippi River when they crossed it between East St. Louis, Illinois and St. Louis, Missouri. With their arrival in Springfield, they were now in the beautiful Ozark region of southwestern Missouri. The scenery had changed from the rolling farmlands of the

Midwest to the more rugged and hilly country of this geological peculiarity.

As they left Springfield for Tulsa, Oklahoma, the Ozark hills and forests were replaced with plains that got flatter with every mile traveled west. They pounded I-44 hard on the third day of travel. They saw Jack pumps rocking up and down as they extracted oil here and there throughout their time in Oklahoma. When they got to the state capitol, Oklahoma City, they picked up Interstate 40 west. At the end of this long day, they stopped in Santa Rosa, New Mexico at the junction of U.S. 54. They ate, hugged and went to their rooms with minimal conversation.

Bill whispered to Gerry, "Just keep thinking about how wonderful our first night in our new home will be."

"Yeah. Well, I'm looking forward to it. Do you think our furniture and stuff will arrive the same day or the next?"

"Good question. I should call the shipping and scheduling office tomorrow and see—be sure to remind me to do that. When we get confirmation, I'll call Norma Faust so we can get our keys. I don't want to sleep in the car or on the floor."

Bill had done research on some scenic driving routes prior to leaving Cleveland. U.S. 54 through New Mexico to Alamogordo wove its way through some very spectacular, extinct volcano country. Bill drove this part so Benny could get his fill of the magnificent beauty of the southwest. In Alamogordo, they turned west again on U.S. 70 to Las Cruces, a town straddling the Rio Grande River. Benny commented the whole way that this was better than watching western movies. That night, they stayed in Tucson, Arizona. The Sonoran Desert had captivated them all as they approached that city at the foot of the Catalina Mountains. They even pulled over at a rest area and just marveled at the beauty of this highly diverse ecosystem, despite the fact that the temperature was well over 100 degrees. They were now six hours away—just along I-10 and I-8—from their new home in San Diego. The last day of caravan would not be as long, but anxiousness and expectations rode with them all the way.

They were on the road out of Tucson at six-thirty, anxious to get to their new home. The moving company dispatcher told them that the truck would be at their home, waiting for them. They would gain an hour crossing into the Pacific Time Zone… Oh, wait, Arizona didn't recognize daylight savings time, so they would be in the PDT zone all day. The drive across Arizona in the early morning was magnificent. The desert and the mountains created endless visual imagery that changed between saguaro cactus forests to boulder-strewn canyons. All the while, the deep blue sky perfectly offset the tan, brown and red rock formations they marveled at along the way. They crossed the Colorado River in Yuma, Arizona and smiled at seeing the "Welcome to California" sign.

Just after crossing the state line, massive sand dunes extended along I-8 for several miles. They learned later that these dunes were often used as movie-making locations for various films. The desert floor along the subsequent stretch of highway was very flat and uninspiring. When they drove past a small town in the Imperial Valley named El Centro, they noticed that the highway was several feet *below* sea level. They all knew from their geography lessons that Death Valley, a couple of hundred miles north, held the lowest elevation point in the United States. However, they didn't know about the Imperial Valley, from which most of the winter vegetables were grown and distributed around the country.

As they left El Centro's low point, a bluish line of hills to the west loomed ahead. The desert here was not nearly as beautiful as in Arizona, and the humidity was much higher due to the irrigation. The more they drove, the bigger the hills became until they were mountains.

The Laguna Mountains offered dramatic geological change from low desert to high desert to true mountains. The visual drama began with a very steep and winding section that was just over twenty miles long. They saw several cars pulled over with their hoods raised. Bill watched his own temperature gauge, but it had moved only slightly toward "HOT". The road leveled off some and they found themselves traveling through more switchbacks in a section called *Devil's Canyon*. Huge boulders the size of houses were everywhere. It looked like a giant child had spilled his bag of granite marbles and let them cascade across the landscape.

As they crested a hilltop where the sign said '4,000 feet above sea level', the air became noticeably cooler. Still, it was a relative term. By Ohio standards, it was still damned hot! Their air-conditioning prevented them from experiencing the 102 degrees of dry heat outside that registered on the exterior thermometer on Bill's car. The interior temperature of seventy-eight degrees kept them comfortable during this transit across the hot landscape.

The caravan kept heading west, and the lay of the land along I-8 became less barren. Off to the side of the road, they saw valleys interlaced with small drainages containing lines of oak trees and other vegetation that belonged to a unique, west-coast ecosystem known as *chaparral*.

In the distance, to the west, they could see a kind of gray layer that blended into the stark blue, cloudless skies overhead. They passed towns with odd names like Jacumba (Ha-coom-ba) and Boulevard, until arriving in Alpine. The highway descended from Alpine down to a valley, with another, much larger town named El Cajon - "the box". It was called the box because it was surrounded on three sides by high hills. It was still very hot.

They drove up, out of this valley and found their exit to the San Carlos area, where their home—and the moving van—awaited their arrival. Norma handed them the sets of keys, congratulated them, and left them to the unpacking. The sea air was now in their nostrils, and a gentle, westerly breeze brought it to them. They were home.

Chapter 30

The Welcome Mat

The movers quickly and efficiently stacked the labeled boxes in the correct rooms. Bill and Gerry hand-waved the placement of furniture, having made a layout beforehand. The first box they opened contained the glassware.

Gerry said, "Darling, we need a grocery run. I need dishwasher detergent and liquid soap so I can clean all our cooking and eating necessities. And we probably should get some food for tonight and for breakfast tomorrow. Let me have that box knife. I'll start on things here while you're away."

Alice and Benny were upstairs in their new rooms, unpacking clothes, books and the things that made their rooms feel like theirs. The master suite had its own bathroom, complete with shower stall. The kids picked theirs from the other two side-by-side bathrooms outside their bedroom doors. Bill could hear them moving things around, opening boxes and then:

"Mom! Where are the sheets and pillowcases?"

"They should be up there. Look through all the boxes."

"Here they are. They are in several boxes. One is called a

'wardrobe'. Weird."

It took Bill an hour to buy what he felt was needed to get the pantry started, put some beer in the refrigerator, and find some nice steaks for the outdoor grill. The previous owners had been kind enough to leave a bag of charcoal and lighter fluid. Baked potatoes, of course. After putting the groceries away, Gerry, having filled the dishwasher, started the first load. Bill pulled a couple of glasses out before she started the machine, washed them by hand and dried them with a paper towel from the roll on the wall mount by the sink.

"Be right back," he said. He scurried out to the garage and brought back a couple of folding lawn chairs.

"What do we need those for?" Gerry asked.

"I thought we'd take a break and wash some of the dust out of our throats. Cold beer? We have clean glasses."

Gerry had a bandana wrapped around her head in an attempt to keep the unpacking dust out of her hair.

"Yes, my dear. A cold beer sounds great, but why the chairs?"

"Let's go sit out front and enjoy the sea breeze."

"Good idea. The dishwasher is working, but the spices and second load can wait. Let's go."

The first gulps from the ice-cold beer tasted wonderful. Bill had asked about a good west coast beer, and the clerk said that Olympia was pretty good.

"M-m-m. This beer tastes very nice. Not too heavy. Quenches my thirst nicely," Gerry said. "Good choice."

While they were savoring their cold beer, up the driveway walked a diminutive woman in shorts, a bright, striped blouse and flip-flops. "Hello. You must be the Bannocks, our new neighbors. I'm Kimoko Martin and I live next door. Norma told me you were moving in, so I made this for you as a welcoming present."

She handed Bill a package wrapped in textured paper with a silver ribbon. He handed it to Gerry, who carefully opened it to find a decorative box. Inside was a framed painting of two stylized white cranes leaping into the air with wings spread. There was a touch of light peach on the foreheads of the birds. The extended legs, the bills and the tail feathers were painted gold.

"Oh, Kimoko!" Gerry exclaimed. "It's absolutely gorgeous. Where did you get this?"

"Oh, I painted it just for you. When I knew you were coming, I thought it would be just right as a welcoming gift from a neighbor. The crane, you see, is the Japanese symbol of good health, love and prosperity in a home. The signatures at the bottom are my name in English and Japanese. I'm glad you like it. It should probably go in your bedroom so you both can see it every day."

"It will be placed in that manner. It's too beautiful and thoughtful a gift not to be viewed every day. May I get you a beer, Kimoko?" Bill asked.

"Oh, no, thank you. When my husband Shane gets home from the golf course, I'll send him over to introduce himself. I'm sure he'll drink a beer with you."

They thanked Kimoko again and she walked back to her house.

"Oh, Bill, this painting is exquisite. Let's take it up to the bedroom and put it in a safe place until we're ready to hang pictures. What a nice gesture of welcome."

"I'll say! I hope our other neighbors are as nice as Kimoko seems to be."

Around four o'clock, the doorbell chimed and Bill opened it to see a sturdy-looking man with a crew cut and the most dazzling blue eyes he'd ever seen staring back at him.

"Hi. I'm Shane Martin. Kimoko told me she met you today,

so I thought I'd drop by to welcome you also." They shook hands.

Gerry emerged from the kitchen and Shane greeted her with a firm handshake. '

'You're Gerry, right?" She nodded. "Here's a nice bottle of wine for your first dinner in San Diego. I hope you like it."

"Wow, Shane. Thank you," Bill said. Gerry dazzled him with her smile of thanks.

"So, you moved all the way here from Cleveland, Ohio, right?"

"Yep. We managed to get across the desert and through the mountains without blowing a hose or radiator. Man, it was hot!"

"Yeah. Well, this side of the mountains is blessed with the sea breeze. You're gonna be surprised how chilly the ocean water is. When you decide to go swimming, wait until August to early October. See, there's the Japanese current that brings cold water down from the Gulf of Alaska. In late summer, there is an eddy that comes up from the south that warms the coastal water temperatures somewhat, maybe up to the high 60s or low 70s. Most of the time, the water temperature stays in the mid to high fifties. That's what keeps us cool here."

"That's good to know. I won't tell the kids. Let them be surprised. I'm sure they'll want to go to the beach any day now," Bill said. "So, where do you play golf, Shane?"

"Well, today, I was out at Singing Hills, past El Cajon. It was pretty hot, but the course was in good shape. Shot an eighty-two, my best of the year so far. Do you play?"

"I do. Our daughter Alice plays a pretty good game too. We should make plans to play sometime soon. We gotta unpack and get settled first."

"You bet. Sure. Well, you bought a really nice place. The previous owners were also retired Navy like me, but wanted to go back east. Not us. I'm originally from Richmond, Virginia, but this is where I plan to spend the rest of my days."

"What did you do in the Navy?"

"I flew F-4s off of a couple carrier decks during the early days of the war. That goddamned war made me realize that I'd rather do something else. I had enough time in the Navy to get some part of the retirement package, especially with combat credit. In case you were wondering, I met Kimoko in Yokosuka when I was stationed there. She comes from a very good family in Japan that owned and operated several businesses. Her parents were both survivors of the Hiroshima bomb and moved to Tokyo after they recovered from their injuries. They were fortunate not to get radiation poisoning."

"Forgive me for asking an impolite question, but weren't they a little put off with you seeing, then marrying their daughter?" Gerry asked.

"At first, yes. But then they saw that I was not there to find me a war bride. I mustered out as a lieutenant in '68 and stayed there for almost a year. Kimmy and I were inseparable and her parents finally realized that I was good to go as a son-in-law. I took a job as an instructor pilot here to make a little more money, so we could fly her parents here to visit. They ended up staying. They live in the guest house behind ours. They've learned to speak English very well and are currently setting up a grocery business in El Cajon.

"Say, I'm bending your ears. Sorry about that. I'll give you two the third degree when we have you over for dinner. I think we're gonna be good neighbors. You'll find that most people in our general neighborhood are pretty cool. Bunch of old hippies...

"Oh. Here's my phone number. When you get yours installed, give us a ring and we'll set things up. So, is your daughter any good?"

"Let's say that the San Diego State women's golf team is glad to have her on the team."

"Ah. Hmm. Maybe she can be our ringer when we play some of the guys at Singing Hills or Ivanhoe courses."

"You may not ever have to buy another beer in your life. She's pretty damned good—a natural. You'll soon see."

"Great. Okay, I'll let you people get back to this tough work. Thanks for the beer. Talk to you soon."

Shane left and Gerry and Bill looked at each other. "This is going to be interesting. Shane and Kimoko seem genuine. I'm looking forward to everything. Aren't you excited?" Bill said.

"Yes. Excitement. It's bordering on overwhelming. I'm glad to have you as a steadying influence. We've already been through some unpleasant stuff, but I don't get that feeling here. Shane and Kimoko were a terrific welcoming party. I can't wait to hang that painting.

"Well, it's getting on toward dinner time. I'd better put the potatoes on. Let me unload the dishwasher and we can put stuff up. Too bad we don't have time for a group shower before dinner. That'll have to come later."

Chapter 31

Aztec Alice

Gerry instantly became the chauffeur for the kids because the directions of travel for both parents dictated those arrangements... That is, until they decided that Alice needed her own transportation. They bought her a three-year-old Ford compact station wagon. It had to have room for her golf clubs, after all. Hers and Benny's class and practice schedules coincided, mostly, so Benny had himself driven to and from school by his big sister. He didn't mind, it seemed, because he told everyone how many good-looking girls wearing next-to-nothing he saw while riding to and from class. Eye rolls all around...

The downside was the fact that Benny had to tag along to Alice's golf practices at Cottonwood golf club over the hill from El Cajon. While Alice beat balls and practiced her short game, Benny went into the restaurant and did homework, read, and otherwise kept out of the way... That was until baseball practice started. Even though Benny was a freshman, that team seemed loaded with good players, and pitchers who could throw the ball through a brick wall. He was a little awed by his new teammates and worried about being cut before the fall league games started. His fielding, though, was the talk of the coaching staff.

Before they moved to Cleveland Heights, Bill had taken Benny and a five-gallon bucket of baseballs to the sports field behind Mayfair Elementary School. He put Benny's back to the big brick building wall and hit him grounder after grounder to all sides. They practiced footwork almost as if he were in ballet class, but when a ball was directed to one side of Benny or the other, he glided to the place he needed to be to scoop up the grounder. The field's surface was not smooth, and many an evening saw Benny coming home with a fat lip or a bruised chest and legs.

"Hit it harder!" he would yell, as if it was a challenge he was making for himself.

One day, Bill gave Benny a few used golf balls to sharpen his reflexes and react more quickly to bad hops.

"What are these for? I'm not going to play golf. That's for you sissies," he joked.

"No, wise guy, you aren't going to play golf, but what you're gonna do with these is take them to that schoolyard along with your glove and throw them against that brick wall. You'll soon discover that your reaction time will improve after a few of these things bounce off your body. Come on. Let's try it and I'll coach you up."

Benny Morgan had grown into a sturdily built six-footer. He'd used the weights Bill bought for Alice, so his muscles bulged significantly, while he continually developed his agility as a baseball player. He kept his hair cut close to his scalp. He told everyone he didn't want to have all the fuss associated with keeping an afro hairstyle looking good. "People only have to look at me to know I'm black. I just don't care about identity or cultural hairstyles. I don't have to send any messages by what I look like. My big thing is hitting these great curveballs the college pitchers will throw at me," he'd say.

Alice, being classified as a sophomore because all her credits from Wilberforce were accepted by SDSU, became an instant sensation with the golf team. She could outdrive everyone, including Coach Mason, a former LPGA player. But it was her scoring game that had everyone buzzing. She rarely had more than thirty putts for a round of eighteen holes, and her iron play was crisp, consistent and accurate. By November, her handicap was "scratch", meaning she didn't need any strokes from anyone she was playing. Once she figured out the lay of the course at Cottonwood, she threatened or broke par regularly.

She also decided she wanted to pursue sports medicine as her major. The head trainer for the Aztec sports teams recently obtained the chairmanship and budget to develop and implement that curriculum. Alice created joy among her professors in all her classes because she was so disciplined — a trait that complimented her innate intelligence. Her presentations in speech class were often met with applause by her classmates and her instructors. Of course, her brilliant smile and physical presence contributed to her acceptance by her peers too.

The fall collegiate golf competition put Alice into the realm of playing with people as good as or better than she. Coach Mason, trying not to put too much pressure on Alice at first, placed her as the third player on the Aztec team. In her first match, played at the toney Los Angeles Country Club, she trounced her University of Southern California (USC sponsored this triangular match that included UCLA) opponent with a stunning 70 – 77 win.

"Not bad for not having seen the course before," she deadpanned. "Pretty nice layout too. Is there an army of groomers there who made that golf course look like a painting?"

San Diego State returned the favor two weeks later with their invitational at Torrey Pines. Alice played in the number two slot this time, and proceeded to take medalist honors with a brilliant 68. Bill caddied for her on that occasion. They'd played Torrey together a few times, so she knew the nuances and had an excellent 'book' on the course.

She hit the ball so solidly that day, Bill had to work at not cheering. Number six on the South Course was a nice par five. She hit driver, 4-iron to the green and sank a twenty-six-footer for eagle. They could see her UCLA opponent just wilt. And they still had twelve holes to play.

The San Diego Union-Tribune ran a feature article about the SDSU women's team that emphasized Alice's brilliant contribution. Because she presented such a striking figure, she was also recognized all across the campus. It would have been easy for her to become the prima donna if not for the other three in her family who kept her grounded. Benny always found a way to bring her back to earth with some snide remark.

"I hit two doubles today and drove in three runs for our team's win. What did you do? Three putt?"

Gerry kept Alice involved with chores around the house, running errands now that she had her own car and reminding her that she was just an equal partner among the four.

She and Bill would often sit on the bench out back and just chat. Sure, golf was a big topic, but so was her schooling. They talked about his teaching job and the kinds of kids he was seeing. He shared some of the anecdotes about hero worship in the school, and how the most popular kids – especially the athletes – often wallowed in their stardom.

"My dear Alice, fame is a fleeting thing. Golf will be with

you for most of your life, but so will being a contributing and purposeful citizen. Right now, we're pretty lucky to be living in a city where race relations are better than in Cleveland. When you travel outside our protective bubble, it won't always be that way. But to your advantage, you've experienced both sides of that. Your teammates don't see you as a beautiful black girl, just someone who makes twenty-footers for birdie all day long. I can see it by the way they talk to you and with you. You're a lady Aztec, for sure. Coach tells me that you're doing very well in class too. There's even buzz around campus about running you for student council next year. That, my precious Alice, is what leaders are made of. You know, of course, what the single most important descriptive noun is for those great leaders?"

"I can think of quite a few. What do you have in mind?"

"Humility. In leadership, that means being able to think and act like a queen and still be able to communicate with everyone from everywhere on their terms. We can talk to Shane about the different kinds of leadership he experienced in the Navy. My point is that you should be very cautious about having your successes make you feel superior to anyone else. Especially not me."

That brought a laugh from her. "Bill, next to Momma, you are the most important person in my life. Your advice has always been spot on. We think very much alike on so many levels about so many things. I know I'm doing well in everything, and I do want you to be proud of me and respect my hard work. You know I'm not lazy or a slacker. I also recognize that I have a special kind of drive. I don't know where it comes from, but I just seem to know when it's time to focus on what is at hand.

"Let 'em take the pictures. I know I'm photogenic, but if it helps promote the team and attract better recruits, so be it. I also think it would be better for the game of golf overall if more black boys and girls, men and women, were able to play. It would sure get them off the corner and into some fresh air. Maybe someday I'll be able to make that a goal as a result of what I'm doing."

This discussion turned out to be one of Alice's and Bill's most important so far. The four of them were now completely intertwined. Gerry and Bill were delighted to see the lights come on in Benny when he finally realized that he was smart, and that baseball was just another vehicle for him to express himself. Yes, he was handsome, well-spoken and attentive to things that needed attention He was finding girlfriends from every race but was wise enough to constrain his natural instincts so that he made mature choices with the women he met.

Alice had a few dates with young men of different races too. In a way, her whole being was a two-sided coin, socially. On the one side, her size, beauty, intelligence and notoriety intimidated the majority of the men. The other side of that coin used those same traits as a filter to help Alice appreciate those men who were more secure and possessed the characteristics and capabilities that were compatible with hers. As time went by, her complaints about lousy dates were increasingly replaced by favorable reports.

Alice Morgan, the champion golfer, wore her Aztec red and black outfits with great pride. Her blood was as red as that of her teammates and her skin was dark. She was all Aztec on campus and while playing golf for the team, but she was also becoming a whole woman, a budding intellectual while remaining the loving daughter to Gerry and Bill Bannock.

Chapter 32

Neighbors

Bill and Gerry's first call came the day after the phone's installation. In their infinite wisdom, they also purchased separate phone lines for Alice and Benny. That first call was from the Martins next door.

"Bill. It's Shane. We'd like to have you and Gerry over for dinner this coming Friday evening. Are you available?"

Bill looked at Gerry while covering the phone: "Shane has invited us over for dinner on Friday. Are we good with that?"

"Oh, sure. Ask him what time and what we should bring."

"Shane, we'd be delighted to come over. What time Friday and what should we bring? Wine? Dessert?"

"Come over at 6:30. Don't bring anything. We've got the whole thing planned. Or, I should say, Kimmy has it all planned. She just loves doing this sort of thing. See you Friday."

Kimmy indeed had everything planned. She was dressed in what she described as traditional Japanese hostess attire. The silk robe sported a lavishly bright flower design with maroon turned-back cuffs at the sleeves. The *obi* (sash) was a matching maroon.

She also brought them up to speed on some Japanese traditions before dinner. They sat on *tatamis* (woven rice mats) instead of chairs. The low, black-lacquered dinner table served to hold all the dishes. It had a small spray of various flowers in the middle to accentuate the black color of the top.

Saki was served warm and in tiny porcelain cups. There were three kinds of raw fish presentations that she called *sushi*. This was just the beginning. She served some delicious deep-fried shrimp that tasted like nothing they'd ever eaten. She served everyone a heap of gummy rice to accompany the main course of steamed vegetables and small, pickled fish morsels. Gerry and Bill were so busy remembering how to use chopsticks that their conversation efforts were limited to telling Kimmy how tasty everything was. She smiled shyly and kept the good dishes coming. Finally, for dessert, she served mango sherbet in what looked like hand-painted bowls. For this, they used the small silver spoons. The word that kept popping into the minds of Bill and Gerry was *elegant*. Everything was presented artistically and in a precise manner. Even the floral designs on the serving dishes were positioned so that the diners could see them as Kimmy doled out the food. She was meticulous in assuring that everyone received what looked to them to be exactly the same amount of each item.

Kimmy would not hear of them helping her clear the dishes. She shooed Shane, Gerry and Bill into the living room while she filled the dishwasher.

"How about a little cognac to tamp down that dinner?" Shane asked.

"That would be wonderful," Bill said.

"Kimmy knows how to put on a great Japanese-style dinner. She enjoys it very much, and to have new neighbors as an excuse to put on her best moves is a special treat for her. You two were properly polite and seemed to be able to handle the chopsticks and such pretty well. Not bad for mere Americans," he said laughing.

Gerry said, "Shane that painting of the cranes was just so beautiful. It also gave us a sense of what sort of grace Kimmy possesses. You being married to her says a lot about you too."

"Thanks. Even though I had to overcome severe bouts of testosterone poisoning while flying jets, her calm and placidness helped me come back to earth. She read me a few stories from some World War II Japanese airmen's diaries about their struggle with the duality of living through intense combat and then returning to the quiet, gracious moments like we just had at dinner. There is a concept of balance in Japanese culture that we Americans tend not to have."

"Interesting to hear you say that, Shane. My parents were from Ethiopia and raised me in a household of grace and respect for peaceful times too. There were lots of similarities to tonight, and many differences too, but my parents always tried to project a sense of calm and grace.

"My father was a physician, and he told me stories from Ethiopia of how he would often come home drained from working hard on so many cases of disease with minimal equipment and medical supplies. What broke his heart was that he knew he could cure so many maladies if he had the right treatments available. My mother always tried to lighten his emotional load and, at the same time, pass on that sense of calm and respect. They were gentle people and also genteel."

Kimoko came back into the living room and sat next to Shane on the couch. Gerry and Bill showered her with compliments and thanks for a wonderful dinner.

She bowed her head shyly. "It is my pleasure to do such things for nice people."

"Thank you for saying so. We try," Bill said.

Shane spoke after a brief silence. "San Diego has long been a Navy town, as you know. And many sailors have come home with what we used to call 'war brides' from different countries. Many of our sailors were just kids away from home for the first time and they became enthralled with the exotic beauty of oriental women. Of course, after World War II, Japan was a burned-out shambles – at least in the major population centers. So, many of the survivors latched on to our kids during the occupation. A few of our older chiefs who were there told us how wretched things were right after the war. Apart from the basic biology, many of our guys felt great compassion. And biology, being what it is, took it from there.

"Some of our quartermasters there simply looked the other way as many of our soldiers and sailors took food, clothing and medical supplies to give to the refugees who were living, literally, in the street and hand-to-mouth. We weren't like the Japanese, Germans or Russians, who abused their conquered people. Oh, there was prejudice, of course. The Japanese military treated our prisoners horrifically throughout the war. They helped re-define and validate General Sherman's comments after the battle of Atlanta: 'War is all Hell.'

"We also have to keep in mind that the warrior code in Japan, *Bushido*, is much older than our country. That code of warrior conduct hadn't changed much over the centuries and the enemies were treated brutally, as were the conquered people. To the Japanese soldier, there was no honor in defeat and even less in surrender. Abuse of the enemy was normal for the Japanese soldier."

"How are the so-called war brides treated here now? What about the American servicemen? Do they get lumped into the bigoted abuse too?" Bill asked.

"Good questions, Bill. The best answer to the second

question is 'sometimes'. But most of the Americans who have their Asian spouses get insulted or accosted usually make sure that the bigots take home a fat lip or something. Now, of course, we're seeing Korean, Vietnamese, Thai and Filipino women here on the west coast. That has created a plethora of Asian cultures that have the bigots confused as they don't know how to place their hate specifically. Pretty soon, I suspect, they'll just lump all Asians together as 'them'."

"So, you mentioned earlier that this neighborhood is filled with old hippies. How do they respond to mixed marriages of our type?"

"Yeah, the couple across the street and two doors down features a black San Diego Charger football player and his white wife. She is a real beauty and their two kids are simply gorgeous. Up the other way is a mixed couple like you two. They still wear beads and lots of loose, tie-dyed clothing. She's a lawyer and the guy is a gardener. Now there's us four.

"There are a few on this street who won't even look at us, of course. If I go shopping with Kimmy, we get stares. When she goes by herself, the white people think she is a housekeeper for somebody." That brought a groan and a laugh.

Kimmy said, "I even had one lady at a store ask me who I worked for and did I have room in my schedule to work in her garden."

"What did you tell her?" Gerry asked.

"I told her that my husband was a Navy bomber pilot and wouldn't allow me to work for somebody else. She looked at me like I was from Mars and walked away."

"Well, it's good to hear that we are in a community that has some diversity. Is that why the people who lived in our house moved?" Gerry asked.

"No. The guy was retiring as a captain and just wanted to

get back home to Pennsylvania where his family lived. He and his wife were all Navy, so Kimmy was, to them, a normal situation."

"Gerry lived in a part of Cleveland where there were very few white or Asian people. I was raised in an almost all-white suburb. We met through our daughter, Alice. Alice was out looking for a caddying job at the course I used to play regularly. We got along great; the girl – now a young woman – knew how to read greens and give yardages, so I was intrigued. Then, I met her mother, who'd come to pick her up, and I was a goner. Alice became my permanent caddy and it served as a way to see her mother more often. One thing led to another, and here we are."

"How did your families feel about your marriage?" Kimoko asked.

Bill said, "Well, my parents were killed in an auto accident when I was thirty. I have one uncle who is all redneck all the time, so he doesn't even know I exist; my call. My golfing pals didn't take kindly to having Alice on my bag and started shooting off their mouths. I closed one of them. I had to buy the Cadillac from him to keep him from suing me. So, I haven't really had to deal with family or friends in that way. This is a fresh start for both of us."

He looked at Gerry and she told her story. "My parents were run over by a drunk driver after I was out of college. If I have any relatives, they're still in Ethiopia. I made a few friends while teaching, but I was pretty busy as a single mom raising two children by myself. My husband was murdered by muggers in Cleveland, so until Bill came along, I was on my own. No time for friends.

"Bill and I have talked about the impact our presence might elicit in others, but we're so used to being stared at by white and black people alike that it no longer bothers us. We are in love and we have two beautiful children to help become adults. Bill has told you about Alice, but Benny, our son, is growing into a fine young man. He's a very good baseball player and is on the Aztec freshman team as their starting shortstop. He's just discovering his intelligence and will soon decide how he will save the world." Everyone smiled at Gerry's obvious pride.

"Our romance is, of course, very special and precious to us. Bill's right. We did fall in love at first sight. Racial differences were never a part of that. We know the reality, of course, but between us, it's been Bill and Gerry, the lovers—nothing else."

"Well, that's wonderful. We're very happy that you are our new neighbors," Shane said. "I can't wait to see this great daughter play golf. Also, maybe we four can pack up and go watch Benny play baseball? I'll bet he'd love having us cheering for him."

That brought a big laugh from Gerry and Bill.

"Okay, Shane. Look, would you please make a tee time for us three? Oh, wait, I'd better ask Alice when she's free. I'll call. Meanwhile, I'm planning an outdoor barbecue on Sunday afternoon. Please come. You'll be able to meet Alice and Benny. Sorry, Kimmy. No saki, just bourbon and beer."

"I drink beer now and then. Let me bring you a Japanese beer that is just now being sold here."

"Great," Bill said. "Thanks for a very lovely evening. Talk to you tomorrow."

"Oh, darling, I'm so glad our new neighbors are nice and interesting," Gerry said as she twined her slender fingers with Bill's while walking back home. "I love our new life here so far."

That feeling of love persisted through the next two hours until their glistening bodies finally ran out of energy and allowed them to sleep with limbs, brown and white, entwined in beautiful harmony.

Chapter 33
Alice and Benny

Bill and Gerry celebrated New Year with a few other couples at Shane's house. Alice and Benny also came to the party with dates ... for a while. They sipped some champagne, rang in the New Year with everyone, and then took off for parties they'd been invited to. Bill and Gerry stood on Shane's second-floor deck and watched fireworks dot the night sky. There was lots of red, white and blue.

As they stood there, Shane and Bill locked eyes. He said, "Look at all of us. I'll bet our founding fathers never anticipated the multi-racial culture that we all represent. Do you see what I mean?"

"I do. What I see are people in love who are loving life with their partners and spouses. Let's see. What do we have here on this deck? I see Caucasians, of course, but there is a Hispanic couple, three different brands of Asians, two African descendants, and even that enjoyable couple with Indian backgrounds. Good job at forming the true representation of our peoples—all in one city. I seriously doubt the folks back in Cleveland are doing anything like this."

"Not in Virginia either, I can say for certain. Where do you suppose we're headed in the multi-racial culture, Bill? I think there are a lot of suppressed hateful people still. Is history so immutable that change and adaptation are out of the question for certain folks? Your kids, for example, are terrific, smart and really good-looking. Will society treat them as functional equals, or will they have to endure all that antebellum bullshit?"

"I expect them to have to endure the bullshit. The thing is, Alice is a superior athlete and an honor roll student. Benny looks like he's going places with his baseball and academics too. I say that only in the context of publicity. What they both also have are strong drives to excel. I look forward to great things from them, whether or not they become professional athletes. I think Alice will end up being a pro golfer. Baseball is harder to crack into and takes a long time. As black athletes, they'll both have to be way better than average at everything else to achieve any high-level goals.

"Gerry and I talk with them both all the time about the limits that athletics has, and that their education and knowledge base will serve them for the better part of their adult lives. Right now, though, we're letting them enjoy what they're doing. I can't wait for you to see Alice play golf next Saturday."

Next Saturday was a beautiful mid-winter day with no clouds and a predicted high temperature of seventy degrees. The golf course was situated in a semi-dry riverbed surrounded by hills dotted with live oak trees and the various plants constituting the southern California *chaparral* ecosystem. In addition to the live oaks, willows and sycamores were scattered around the course layout. One could hear Downy Woodpeckers drilling tree trunks everywhere.

Their tee time was for 12:30 P.M. Shane and Bill rented a

cart, but Alice said she'd walk and carry her SDSU golf bag.

"We play here a lot. I'll help you read the greens if you need me to," she offered.

A fourth player was assigned to the group. He was a strapping fellow who introduced himself as Andy West. He was carrying his bag too. Bill smiled to himself. It was going to be fun watching things unfold.

Shane flipped a tee to see who would hit first. Andy won and striped a big drive down the middle of the first fairway. Alice followed with one of her own – playing from the back tees. Bill had to cover his mouth to keep Andy from seeing him laugh. Then, Andy noticed her bag and nodded. "So, you play for the Aztecs, huh, Alice?"

"Yes. You hit it pretty well. Where do you play?"

"Oh, I belong to San Diego CC and am playing here today because there's a club tournament there this weekend. The *Winter Classic*, they call it. I'm not really that interested in all the club stuff."

The men teed off from the back tees too, and Bill's drive ended up being about ten yards short of Alice's. Shane pushed his drive into the rough, so played the second shot first. Number one was a medium-length par four, so all of them had short irons to the green. Shane's second shot fell short and to the left of the green, leaving him a difficult chip to a short-side pin. Bill hit 9-iron to fifteen feet. Alice hit her wedge to ten feet. Andy skulled his wedge and the ball scampered over the green. Alice rolled in her putt for birdie, while Andy's comeback chip was short. He two-putted for bogey. Shane chipped up, but the ball had little bite and rolled twenty feet past. He also two-putted. Bill's first putt lipped out and he tapped in for par.

The next few holes were played in relative silence as all the players were trying to get into concentration mode. Alice, of course, was in that state of mind from the time she stepped out of the car. She and Andy walked and talked a little, but Alice wasn't having any flirtation. She was focused. Bill had seen this before. Andy had no chance of getting to know Alice on the golf course.

Shane and Bill, however, soon began jabbering away as they rode along by themselves. Shane finally got his timing together by the fourth hole and started making pars and even a birdie. Bill played his usual game and made the turn to number ten at one over par. Alice was two under and Andy finished number nine with a three over thirty-nine. He seemed mesmerized by Alice's play. *No kidding!*

As Bill and Shane came back to their cart with soft drinks, Shane said, "You were right about Alice. She can really play. Once Andy cooled off, she started hitting her drives past his. She also putts like a champ. Without those lip-outs, she could have had a 32. Man! Are you gonna caddy for her when she turns pro?"

They laughed at that, and Bill said, "Maybe I will. We have a good rapport when I'm on her bag. Why not? You mean IF she turns pro."

"Yeah. But she seems good enough. I followed the women pros around when they played at Torrey. She's as good as most of them."

"Well, I want her to finish her degree at the university before we entertain any of that. I agree that she's got all the shots and the right mental strength to stay with them, but she needs to have a fallback plan. One slipped disc and she's teaching school."

"Of course. You're right. But watch out for the publicity hounds and the media who want to promote this beautiful brown girl as breaking through color barriers on the LPGA tour and all that shit."

"I know. We've discussed it with her. She realizes what's coming. Look at poor Andy there. He's totally taken by Alice. Her aloofness has him totally befuddled. I'll bet few girls or women have ever resisted him, what with his looks and money. Alice is a leader, and she's strong-willed. The guy she ends up with will be a very excellent fellow. At least, that's what I expect. She's in no hurry to rush that situation. As she realizes what and who she is compared to her peers, I can see her wondering what she's going to do with it all. Again, I expect big things, but I'm not pushing. I'm just the caddy."

Shane laughed at that and they drove over to the tenth tee. Alice and Andy had already hit and were waiting impatiently. Shane and Bill both hurried too much and hit their worst drives of the day. They recovered, but watched Alice carve up the back nine with a thirty-three to go with her thirty-four on the front nine. Andy shot an eighty and was gracious enough to buy everyone a beer after they finished. Shane shot an eighty-two and Bill a pedestrian seventy-eight. They chatted and laughed together as Andy shifted gears and extolled Alice's golf game.

"Even our club champion woman player doesn't come close to you, Alice," he said. "You are amazing! In fact, I've never seen anyone—man or woman—who focuses like you do. It felt that you didn't realize that the rest of us existed ... except when your etiquette kicked in. It was truly a pleasure to play with you three. I wish you, Alice, nothing but greatness. I look forward to seeing your name in the papers." With that, he left a $50 bill on the table, shook hands and left. Alice just rolled her eyes.

"Well, he was a nice guy and didn't step in my line, so all-in-all it was a pretty good day," she said.

After a beat, Shane and Bill shared a look and burst out laughing. "No angel, you just do that to people. You should have seen the look on his face after you hit the first drive. He knew that his charming self was not in play today."

They all laughed, finished their beers and drove home.

School classes had resumed, of course, so the four were hard at work during the fall and into winter. Alice and the golf team went to Tucson, AZ for a winter tournament at the University of Arizona. While she was away, the Aztec freshman baseball team played a weekend series with USD's team that was coached by a former major league pitcher. Shane, Kimoko, Gerry and Bill decided to have a backyard cookout before going to one of the games played on SDSU's campus. The game started a one o'clock that Saturday, so lunch was early. In fact, they got there early enough to see the end of batting practice and the infield warm-up drills.

It was clear to everyone that Benny's smooth movements at shortstop were unique. The footwork practices over the last couple of years with Bill created a smooth and balanced fielder who seemed to glide to the ball. His hands were, as the saying goes, golden. They just seemed to absorb the balls that were hit to him. It was their first look at Benny actually playing baseball in a competitive environment. They didn't tell him they were coming, and he didn't see them in the stands behind third base either.

The Aztecs romped. The final score was 9-3. Benny had three hits, including a long home run to left field. The four interested spectators threw off their constraints and whooped and hollered. As Benny was rounding third, he glanced their way, saw them waving and cheering, and let a little smile show his recognition. He also made three very nice plays at shortstop, including initiating a spectacular double play-off of a hard grounder deep in the hole between second and third bases.

Shane and Kimmy were both very impressed with Benny's

play. Kimmy said that baseball had become a national madness in Japan and her father insisted on taking his family to some games. It was unusual for women to attend baseball games, but her father was enough of an iconoclast to ignore that backward-thinking restriction

"He made sure we understood the game and what was happening on the field," she said. "He wanted us to be as knowledgeable as anyone in the audience. We knew when to cheer and groan too." Everyone chuckled at that comment.

"Bill, Benny is a very slick fielder and it looks like he can hit. Do you think he has a future in baseball?" Shane asked.

"Who knows? Baseball is weird and depends a lot on coaches' favorites. I've known some good players who couldn't even make their high school teams, but played all-star caliber ball in summer leagues. Go figure. Benny is beginning to really like school and is taking an interest in political science. He does not suffer fools gladly, so that automatically excludes him from running for office."

That brought a good laugh.

Gerry said, "Benny took his father's murder very hard. It took a couple years for him to take the edge off his attitude. Bill has had a lot to do with getting him to overcome the past's pain and have vision for the future. Of course, there is this really cute girl in his government class with whom he seems enthralled. We've met her a couple of times and she really is very pretty and smart. We've had to stifle laughs when she stops Benny in his tracks."

Bill followed with, "Even if he hits .400 this year, he's still just a freshman. Let's see what happens next year before we get too excited about Benny's baseball future."

Chapter 34
High and Inside

Winter gave way to spring, and the famous marine layer started bathing the beaches and the city of San Diego with its misty shroud. With the deserts heating up, the thermal low-pressure area out there drew the cooler air in from the still chilly Pacific Ocean. Sometimes the clouds moved all the way out to El Cajon, twenty miles inland, but most of the time that part of the county was sunny and nice.

Gerry's teaching job was going very well and her students were rising to the expectations she had for them. She soon realized that her English department seemed satisfied if the students could read a paragraph without stumbling across words, or write a one-page essay that conveyed a coherent thought. Little consideration was given to good, legible cursive writing, grammar rules, and the mechanics of punctuation and sentence structure. Even her advanced composition students struggled at the point of Gerry's editing pencil. Gerry Bannock demanded much more. Her teaching experience from the inner city allowed her to implement her lessons so that her students developed rapidly. She told Bill that the lack of language discipline she saw must have been going on for years in the lower grades as well.

It seemed natural for Bill to be teaching science. He had to do some extra research—especially for the one section of biology that he taught. The biology teacher that was scheduled to teach the second semester had her husband move away to a Florida Naval air station. She and the kids chose to move with him. Bill had to brush up on his chemistry and physics too, but the labs still challenged him most in setting them up to work so that real learning occurred. His use of the Socratic Method prompted more of them to study, and put some effort into their homework assignments too.

Alice continued to dominate the field in every golf tournament she played. Benny was indeed hitting close to .400 and both of their scholastic grades were at or near the top of their class. Gerry and Bill had never been happier together, as the children and their lives seemed to be completely headed in the right direction. Their children worked their butts off as much as they did. Their house was often a comfortable study hall during evenings and on weekends as Gerry and Bill graded papers, wrote exams and planned lessons. Alice and Benny were busy reading, writing, re-copying their class notes and studying them.

One day, he was teaching a class on basic mechanical advantages and machines in physics when his classroom phone rang. This was a rare occurrence as the front office screened calls and only allowed the most important ones through. The ringing of the phone sounded extra loud since everyone knew that this was no fluke.

It was Gerry. "Oh, Bill! Benny is in the hospital. He was hit by a pitch and is still unconscious. I'm headed over to Grossmont Hospital right now. I got somebody to fill in for my last class. Can you come right away? It sounds serious. I'm out of my mind with worry. Please hurry."

"I'll be there as soon as I can," he said.

His students noticed the stricken look on his face as he put the phone down. They were silent for a moment, then somebody asked what had happened.

"My son was hit by a pitch at his game today and is in the hospital right now. Thanks for asking. Look, I've gotta find a fill-in. Start working on the questions at the end of chapter twenty-three while I try to sort this out. Thanks for your patience."

"Sure thing, Mr. Bannock. I hope your son is okay," said the senior class president.

The office found a teacher who had a planning period during Bill's last class. She came to his room shortly after the bell rang for dismissal of the current period.

"Oh, thanks, Ms. Spencer. Here is the lesson plan. They're working on balancing equations for this chemistry class. Here's their worksheet. It's chapter seventeen. Thanks so much. Anytime I can return the favor, just ask."

Bill got to the hospital ER without any mishaps. He found Gerry in the waiting room, looking like she was going to fall apart. Her eyes were red, her cheeks streaked with tears. Her hands were clutched but still trembled. When she saw him, she leaped up from her chair and threw her arms around him, sobbing words he could barely understand.

"Oh, Bill, he got hit in the head by a pitched ball. They rushed him upstairs to surgery after stabilizing him here." She stepped back and started to regain her composure. "I waited for you to get here. We can wait for him up on the fifth floor. Let's go. I don't know when he'll be out of surgery. Oh, God! My baby boy! This just can't happen. No. No. No."

"Easy, baby. Let's not rush to any conclusions. Let me ask the ER nurse what she knows."

Bill found a nurse, who pointed him to another nurse

resting behind a desk. Her name was Sophie McFadden.

"Nurse McFadden. I'm Bill Bannock, the stepfather and guardian of Benny Morgan. He was brought in with a head injury from the baseball game over at the university. What do you know?"

"I spoke with your wife, but I don't know how much registered. We were pretty busy getting him upstairs by the time she got here. What I know is that Benjamin suffered a serious contusion to his left zygomatic arch and bone; the bones that surround the eyeball. He was unconscious, so I expect he has a serious concussion as well. The ER doctor got him right up to surgery after X-rays. Fortunately, we have a specialist on call, and he got right to work. The last thing I heard was that they were trying to save his eye. That's all I know. You should take your wife up to the waiting room on five. The surgeon's name is Dr. Alvarez. He's one of the best in the state. Your son is in good hands here."

"Thank you so much, nurse. We'll go upstairs and wait for news."

He led Gerry to the elevators and they found the waiting room on the fifth floor. He told the desk nurse who they were.

"Dr. Alvarez is working on your boy now. Please have a seat. There's a coffee machine in the hallway just there." She pointed down the hall.

They sat, and Gerry wouldn't let go of Bill. He could see that she was fighting to remain calm and composed. After a couple of hours, Bill got up and asked the nurse where there was a telephone he could use. She directed him to the pay phone next to the coffee machine. He bought a cup of coffee, but Gerry didn't want any. He called Alice at home and told her what had happened and where they were.

"Oh my God, Bill! I'll be right there. Should I bring something?"

"Bring a thermos of ice water and lots of good coffee. The stuff from the machine here is shit. I don't know how long it'll be, so the coffee would be a big help. We're on the fifth floor. Take your time and drive safely. The emergency part is over, now it's just how well Dr. Alvarez can fix Benny's injury. See you soon."

Just as he hung up, there was a clatter of spiked shoes coming down the hallway. It was Benny's baseball coach Silas Bauer.

"Hey, coach. How'd this happen?"

"First, bring me up to speed about Benny's injury."

"The ER nurse said it looked like the orbital bones surrounding his left eye were in pretty bad shape and that he had a concussion. He's been in surgery for a couple of hours now."

"Thanks. Well, it was one of those weird plays. The Montana State pitcher was throwing very fast pitches, but he was also wild. Just as this kid was ready to wind up, Benny asked for time. The pitcher threw it anyway even after time was called. I saw Benny glance back at the umpire to make sure he got timeout, but when he turned back, the ball was on him, high and inside. I wanted to run out there and strangle that kid."

"So, you had to finish the game?"

"Yeah. The MSU pitcher was so shaken up, they had to take him out. Benny looked like he'd never move again. There is a phone by the concessions stand, and our trainer called the ambulance. It only took about ten minutes for it to get there. After they took Benny away, both teams sort of went through the motions. After five innings, their coach and I decided to end the game right there. The teams were tied at four, so it didn't matter.

"Do you mind if I wait with you for the report? I'll have to tell the Dean of Students and the Athletic Director, of course."

"Sure. This is my wife, Gerry, Benny's mother."

"I'm sorry we have to meet under these circumstances Mrs. Bannock." He held her hand as she nodded. Just as coach Bauer finished talking to Gerry, Alice came striding down the hall with arms filled with thermos bottles.

"Coach, this is Benny's sister, Alice. She's on the golf team."

"I know all about Alice. She's the talk of the campus. Nice to meet you in person. I'm so sorry about Benny. Let's hope for a full and speedy recovery. I'll just sit over there and let you folks talk."

"It was good of you to come, Coach Bauer," Gerry said. "Benny thinks very highly of you."

They drank some coffee. Alice asked the coach if he'd like some iced water.

"That would be great. It feels like I've been chewing tissue paper." That brought a chuckle from Alice.

A half-hour after Bauer arrived, a slender, medium-height man in scrubs pushed through a door into the hallway. As he turned toward the waiting group, he pulled his mask down so that just the two lower laces held it around his neck.

"Are you the family for Benjamin Morgan?" he asked. His dark eyes flashed, but they could see fatigue in them too.

"Yes, I'm his mother. How is he? Are you Doctor Alvarez?"

"Yes. Sorry, I should have introduced myself." He shook everyone's hands. "Well, Benjamin has suffered a fractured zygomatic bone and arch on the left side of his face. There was quite a bit of bleeding that seeped into his eye socket and put a lot of pressure on his eyeball. It took me some time to remove the hematoma and reconstruct the socket. Fortunately, there were only four bone fragments and none of them pierced the eyeball itself. Our biggest concern here will be damage to the retina from the hematoma, or blood clot behind the eyeball. I couldn't relieve that pressure until I had made certain that no bone fragments were in the narrow area behind the eye.

"He also received a concussion – as you might imagine – but all his reflexes and vitals seem to be in the normal range. I expect he will regain consciousness in the next few hours. He's resting comfortably in recovery and all his numbers look good. He's a very healthy young man, so I have high hopes for his full recovery. I don't know if he'll want to stand in against any more fastballs, but if I've done my job, his eyesight should be very close to normal after he heals up."

"Thank you doctor," everyone said in a relay of voices. Silas Bauer thanked the doctor, shook everyone's hands and scurried back down the hallway.

Bill said, "Should we stay here in relays and when Benny wakes up, call the others?"

"That sounds good, darling." I'll take the first shift. When I'm not able to stay awake, I'll call and somebody can come and relieve me."

"Okay. C'mon, Alice. Let's go home, have some dinner and get some rest. It might be a long night. Gerry, you should go down to the hospital cafeteria when you can and get something to eat. You're gonna want to stay strong and minimize your stress."

Gerry hugged Bill hard, kissed him softly and stroked his cheek with her long, graceful fingers. "I will. Thank you for being strong for me and for Benny. Go rest now. See you soon."

Chapter 35

Recovery and Moving Ahead

Bill awoke just after midnight. He turned on the coffee pot, showered, ate some scrambled eggs and filled his travel cup with the fresh coffee. He got to the hospital just after one o'clock and found Gerry snoozing on the waiting room couch. He stroked her arm gently until her eyes snapped open.

"Any word yet?" she asked groggily.

"Not yet. I'm here now. Go home, eat something and get to bed. I'll be fine. Alice said she would relieve me around eight."

Gerry stood up and hugged him, mumbled "okay" in his ear, picked up her purse and walked somewhat unsteadily down the hallway.

At about six-thirty, a nurse came up to Bill while he was reading an old sports magazine, and asked him if he was related to Benjamin Morgan.

"I'm his stepfather."

"Benjamin is awake and asking for you or his mother. Would you like to see him?"

"Yes. Let me call his mother first and get her here too."

"Okay, but you can't stay in his room too long. He's had a pretty rough time."

When he returned from making the call, he followed the nurse to the recovery room where Benny was resting. Both eyes were bandaged to prevent eye movement. When Bill spoke, Benny reached for him and smiled. Bill grabbed his hand and squeezed.

"What's the doctor say, Bill? Am I gonna be blind?" He had to speak through his teeth because his jaw appeared to be wired shut too. That made sense, since the reconstruction of his bones was a delicate procedure, and any movement of his jaw would hinder healing.

"He told us what he did to save your eye. He said he put the pieces back together and removed the blood clot from behind your eyeball. As far as he could tell, your eyeball didn't get damaged."

Benny drifted off. After a few minutes, he asked, "Is Momma here?"

"Not yet. She's on her way. The nurse says you shouldn't talk too much. It looks like it's gonna be milkshakes for you for a while."

"Chocolate. Add some of that new protein powder so I don't get too weak," he said with a little smile.

"Sure. Anything you want."

Just then, Gerry came into the room and went to the bed. "How are you feeling, baby?"

"Kinda groggy. Don't worry, Momma. I'm gonna be fine. Gotta heal. Looks like my baseball season is over for now." He reached for her, and Gerry took his hand in both of hers.

"We're here for you, Benny. We'll do everything we need to do to get you back to health. We love you."

"I'm glad. I love you too. But I'm feelin' sleepy right now. Thanks for coming." With those words, his grip on Gerry's hands slackened and he went back to sleep.

Gerry wiped the tears from her cheek and turned toward

Bill with a look he'd never seen from her before: desperate worry.

"I don't know what the outcome will be for Benny's baseball career, but he has a very good brain. Of course, we'll be there for him at every turn," he said, reassuringly.

Benny was discharged from the hospital a week later. X-rays showed his facial bones healing in place after the reconstruction. There appeared to be no hematoma developing behind his eyeball, so Dr. Alvarez was very confident that Benny's vision would return and become close to normal. "He'll have to have both eyes immobilized as well as his jaw for a couple more weeks until the bones start to knit. We'll take pictures every week."

Meanwhile, Alice continued to tear up the Mountain West golf world with a string of victories both in San Diego and on the road. SDSU played Air Force in Colorado Springs during the last week of April—the week of spring break. On the day of the tournament, it snowed a foot. The golfers and the cadets worked to clear the greens, but they all had to wait two days for the sun to melt the snow. At over 7,000 feet, the snow sublimes as well as melts, so the fairways became playable by the second day. When she got home, she said that at that altitude everyone was breathless much of the time, but the academy golf course was magnificent.

"The course was carved into a pine forest and was pretty hilly," she said. "Oh, and I shot 65; my lowest score ever. Well, the ball was flying so far, that most of the time I was hitting driver-wedge. I was able to reach every par five, so I made a lot of birdies. Even after the snow melted, the course was immaculate. We all stood around looking at the snow-covered mountains right next to the campus. Spectacular."

After two months, Benny's bandages were removed for good.

X-rays showed that the bone fragments had healed together just as expected. His vision in his left eye was still blurry, but Dr. Alvarez said it would take a few days for everything to start working again, including how Benny's brain realized that it had two eyes in binocular association and had to get back to work. They took him to an ophthalmologist for an eye examination and vision testing. Benny said that the blurriness was lessening each day. The overall eyeball health was very close to normal.

The doctor, Sandra Walsh, said: "Don't worry about the discoloration in the white of the eye. There are cells called *phagocytes* that will eventually eat the escaped blood. I expect it will be another couple of weeks for that to clear up. At that time, I want you to bring Benny back in for a vision test to see if he'll need corrective lenses."

Benny's vision returned to normal, but when he looked quickly at something at the other end of his field of view, there was a troubling flash. The ophthalmologist said that it may or may not disperse with time, but she recommended that Benny stay away from baseball for a year. To say he was disappointed at that news would be a gross understatement, but his mother and Bill kept positive and helped him realize that he had so much more to offer the world.

"I know, mom, but I love baseball. It'll be hard for me to go to Padres' games and watch."

"Yes, I understand, baby. But at least you'll have two working eyes to prepare you to be a Senator or something similar," Gerry consoled.

In June, the NCAA announced their all-Americans for spring sports. Alice Morgan was named first-team all-American in golf. It didn't take long for the phone to start ringing. Sports agents were trying to talk her into turning pro so they could get rich on the prospects of her winnings. She asked Bill for advice, and he told her that turning pro would mean she would be very hard-pressed to finish her college degree and play in enough tournaments around the world to make it worth her while.

"As we discussed, you'll always have golf, but your education is necessary for the part of your life after professional golf ... if you go that way," he reminded her.

They talked with Coach Mason about deciding whether or not to turn pro. She went into great detail, explaining what being on tour was like.

"Well, let's say you arrive at the Los Angeles tournament site on Monday morning. Now, you've just flown in from Boston on a red-eye, and the pro-am in L.A. starts on Tuesday. You make sure your clubs made it off the airplane and take a taxi to your hotel, check-in and change into your practice clothes. Next, it's a taxi ride to the course, where you play some practice holes, get a feel for the greens and meet all the LPGA and local officials.

"After that, you try to find a caddy—if you don't have your own personal one—and secure him or her for the week, leave your clubs in the course locker room. Then you find another taxi to take you back to your hotel for dinner. You will probably run into some players you know and go to the restaurant together.

"Let's say that one of your friends is a well-known player. During your dinner, you are accosted by fans and maybe a hustler or two for autographs or even phone numbers.

"You are out of your mind with jet lag, so you turn in early. After getting back to your room, you shower and collapse. Your wake-up call is for six o'clock and then it's breakfast and another taxi ride over to the golf course. Of course, if you're a top twenty player, the tournament will have a courtesy car for you to use. When you get there, you go to the range and start hitting balls, trying to get rid of that annoying push-fade you had last week. Let's say that your tee time for the pro-am is at ten o'clock.

"You meet your three playing partners and try to avoid the cigar smoke and the fawning. Most of the players will be men with lots of money and have never been told 'no'. Your players will play from the back tees to show you how powerful they are. After the third hole, you and your caddy are sharing eye rolls after just about every shot. Sometimes you get lucky and are matched with a good player who at least respects the game, the course and etiquette. Mostly, though, the other players are trying to show off their power and are making bets with each other. Do NOT get involved with betting with these people.

"Okay. So, after you finish your round, they'll invite you in for a beer or drink. I'd strongly advise against that. Tell them you've gotta practice. Then, go hit balls and chip and putt until dinner time. The next day is a practice round day. This is the time where you'll make your 'book' on the course if you haven't played there before. It will take almost all day, but you still want to hit balls and practice the short game afterwards.

"If you're lucky, you'll get an early tee time on Thursday morning, when the course is not spiked up and the greens are the smoothest. You'll be able to refine your book too. Be sure to warm up good before you tee off. When you're finished playing, practice those shots you weren't happy with during the round. This is where your caddy earns his or her keep. They have to hang with you the whole time. It's a long day for them too. When you leave for the day, they have to clean your clubs, make sure you have a dozen or so balls in the bag, clean your shoes, etc."

"So, you make the cut on Friday and play the weekend. You're gonna make some money. But if you finish in the bottom half of the field on Sunday—or Saturday if it's a fifty-four-hole tournament—you'll be lucky to get a check for a thousand dollars. You must pay your caddy the going rate and tip generously if he or she has done their job.

"If you're smart and organized, you've made your travel and lodging arrangements for the next stop on the tour after you know you made the cut. So, after you finish up at the course on Sunday, you go back to the hotel, clean up, pack and take a cab to the airport, making sure that your clubs are checked through to the right destination. Now, you're ready to do it all again. Does that sound like something you want to do, Alice?"

"What a grind! So much for glamour. I had no idea it would be such a grueling routine. Wow! I honestly don't know. Thing is, I like school. I want to get my degree. I love the sports medicine curriculum and would love to be a trainer someday.

"You've given me a lot to think about, Coach Mason. I really appreciate you spending the time."

"Well, every time one of my girls talks about turning pro, I give them this little 'day in the life' talk. If you look closely, you'll see that there are maybe two dozen women golfers who ride first class in this business. And if you don't keep winning or making lots of money, your sponsors dry up and you end up like a good friend of mine. Kathy Bixby won a U.S. Open quite a few years ago, but that was her moment in the sun. She did have the foresight to buy into a driving range in Tucson where she now teaches and operates the business. So, it's a matter of what you want out of whatever you end up doing as a professional golfer."

"I understand. I don't think I want to be around the clubhouse for fourteen hours a day. I will try out the pro game when I graduate, but if it doesn't pan out, I'll have my degree and some good experience."

"Good thinking, Alice," Mason said. "You're a very bright young lady and wherever you end up, that place will benefit. Oh, and you're also a hell of a golfer. Everyone around here drools at how far and how straight you hit everything. I thought you were going to drive some of the greens at Air Force."

Everyone laughed.

Bill thanked Coach Mason for her time and the three of them left.

"Let's stop at the ice cream shop, Bill," Alice said. "I think I deserve a banana split."

Chapter 36

Pro Alice

Everyone passed the next two years in a manner to which they quickly became accustomed: *routinely*. It wasn't that it was boring, by any means, it was just that they all seemed to have put their heads down and done their jobs. Alice ground through college with very high grades and letters of recommendation from her professors that were almost embarrassing in their unbridled praise for her dedication, brilliance and hard work... Especially the hard work. The girl just didn't seem to ever run out of focus and energy to do what needed to be done. The family endured the publicity and notoriety that the media heaped on her—and them—for her all-American performances in golf. San Diego, being a golfing mecca, was totally enthralled with this tall, beautiful brown woman who was setting the golfing world on its ear.

Breaking the color barrier at most of the country clubs seemed to be an emerging movement, and Alice was the leader without portfolio for that movement. Her photogenic face and form didn't hurt it either. Alice began to see that as a kind of mission in her young life. The day after she received her diploma from San Diego State University, she filled out the paperwork for turning professional and applied for LPGA qualifying school.

Bill suggested to Alice that she cast her net toward acquiring a caddy that really knew a lot about golf and even, perhaps, life on tour.

"Good idea. I guess you won't want to quit your teaching job and be my caddy on tour," she joked.

"No. Besides, I'd probably end up being your bodyguard too, and I'm too old for that. Seriously, not everyone is going to be nice to you once you're outside the comfort of San Diego and college golf."

"Yeah, I felt some of it when we went to places like Montana State or Wyoming. It seems some people just can't tolerate a brown woman playing good golf on their precious, hallowed turf. Well, I can ignore that stuff while on the golf course, and I know I'll have to keep my mouth shut for a while. I also know I'm going to be the only non-white player on the tour. Oh, there are some girls with Hispanic names, but they just look like Italians to those who carry prejudice and bigotry." They both chuckled at that analysis. "Someday, though, I'll have my say. I'll wait for the time when, like Babe Didrickson, I can get away with saying anything because I'm so good as to be untouchable. I've thought about this a lot, Bill. Will you always be there for me when I need to talk things through?"

"Of course, Alice. I only want the best for you. I'll always love you and be there for you." She flashed him that impossible, Sports-Illustrated-cover smile and wrapped her long, strong arms around his neck, squeezing him for long seconds.

"I love you too, Bill. Having Momma be so happy removes a lot of worry from me, and you make her VERY happy. Now, I gotta go find a caddy."

Alice asked around the athletic department, and a few people showed interest. One day, as Alice was saying goodbye to Coach Mason, one of the male golf team members intercepted her outside the coach's office.

"Alice, I hear you're looking for a caddy."

"Oh, hi, Connor. Yeah. I need somebody with as much experience as I can find. Do you know anybody who I could hire?"

"I do. Me. I don't know if you know, but my family have been long-time members of Mission Bay Country Club. The club has produced three PGA touring pros over the years, some of whom I've caddied for at the club. One of those guys, Billy Collins, trained me to be a tour caddy. We'd go out at first light and he'd pretend we were playing the U.S. Open. So, I have a pretty good idea about what to do."

"Tell you what, Connor, take me to your club and we'll play a round. You caddy and show me what Billy Collins taught you. I really do need that kind of support while I'm finding my way."

"Sure. Give me your phone number and I'll call you when I get a tee time. Let me get going on that right away. Talk soon." And Connor Gaylord was gone.

Connor Gaylord was the son of one of San Diego's industrial scions. They were old money from the earliest 20th-Century service industries and helped found the Mission Bay Golf and Country Club located up the hill from the shores of La Jolla and Pacific Beach. Connor had a golf club put into his hands from the time he could walk. But, like Bill, he couldn't get any better than a one or two handicap. Golf, it seemed, was in his blood, and though he played sporadically for the SDSU men's team, his golf future was going to be elsewhere.

He was tall and handsome at 6'3", but was refined, polite and well-read. His steely blue eyes could look right through a person, but with his infectious smile, it was easy to feel comfortable around him. Bill met him while Alice and he toured the club course. Bill walked along that day and saw that as the holes progressed and Connor learned her club performances, they started looking like a real team. He did all the little things just right and even talked Alice out of a couple of shots because she'd picked the wrong club for the particular situation. They finished the round at even par, not bad considering they had never seen the hilly, and difficult-to-walk golf course with lightning-fast greens. Alice only made three birdies, but the three bogies came early before she got a feel for the sloping and contoured greens. Bill was pleased with what he saw.

After the round, Connor bought everyone lunch at the club. There were more than a few looks from the other patrons, but one lady came over to shake Alice's hand.

"Hi. I'm Dorothy Etheridge. I've seen your picture in the paper and in golf magazines. Congratulations on being all-American. Connor is a terrific caddy. Did he caddy for you today?"

"Yes, ma'am. He IS very good. Thank you for your compliments."

"Oh, I hate to sound like a celebrity hound – we get quite a few through here – but would you be kind enough to give me an autograph? Here's a clean napkin."

"Of course."

"That's sweet. What are your plans, if I may ask?"

"Well, I'm turning pro and going to the Q-School sectional tournament in September. Connor is going to be my caddy."

Connor's eyes popped out of his head and the fork stopped halfway to his mouth.

"Well, I hope you do well. I'll look for your scores in the paper. It's five really tough rounds, from what I hear. Be sure to drink lots of water out there in Palm Springs. It was so nice meeting you, Alice. Good luck."

"You'd better get used to that, baby," Bill said.

"Did you just hire me to be your caddy, Alice?"

"I did. I was meaning to tell you after lunch, but the celebrity moment just intruded itself."

Everyone chuckled.

"I can't pay you anything until I start winning money."

"No worries. I have more money than I can ever spend. Heck, I might even subsidize you until you start drawing a paycheck. After all, it's gonna cost a few thousand dollars just to get you through the Q-School stages. Would that work for you?"

Now it was Alice's turn to have a slack jaw. "Wow, Connor! That would be wonderful. Thank you. It will give me even more incentive to succeed. Don't worry, I'll pay you back as soon as I can."

"Aw, no rush. Tell you what, why don't we drive out to Palm Springs early tomorrow so you can see the course you're going to play? I've played it a couple of times, so making a book should be pretty easy. I'll pick you and your sticks up at five o'clock tomorrow morning. It's just over two hours and we'll be ahead of traffic. Besides, we might get a round in before the temperature tops a hundred." He smiled at his own audacity. Alice and Bill smiled back.

"Mind if Gerry and I tag along, Connor? We could be her first gallery."

"No problem. My station wagon has plenty of room. See you tomorrow morning. Bring coffee."

Alice and Connor worked the course at Indian Flats while Gerry and Bill scurried from one shady spot to the next, clutching their canteens. The really good news was that Alice got to play by herself and took putts from all spots on the green to build her 'book'. Her length off the tee allowed her to hit all but one of the par five holes in two shots. That one had a nasty water hazard that required a layup for a third shot to the green. She played well but was more intent on making her course book for next week. She and Connor didn't even keep score.

The course was nestled right up against the San Jacinto Mountains which loomed tall and multi-colored as they rose above the near-sea-level desert floor. It was a beautiful setting, and they even saw some rare desert bighorn sheep cavorting up the mountainside. The golf course, of course, was immaculate. The greens were Bermuda grass, so Alice had to learn to read the grain because it was so different from the Poa Annua greens she was more used to along the coast.

After the round, they ate a light lunch and drove back home.

As he dropped them off, Connor said to Alice, "Where do you want to meet for practice tomorrow?"

"How about Singing Hills? They have a good range and short game area."

"Sure thing. See you there at seven tomorrow morning."

The three stood there looking at each other. "Well, my dear, your 'employee'—or should I say *employer*—seems to be taking charge of your life," Bill said. "I think he wants you to be a winner."

"Good. So do I! If he's going to remove the burden of scheduling and logistics, I'm glad he's doing it. I can't wait to get started."

Chapter 37

The Pro Game

Gerry had classes to teach and Benny was still recovering his eyesight, so Bill took some personal days to watch Alice participate in the Q-School rounds that, if she finished in the top forty-five players, would go to Florida for the finals. The top twenty players from those grueling five rounds would get their qualified tour cards and be on their way to a paycheck and, hopefully, a career.

It was hot in Palm Springs. The sparse gallery allowed in was mostly family and friends of the golfers. Each player was limited to six guests. Bill kept filling his canteen and, with his floppy hat and wet neck scarf, managed to keep from dropping over from heat exhaustion.

Alice had no such problems. The school made sure that the water stations were kept filled on every tee box. She attacked the course for five straight days and finished fourth overall. The three women ahead of her all had major college and amateur credentials too, and were not intimidated by the pressure.

"Did you see that lip-out on the last hole?" Alice snarled. "That would have given me third. That remark confirmed the part of Alice Morgan her family loved: She was focused, determined and always seeking improvement.

After everyone showered and changed at the hotel, they all went to the fanciest steakhouse in Palm Springs for dinner. Bill sat back and just listened to the excited chatter, teasing and comments from the week's work by Alice and Connor. Clearly, Alice was in great shape and showed little or no fatigue. Even Bill was amazed that she was hitting the ball the same distances off the tee on day five as on day one. She was clearly in a groove. She and Connor worked smoothly and quietly together without a lot of chatter or indecision between them. The weather had been hot but relatively calm, with only one day of wind that required extra shot planning.

Watching the fire in Alice's eyes brought smiles to Bill's face even when she wasn't saying anything.

I don't think anything will stop her. She's going to wring everything she can out of this career. Her being a black woman is going to drive the news people wild. I can't wait to see how the racists will react when she makes the turnstiles sing at their lily-white golf clubs. From what we saw and heard from the sports journalists when she was still in college, if she goes out there and starts winning golf tournaments... Well, it will be something to behold. But if anybody can handle the pressure, our dear Alice can.

When he got home, Bill shared these thoughts with Gerry.

"Yes. I'm so glad we raised her to be fearless and to not suffer fools gladly," she said. "You, my love, have been a wonderful influence on her golf game as well as helping her develop a philosophy where she could accept her gifts and just work to be better every day. Golf is a really hard game with so many variables; I'm sure it drives her nuts when she gets a bad bounce."

"It does. She grouses very well too. I saw that when we played together. But I helped her to move past the bad breaks quickly. I pointed out that a negative memory has to be quickly discarded, or it will carry over into the next shot. She got that right away. As you've heard, she saves the grousing for post-round debriefings."

They both laughed. "My God, Bill. We may have a real star on our hands. How are *we* going to deal with that?"

"Well, I think she wants me to be her business manager. I'll probably have to quit teaching once she gets going. When I worked in industry I learned to negotiate vendor contracts, so that will be important when the sponsors start calling in earnest. I guess we're going to have to be the gracious, somewhat stunned parents who continue to be supportive and loving. That shouldn't be too hard to sell to the media, since we do that sort of thing every day anyway."

During the next month, before traveling to Florida, Alice and Connor practiced diligently. Bill sent them to the Sarasota area a week early so they could adapt to the late autumn climate there, as well as to the different strains of Bermuda grass on the greens. The school year was in full swing for Gerry, Benny and Bill. Benny had recovered most of his visual acuity and returned to his second-year classes.

There was no television for the second level of Q-School for Alice, so she called home every day after her round to report the outcome. On her first day, she was four under par and only one shot behind the leader, who'd been trying to get her card for a few years. She added that Connor was doing a great job of caddying and had her routine figured out perfectly.

"He's been nothing but a gentleman and a great supporting voice during and after our rounds," she said. "He makes me practice what I need to practice and when. But when I start getting too tired on the range, he just takes the bag and walks away. He says that over-practice is as bad as not enough practice. That has helped me with saving my mental energy too.

"Not that I need it, but he bangs on my door in the morning to make sure I'm up, showered and dressed for breakfast. He even keeps me away from eating sweets, jellies and jams. He'll say that sugar highs are followed by low blood sugar mood changes. He puts fresh bananas and peanut butter sandwiches in the bag every day. I asked him how he knew all this stuff, and he told me that he learned it from Billy when they discussed life on tour. He said that the most important thing is to keep an even emotional status throughout the round. I've limited my birdie reactions to a single fist pump."

That made Bill and Gerry laugh, since they remembered her doing happy dances and yelling from years ago.

"So, are you getting any social life in Florida?" Bill teased.

"Naw. Connor sends me to my room by nine. He started that routine all last week. We went to a movie once, but he had me back at the hotel by eight forty-five. He's more controlling than you were, Momma. Don't worry, you two. He calls his girlfriend every night. She and he have been locked in since elementary school days."

"Was I really that much on your case?" Gerry asked plaintively.

"Only kidding. Connor says that the routine has to be part of my life during tournaments so that my mental energy is saved for the game. No distractions. No worries. He is, of course, playing right into my focus strengths. He says it may be what makes me a champion rather than just a great golfer. Pretty heady stuff.

"Okay, it's late here. Gotta get to sleep. Call you tomorrow. I love you both. Good night."

Gerry and Bill hung up the phone and just grinned at each other. She came over and absorbed him in one of her full body embraces. Benny was in his room down the hall, studying with the door closed. The embrace with clothes on evolved into an embrace with no clothes. Then they made sweet, satisfying love with joy in their hearts, knowing their dear Alice was on her way to great things.

Alice's first LPGA tournament slot came as a sponsor's exemption at a course outside Memphis, Tennessee. She would be, of course, the only black player at this all-white exclusive country club. The company that signed Alice up for an equipment contract after she earned her tour card also co-sponsored the Western Tennessee Invitational Championship. Gerry and Bill were teaching, so didn't go with her. They felt good that she was in the capable and strong hands of Connor Gaylord.

Alice called on Wednesday night after her practice round and told everyone that the wait staff working at the club were all black, and quietly told her that they were rooting for her. "They told me who to look out for in order to avoid getting into any confrontations.

"The membership threw the players a pre-tournament banquet and sat me in the back of the room, at a table by myself. Three of the players I'd met earlier at practice noticed and came back to join me. One of the women at our table is a top-ten ranked player whose face you've seen on golf magazine covers.

"She said this was just redneck bullshit and that I shouldn't get too upset. She also told me that even just being a white *woman* at some clubs was grounds for this elitist bigotry. Then another one of the women just said, 'Fuck 'em, Alice Just go out there and win the damned tournament. That will be like sticking a splintered board up their asses'. I had no idea that women could talk like that."

Everyone laughed.

"I've got Connor with me, and he looks like a Greek god

compared to the other caddies. Everyone who is playing in the tournament has been really nice to me. Some of the other caddies told me to be aware of purposeful distractions from the gallery. Apparently, some men do and say things to distract the players they don't like. They said that my focus was going to be tested like never before. I told them that I was thankful for the warning, but that I'd have Connor go over and sort those people out. They just laughed and wished me good luck."

So, as the most talked-about rookie in LPGA history teed it up at eight o'clock on a cool, misty autumn morning, everyone waited somewhat breathlessly for the outcome. Alice called after she'd had lunch and her post-round practice to say that she shot a three under par sixty-nine—two strokes off the opening day leader's sixty-seven.

"The greens were pretty soft, but quick. That caused us to make adjustments with club selection, but after number five, we started hitting it in close. The cups were sharply cut and I had two good putts lip out. Gotta go. I've gotta clean up, have dinner and get to bed. My tee time tomorrow is at eleven, so I have to adjust. I'm feeling good about today and there weren't any people in our gallery that caused trouble. In fact, the other two women in my group only had family and close friends watching them. I kind of expected more press coverage, but the gallery remained small the whole round. My equipment sponsor sent one of their public relations types to watch over us, so I just focused on playing good golf. I feel like I'm gonna tear it up tomorrow.

"G'night, you two. I love you both and I hear your voices in my head often. Talk to you tomorrow, when I'm done playing."

Gerry and Bill went out after school for their own Friday night treat, heading to their local hamburger joint and drinking a couple of beers. Alice said she'd call around six, Pacific Time, so they hustled home to await her news.

"Yeah. Connor and I figured out the course. He's a wizard at reading greens and my stroke has been solid all week. Oh, I shot a sixty-five and am now tied for the lead with the defending champion. I'll be in the last group tomorrow. The gallery was bigger today, and we expect it to be larger still tomorrow. The local government has assigned a couple of Sheriff Deputies to escort me to, from, and around the course. The sponsors put in big money and don't want any idiotic disturbances to spoil their newest great marketing vehicle."

Alice said all this with a fake southern accent, causing Bill and Gerry to laugh a little.

Bill said, "Okay. Forget all that. Those folks who are mean-spirited and trying to distract you are simply prisoners of their own misbegotten culture that refuses to enter the twentieth century. It's pitiful, I know, but the racism and bigotry are not going away any time soon. Your answer to them will be winning the tournament, smiling for the cameras and being a humble, gracious winner. They'll have no response to that and you'll win again."

"Thanks, Bill. I know you're right. Momma, I want to make all of you proud. If I'm gonna be the first black woman to win on this tour, I'm gonna be the best at doing whatever I have to do to make people forget that I'm not white. I'm learning that lesson and gaining more of a sense of purpose each day.

"Well, my tee time tomorrow isn't until noon, so I'm gonna read for a while and get some sleep. Funny thing is, I'm not that nervous about tomorrow. Connor says I have a killer instinct. He makes me laugh. I think his sense of humor and control over my time makes me feel pretty calm. After all, I can't be jerking putts on fast greens, now, can I?"

They said their goodnights and then Gerry and Bill relayed

the conversation to Benny, who emerged from his room.

"Wow! I guess I'm gonna have to learn to treat her like some celebrity pretty soon. To tell you the truth, she's not like any girls I've met. Her focus on her game is amazing. You know, I think she's gonna be the best in the game pretty soon," Benny concluded. Nobody disagreed.

On Saturday, Alice fired a sixty-four, setting the fifty-four-hole record for the tournament. She was clear of the field by three shots going into the final round on Sunday. Her call home that night included some excited recounts of the eagle putt she holed, and a couple of spectacular up-and-in holes she played to avoid making any bogies. Gerry and Bill did their best to calm her down so she could get some good rest.

"Yeah. I know," she said. "I just had to share my excitement. Sixty-four is my all-time best score, and I so wished you could have been here to see it. Okay, I get it. I still have tomorrow's round to go. Connor brought me back to earth today by pointing out the misread putt I missed on number eleven and the bladed chip on number six. I think he'll keep me grounded tomorrow too."

And he did. Alice finished with a sixty-eight playing all four rounds under seventy. It was a spectacular finish as her closest pursuers faded on the back nine and allowed Alice to pull away to a five-shot win. A photographer caught her leaping into Connor's strong arms with her arm raised and her mouth open in a yell. As promised, she posed with the trophy by flashing her most compelling smile.

Gerry and Bill were beside themselves with joy. They jumped around the house while Benny just shook his head.

"It's just one tournament. What did she win—maybe fifty thousand bucks? That'll barely pay Connor back and for the plane tickets to Texas next week."

Alice's actual winnings were sixty-two thousand dollars.

She paid Connor back what she owed him from the Q-School sponsorship and flew them both to Houston for the Texas Open. This would be the last LPGA tournament of the season, and those in San Diego were anxious to have their girl home for a while. She didn't win in Houston, but finished in the top ten, garnering another nice paycheck.

The three of them greeted her at Lindbergh Field, only to find that her former golf team members and several other young women were there too. As Gerry and Bill stood in the background, her mates and new friends fussed, hugged and begged for autographs. They smiled at each other as Alice's poise, grace and presence charmed everyone ... even them.

Connor's parents were there too, and with bodyguards present, they greeted Bill and Gerry and shook Alice's hand vigorously. Jenny Klein, Connor's girlfriend, wrapped her arms around the strapping lad and didn't relinquish her grip as everyone walked out to their cars. Connor made the *call me* sign to Alice as he, Jenny and his parents hustled into the waiting limo.

Bill and Gerry could see the pressure falling away from Alice as she slumped in the back seat of the Cadillac. "Man, does it feel good to be home! I didn't realize how much energy it took to do all this stuff until I saw you three. Then I knew that I didn't have to be *ON* anymore. Momma, is there any champagne on ice at home? I think I deserve a little bit of celebration."

"Yes, baby, we'll drink some champagne. It should go well with the steaks we're gonna barbecue. Do you mind that we invited Shane and Kimoko over too?"

"No, it'll be nice to see them. They've been good neighbors, after all, and should be part of our little celebration."

The dinner and celebration went as planned, and Shane fussed over Alice's performances. She just kept smiling and drinking champagne. Around nine o'clock, Alice excused herself and went to bed. Nobody expected to see her again for at least twelve hours.

These recent events were just the beginning. Alice Morgan was now up to her hips in the pro game and she was quickly learning to fight off the bad stuff. Gerry and Bill were now more than interested spectators. Their roles in being her support system were changing as they adapted to the new paradigm in their lives.

Then, there was Benny...

Chapter 38
Benny

"I don't want you to call me 'Benny' anymore. I'm not a kid, so it's gotta be Ben or Benjamin. Can you two do that for me?"

"Sure. You're always gonna be my baby boy, but I will promise to start using your full name. Benjamin does have a more proper ring to it," Gerry said with all seriousness.

"Does that mean you're gonna get mad at us if we slip up?" Bill deadpanned.

"Naw. But if you call me 'Benny' in public, I'll just pretend that I don't know you."

"That's fair. Why the big change in identity?"

"Well, my poly-sci major has kind of driven me toward wanting to do something in public service. 'Benny' sounds too... I don't know... Too street-corner colored. 'Benjamin' doesn't sound so intimidating. Do you understand?"

"Yeah, I think so. Gerry?"

"Oh, I don't think it matters that much, but if you think it gives you more credibility, I'm okay with it. I'm just glad we didn't name you Horace."

That cracked everybody up, and *Benjamin* came over and gave his mother a big hug and kiss on the cheek.

Benjamin Lester Morgan had just turned twenty-one and was a fully-grown young man of six feet, two inches. After being hit by the baseball, he gave up the game for his growing interests in government and politics. He told them, one day, that the trauma and the recovery gave him time to think about what the rest of his life was going to look like. Like his sister, he became quite popular on campus and was elected to the student council. He kept in shape by running, lifting a few weights (still), and learning to play racquetball. He was a gifted athlete and quickly moved up the ranking ladder at SDSU's racquetball club.

But politics and governing became his new-found intellectual interests. He read everything he could find about the history of the United States, from its earliest, pre-Revolutionary times, to the wretched decisions of the British, Dutch and Portuguese slave traders. This led him to the Revolution, the Constitution's birth, and the evolution of that document up to and through the Civil War. The horror of the antebellum South and the economic imperatives that led to America's bloodiest and most ignoble war caused Benjamin to spend long hours contemplating, then writing his thoughts and summations for his classes and himself.

"Bill, did you know that only one or two percent of the white farmers and plantation owners in the old south owned slaves? The white people were generally poor—though their social status was held in higher esteem than the slaves, of course. Sharecropping was actually white slavery. The alternative for those poor white folks was starvation. The white capitalists of the day kept it that way, because they could maximize profits. See, western capitalism was not that old or mature, so putting rules up against the money men was anathema. That's what started the war: anti-slavery. The concept of having to pay for the labor that made the farmers rich was simply out of the question.

"The thing that I still can't figure out is why all those poor white people were so eager to take up arms against the Union for the sake of defending slavery and the two percent of those southerners getting stinking rich off of it. Didn't they realize that they were being exploited too? Was their perception of their place in society that hard-wired that they were willing to die for the sake of the rich? Makes no sense at all."

"Well, Ben, you're going to find that people often *desire* to remain ignorant. I think that the poor white population in the antebellum South was generally illiterate too. The only 'literature' they knew came from the Bible, and their preachers preached little else but fire and brimstone. They also folded in the superiority thing about whites over blacks in order to cement the mindset for the rich, white farmers. You know, that 'Sons of Ham' thing. Pretty ugly, huh?"

"Sounds like they were brainwashed to the point of not even understanding that getting killed for something they would never see—wealth and comfort—was what that culture was built on. Maybe that's what Karl Marx was talking about when he analyzed capitalism. Our slavery and Civil War periods were truly disgusting, inhuman and un-Christian too. I've read much of the Bible and if you dig deep enough, you're gonna find contradictions and justifications all over the place for making cultural ignorance institutionalized.

"That's why I think I want to get into politics and governance. Somehow, we gotta turn that stone over. I know Reconstruction was a disaster; no surprise that Andrew Johnson, a Tennessean, stopped the 'better angels' who tried to make it right in Dixie, and allowed the carpetbaggers and scoundrels to run roughshod over the countryside. So, I think I want to work for those in office who are gonna actually address the causes, rather than just nibble at the symptoms of our current, persistent racial issues."

"Well said, Benjamin. I'm sure your mother will be supportive of you too. You've got my vote on a number of levels."

When Gerry and Ben sat down together, he repeated his short-term goals after graduation. "Oh, Benjamin. That's really good to hear. You know, Bill and I have had our share of encounters with racists, racism and bigotry over the years. We've been luckier than most mixed-race couples, but you can still feel the eyes and hear the whispers. So far, out here in San Diego, nobody has really accosted us when we've been in public. This neighborhood has been pretty accepting – except for that guy and his wife a couple of doors down who always look angry and run into their house when either Bill or I are outside. It's almost laughable if it weren't so sad and pathetic."

"Okay. Enough of that. What have you got lined up?"

"There is this state representative from National City that is looking for an intern. His chief of staff was on campus last week quietly soliciting the *poly sci* department for people like me, who want to work for the legislator. I should hear something next week. I might have to find a place to live in Sacramento too.

"Don't worry, Mom. All birds fledge from the nest sometimes. I graduate in a couple months and who knows... If I do have to find a temporary place up north, I will behave and not get into any trouble. I've seen what can happen to men and women who don't stick to what they know. I am not interested in booze or drugs. I've never had any trouble attracting girlfriends, but I expect I'd be so busy that that would not be part of my life. I'm young, good-looking and smart. And I have plenty of time for the serious stuff," he said with a straight face.

"Uh, huh. And how can we forget your humility? Well, I

hope I've raised a good son. Some of those 'sophisticated ladies lay in wait for someone just like you. Be very careful of those who get too friendly too soon."

"I understand. You know I have a suspicious gene. Look how long it took me to get close to Bill. You were all fallin' down in love with the guy and I looked at him as if he was from the other side of the moon, or someplace. People have to earn my interest and respect. If not, that respect has no value. I'll be fine. But first I have to get the job."

He got the job. Representative Clyde Bock called personally to ask Ben to be one of his two interns for the coming session of the legislature in Sacramento.

"Great! I'm glad you accepted. You're gonna have to find a studio up there during the session. I plan on having you and Amy Jones running around like scalded cats.

"Okay. I'd like you to come down to the National City office tomorrow to get signed in and acquainted with everyone. I'll sit down with you two interns and fill you in on the agenda. Then, next week, we all go up to Sacramento. I suggest you head up there right away to find a place. Can you do all that?"

"Yessir, Mr. Bock. No problem. See you tomorrow. Oh. What time?"

"When nobody is around, it's Clyde, Ben. Make it ten in the morning."

Gerry and Bill were over the moon with joy that their youngest was on his way to a career in civil service. They agreed that his intelligence and looks would take him a long way.

"I wonder when he'll decide to run for office on his own?" Gerry asked rhetorically.

"I hope it's not until he has learned more of the ropes. I

think he will take a step-by-step approach. Maybe when Bock decides he wants to move up to the senate, Ben will try to run and fill his seat. It's going to be exciting to watch his career flourish. We did a good job at raising that boy and helping him find his own way. It just wouldn't be fair or right if he was doing something because *we* wanted him to do it."

"I agree. As his mother, I will always fret a little. That's the little battle I fight every day, as I've seen him grow into the man I'm proud of. I don't know if I can take any credit for it, but he does think clearly, has a wary eye for bullshit and sees through con jobs."

"Baby, he's gonna be fine. I wonder what the rents are gonna be up in Sacramento. Not to worry, we've got him covered. Did you tell him we'd pay for his apartment up there? How much weekly allowance do you think he'll need? He never said how much—if anything—this internship will pay?"

"Oh, right, um, I think he said that his monthly stipend is about eight hundred dollars. That will probably just barely cover his rent up there. Maybe we can give him another thousand to keep him in groceries?" Gerry suggested hopefully.

"That's not a problem. Wait until I tell you what my stock portfolio has been doing lately. Even with the inflation and other economic bad news, my stocks have grown or stayed stable for the last couple of years. My stock value has already recovered half of what we used to buy this house. We're worth more now than when we first married."

Chapter 39

Fame and Fortune

During the late 1970s and early 1980s, Alice Morgan became the dominant force in women's golf. She avoided the carnival-like requests to play in men's tournaments and stuck to what she did best. And the best was winning golf tournaments and championships around the world on a regular basis. She retained Connor Gaylord as her full-time employee and added the standard percentage of her winnings to his fifty-thousand-dollar annual flat salary. He wanted to marry Jenny, start a family and earn his own way, separate from his family's money. Working for Alice Morgan allowed all that to happen for him.

After she won her second U.S. Open Championship, there wasn't enough room on her golf bag for all the sponsor logos who wanted a piece of her fame. She found herself in the weird position of turning down long-term, seven-figure contracts because there were so many, and the demands of too many sponsors took her away from her game. She was already a multi-millionaire and had things in perspective based on several of her talks with Bill during the course of her run of successes.

He quit teaching and became her full-time manager, even hiring an accountant to help sort out her finances and invest in her newly-emerging brand. He also invested much of Alice's money in steady, can't lose stocks like utilities and energy companies. She would be financially set for life even if she decided to quit playing golf the next day. Alice even did a few TV commercials for golf equipment and clothing lines to go with her photo spreads in various magazines promoting clothing and equipment. Her beauty, charm and personality helped her get all those non-tournament earnings – which exceeded what she won on tour. The Ladies Professional Golf Association only paid a fraction in winnings compared to what the men on the PGA were making.

Alice and Bill insisted that she not disrupt her practice and playing routine. EVERY tournament on the planet wanted Alice Morgan to play, but Connor and Bill made sure that she had rest time away from the frantic pace of tournament life.

Her parents saw her maybe once every other month and during the tour's brief off-season. They had family discussions about recharging emotional batteries and developing a personal life too.

"Yeah. I've thought about that at times. And, yes, I'd like to have a boyfriend. However, with my face on every damned magazine in the country, it's hard to get anything resembling a stable relationship. You wouldn't believe the lounge lizards at the hotels we stay in. The tournament directors provide security for us top players, so I'm pretty safe from those creatures. Some of the lesser-known women just end up eating in their rooms to avoid the predation. Women are still seen as ripe fruit to be picked by these men who have no lives of their own that are worth a damn."

Gerry said, "Well, I guess it's going to have to be someone inside our circle who doesn't care that you're now a multi-millionaire and on TV all the time. One of my fellow teachers, for example, has a twenty-five-year-old son who is single and unattached. It'll have to be something like that, I think. No movie stars for you, baby. You would explode their vanity every day."

Everyone got a good laugh from that.

"It's weird, Momma, in that here I am, a black woman being fawned over by rich white guys who fall all over themselves to pay me huge dollars to sell their products. Am I really breaking down some barriers for black people by being famous? There aren't many black females doing commercials, so maybe I am. I'm still the ONLY black female playing on the women's tour. I know I'm winning almost every other week, but it seems the more I win, the whiter I get."

More laughter.

"Thanks to my cute manager over there, my finances are set for life. I can just live off the interest from a savings account, never mind the stock dividends. So that part of it is taken care of. Bill, I can't thank you enough for setting me free from all that financial stuff. It clutters my mind just to think about it. You have no idea what a luxury it is to say to would-be sponsors, 'Go see my agent'."

"Well, Alice, the color of money doesn't change, but it can change the color of the person who is making a lot of it... As you've just said. I assure you that if you stopped winning and going on TV talk shows, all that fawning by the money people would stop and you'd just be another uppity, uh.... Well, you recall how my former pals at Willow Creek treated you and the names they called you.

"As your manager and chief consultant, my advice is to keep doing what you're doing, but also to continue with the investments you're making. By promoting your brand for things like your own charity foundation and other civic entities like the Boys and Girls Clubs, you will be ensuring your future for when you finally have had enough of touring golf. Making hay while the sun is shining now will enable you to spend the rest of your life with the family you love later.

"If you string the pearls together, look what's happened in just the few years since the day I found you on the caddy bench at Willow Creek. For me, I got to meet the love of my life and also got the humbling pleasure of helping you develop into perhaps the best woman golfer in history. Your brother, Ben, is now on his way into politics and civil service. Your mom and I burst our buttons every day and thank the stars for doing most of the right things by you two. Thing is, though, we didn't really do that much. You and your brother are solid citizens. You had your head on straight when I met you. You've overcome the trauma of losing your father to violent crime, and in so doing have given me the absolute joy of being your friend, mentor and cheerleader."

"Wow, Bill. That's really nice to hear. When I'm done playing competitive golf, I'll still have the foundation that you two helped me build. That's a legacy that I'll take to my grave. Thank you so much."

Alice got up from her chair and landed in his lap, wrapping her long arms around him in a strong hug. He could feel the wetness of her tears on his neck. Next, she got up and did the same with her mother. Her silent emotion of the moment stirred everyone. They unabashedly appreciated each other's love, honesty and decency in this all-too-rare moment of family intimacy. Alice Morgan wasn't the champion golfer at this moment. She was the loving daughter who had just validated her parents' lives. For them, fame and fortune simply couldn't approach the joy of their time with Alice.

But more success, wins and honors followed Alice's

incredible ability to consistently focus on being the best female golfer in the world. She became the first woman of color to win the grand slam of major championships around the world. She won several Vare Trophies for the season's lowest-scoring average. She was also Golf Digest's Woman Golfer of the year for three years in a row, and earned two LPGA championships and many lesser-known events over the following five years. All this put her in the pantheon of the greats like Louise Suggs, Mickey Wright, Kathy Whitworth, Babe Didrickson and Joanne Carner.

And through it all, she was, to Bill and Gerry, still their girl in pigtails. Her stunning smile, great intelligence, poise, politeness and long-suffering patience with the media and sports talking heads had created a special brand of celebrity; one who remained humble.

In her last interview before retiring from the tour, she spoke on the record with the lone woman reporter and editor for a major golf magazine, Kelly Madsen. Alice summarized her career by saying that it was a great ride, but when there were no more hills to climb, it was time to return to the village.

"What do you mean by that?" Madsen asked incredulously.

"It means I'm not going to tour anymore. I'm going to open a golf academy for underprivileged children in the inner city of San Diego. Junior golf is big in San Diego to be sure, but the poor kids don't have anyone to buy them golf clubs, pay for lessons and dress for golf. Heck, I've got six full sets of clubs sitting in my folks' garage that I haven't even taken out of the box. Why not make them available to kids who really want to learn the game?

"Oh, and I want to include tutoring services for the kids in my academies and existing charity foundations so they can become literate and well-spoken when they need to be. See, golf is still pretty much a white man's, elitist game. But it is such a great game that teaches life skills; it should be available to people from all walks of life.

"I was raised, as a child, by my biological father who took me with him to a certain Cleveland public golf course. That course allowed black men and women to play without much prejudice or harassment. I began caddying for him when I was eight. He taught me the mental side of the game and found some used clubs in the pro shop barrel that he cut down for me. He didn't really give me lessons beyond the basics; he just wanted me to have fun hitting the ball. By the time I had grown out of those little clubs, he was playing much less often; he'd lost a couple of jobs and couldn't afford the green fees. Then he was killed by muggers.

"My mother was teaching school and struggled to keep my brother and I fed and clothed. That's when she drove me to golf courses to caddy. And that's where I met my stepfather, Bill Bannock.

"You know, I haven't dwelt on my life story in my other interviews, because I didn't want to allow you people into my parent's lives. As you know, I stuck to golf questions and comments."

"Yeah, I know. It was very frustrating to interview you. We only got your standard cliché answers to questions. How did you manage to stay away from your personal stuff with us hounding you all the time?"

"It wasn't easy, but I felt I had to keep the media out of my house. Now, because I picked you to do this interview, here's the big scoop: I'm going to get married later this year to the son of the course superintendent from my caddy Connor's golf club. We haven't set a date yet, but it's gonna happen later this year. Would you accept an invitation?"

"Of course. I wouldn't miss it for anything! Can I bring a photographer?"

Alice laughed. "Nope. You'll just have to throw rice and confetti like everybody else. I'm sure the San Diego Union will have their society editor there for after-ceremony photos and such."

"Where will you go for your honeymoon?" Madsen teased.

"Good question. I certainly won't tell you or any other media, but it will be to a place where there are no golf courses."

"So, are you set financially so that you can raise a family if that's your intention? Will your fiancé' still work?"

"Yes, we're all set, and yes, Patrick will continue to work for his dad at the golf club. My stepfather and best friend, Bill Bannock, has invested wisely for me and has managed my finances through these difficult financial times. I will use those investments to keep funding and growing my foundations and academies.

"Heck. If we get into trouble, I can always go back to playing golf for a living. I hear you can make good money doing that," she said with a blank expression.

"Nice, snappy answer, Alice. Thank you for the scoop about your upcoming wedding. I wish you nothing but the best, and I will definitely have a crew from our magazine come visit you and your academy when you're up and running. Good luck. You're one hell of a woman, and maybe the greatest female golfer of all time. It's been an honor to interview you over the last few years."

"Thank you. I've enjoyed speaking with you too. Not everyone conducts such a classy interview.

"There's one other bit I want to mention. As you know, my stepfather and best friend is white. He and my mother have been in love from the first moment they met. My fiancé,

Patrick is also white. Before I met him, Connor had to do some serious lobbying to get the Mission Bay Club to let me play golf there. But after a couple years, I finally was allowed to play regularly as Connor's guest. The membership even dragged its feet at honoring my LPGA tour card. As slow as it was, it showed us that people CAN overcome their prejudices.

"It just so happened that I beat their head professional a couple of times while becoming acquainted with the staff. That's how I met Pat. We started dating in secret; you wouldn't believe the things we had to do to keep our interracial selves secret from the membership.

"But when I started winning and getting my picture in the paper and in magazines, things changed. Connor, of course, was also featured. All those things started to weaken the old-school attitudes at the club and after I won the U.S. Open, the membership elected me as an honorary member with full privileges. I know Connor had a lot of influence, but those old racial animosities die hard. Connor used to tease me about helping the club membership join civilized society, but it was really his father, a club co-founder, and the superintendent that apparently swayed the vote. It wasn't unanimous.

"From that day forward, though, the Mission Bay Golf and Country Club was proud to announce my exclusive membership. With that came an influx of membership requests. The club, of course, immediately raised the initiation fees.

"We all laughed about that and I asked Connor if we would get some commission for stimulating the membership revenue train. He just shushed me and told me never to mention anything about it.

"The thing is, it DID change some minds. The 'it', of course, was me being a brown woman with a great putting stroke. I know the camera likes me, so that didn't hurt either. Well, it finally got out that Pat and I were an item, but a funny thing happened. Nothing. The members just smiled and shook our hands and wished us well. Pat and I just looked at each other and laughed a little. We were being something like racial pioneers at one of the most exclusive country clubs in the western United States."

"Okay, Alice. That was an excellent topic to end this interview with. Thanks again. I'm sure your new activities will be successful. Success just seems to follow you around."

Chapter 40

Empty Nest Decisions

Alice Morgan and Patrick O'Neal were married that summer, instead of the fall, by a Justice of the Peace in the main ballroom of The Mission Bay Golf and Country Club. The logic coming from the membership was that it was easier to throw the huge reception party in the same venue as the ceremony. That decision WAS unanimous, including from the bride and groom.

Alice looked stunning in a spectacularly designed dress that didn't hide her athletic figure. It was off-white with sewn-on pearls around the edges, except for the bodice. That was trimmed with a strip of light ochre silk that made the color transition from the dress to her skin seem like the most natural way to present her beauty and stature. She wore low-heel shoes so she and Patrick were about the same height as they took their vows.

Bill looked around and caught Connor's eye. They smiled. He was dressed formally, of course, as was his recent bride Jenny (Don't you dare call me Jennifer!). Gerry wore an elegantly tailored dress with a contrasting floral pattern-on-pattern of café au lait. Everyone else was dressed to the nines, including Sean O'Neal's entire staff of greens keepers and maintenance personnel. Many of them had helped raise young Patrick and kept him away from the mower blades.

The club hired a twelve-piece orchestra that played everything from Tommy Dorsey to the Beatles to Stevie Wonder. Everyone danced until their feet ached. Gerry was the toast of the ball as she and Bill had exactly one dance to themselves. The bridal dance featured the newlyweds, of course, and they were joined by both sets of parents. As Bill looked at the other three couples dancing, he saw a glimpse of the idealism that he and Gerry had so often discussed regarding the blending of the races in their country. When they changed partners, Alice and Bill beamed at each other as he swept her around the floor, and Pat did his best to lead Gerry in their waltz.

After about a minute, people started cutting in and Bill found himself dancing with Patrick's mother, then his aunt, then his cousin. Gerry was hijacked first by Sean Martin, then Connor, then Connor's father... And so it went. Champagne flowed from a crystal fountain, and the most spectacular buffet Bill had ever seen waited for hungry celebrants.

When it came time for the garter snap and bouquet toss, the eligible men and women behaved like children. Alice and Pat finally left the party and were swept away by a stretch limousine to parts unknown to a round of cheers and applause. Yes, rice and confetti were rained upon the joyous couple.

Bill thought: *What's a wedding night that doesn't begin with shaking the rice out of your underwear and shoes?*

Alice told Gerry and Bill where the happy couple were going for their honeymoon. "I wanted to go where there were no golf courses, and we found the ideal trip... I think. We're going to take a cruise with a Canadian outfit that sails into the

Canadian Arctic. We will fly into a little airport on the west coast of Greenland and board the ship there. We then sail up the coast and through the Davis Strait looking for whales and marine wildlife. I saw the pictures, and Pat and I decided that it would be perfect. We're going to end up at seventy-five degrees North, way above the Arctic Circle, where we'll fly home by way of Ottawa, Ontario. I played in the Canadian Open there once and thought it was a beautiful city. There's this really lovely hotel about two blocks from the Canadian Parliament buildings, so we'll stay there for a couple of days, seeing the sights before coming back home."

Prior to the wedding, Alice, Pat, Gerry and Bill helped shop for a new home for the happy couple. Alice and Pat picked out a lovely, rambling ranch-style home on a nice but small lot on the north side of Mt. Soledad in La Jolla. The view from the back of the house was breathtaking. The real estate agent showing the property must have paid off the weatherman that day, because the view up the coast was as clear as it ever got there. They could see all the way north to San Clemente. The "kids" loved the view and wrote a check on the spot. Bill checked out the nuts and bolts of the house beforehand to make sure all the light switches worked and there were no hidden plumbing problems. The house was a gem, a jewel ... just like the name of the town above which it perched.

Gerry and Bill helped arrange the move; they wanted it to be all finished and ready for the honeymooners when they came back to earth in California. They collected Pat and Alice at the airport after they arrived from Canada, and drove them up to their new home. Alice had presented them with a very long shopping list prior to leaving and they'd dutifully stocked the refrigerator and pantry with the items that she'd told them to buy.

"Don't forget a few bottles of champagne on ice for when we get back," were her final instructions.

They toasted the happy but travel-weary couple; kissed, hugged and left them to begin what they hoped would be a terrific and happy life together. Now, it was their turn to celebrate their accomplishments and their time alone together.

***

"So, where do you want to go first?" Bill asked over morning coffee the next day.

"You want to take a trip, huh? Well, let's see... I haven't really been anywhere except to a couple of Alice's tournaments, so maybe we should go around the world. I honestly don't feel like teaching anymore. I'll probably get involved with Alice's academy and such, but I think I've served my communities adequately. If you don't mind, darling, I think I'll submit my resignation tomorrow so the school will have plenty of time to hire a replacement."

"Of course, I don't mind. I've been collecting travel brochures from various places. I've looked at Europe, India and 'down under'. I'd love to go to Africa, but there are few places there without war and civic unrest. Ecuador is starting the tourist business in a big way for visiting the Galapagos Islands too.

"Hmm. Maybe we should buy a wall map of the world and some darts."

"Yeah. Better yet, let's both write places on same-size bits of paper and draw them out of a hat, literally. Let's take several trials and add up the scores to see which place wins."

"That's my darling engineer talking. Sure. Let's get started."

After reading all the brochures and looking up different

places on maps, New Zealand won. Bill called the consulate the next day and had them send information for touring New Zealand. Gerry went to the city library and brought home a stack of books on that country. They entered full research mode and got more excited each day. This was their first week without the children in their daily lives, and they both felt that they were already on a vacation.

Alice and Ben's careers in golf and politics, respectively, set them free. Ben's work in politics started taking off as his boss from National City ran for state senate ... and won! All of representative Bock's local campaign apparatus was shifted to Benjamin, and at age twenty-eight, he started his campaign. Bill and Gerry supported as much of his campaign as they were legally allowed, but he turned out to be a money-raising dynamo. The wind was clearly at his back. He was even dating a very nice professional woman he'd met in Sacramento.

They got their shots and made sure their passports and travel records were up-to-date. The next step involved contacting a travel agency. They gave the very nice and helpful woman their planned itinerary and schedule window.

Since New Zealand's summers coincided with North American winters, they decided to go to the land of kiwis during December.

"Let's take our time," Bill suggested. "Let's go to some out-of-the-way places there and get to know the people and the culture."

"I wouldn't have it any other way. If we spend any time in the southern mountains, it'll still be cool, won't it? We better plan on packing a sweater or two."

With stops in Honolulu and Fiji, the trip time took almost twenty hours. The 747 was not very full and they managed to stretch out across some vacant seats to sleep. It was six o'clock on Thursday morning when the massive aircraft touched down. The couple were pretty shattered even after sleeping on the plane.

Clive Harris from Two Island Tours was waiting for them at the Auckland International Airport. Clive was a ruddy-faced fellow with haystack red hair, bright blue eyes and a ready smile that showed a lot of teeth, two of which had gold caps.

"Welcome to New Zealand, folks. I'm Clive Harris and I will be your driver and guide for your entire visit to our beautiful country. Right, let's get your bags."

After they cleared customs, Clive helped them load their luggage into the back of his Range Rover, and drove them through Auckland up to their hotel that was right on the harbor.

"I'm sure you folks would like to have a proper breakfast and a nap before heading out to the Bay of Islands. That's where we'll spend the afternoon, before we get you back to the hotel for dinner. Remember, today is tomorrow for you. When you flew over the International Dateline last night, you entered Thursday. Right. Here we are. I'll make sure you're checked in properly."

They were checked in by a desk clerk named Mary from Edmonton, Canada. "You'll be in room seven-twelve, Mr. and Mrs. Bannock. Breakfast will be served for another two hours. Welcome to New Zealand."

Clive said he'd meet them in the lobby at eleven. "That'll give us time to get up to the Bay of Islands and a nice lunch of local seafood. Off you go. Rest up. See you soon."

Clive's cheeriness did manage to penetrate their travel fog. A bellman loaded their stuff on a cart and elevated them up to the seventh floor. Bill tipped him and they unpacked their bathroom kits and a change of clothes.

"Let's go have breakfast, shower and take that nap. I could use having my batteries recharged," said Bill

"Me too. Let's go."

They ate a hearty breakfast from a long buffet and managed to shower, undress and land in bed before their eyes shut completely. Bill had set the travel alarm for 10:30 A.M., so they managed a couple hours of sleep.

North Island, New Zealand lay closer to the equator than South Island, so the weather felt a lot like San Diego in late June. They dressed in shorts, sandals and golf shirts.

"Good to see you brought your camera and sunglasses" Clive said as the couple entered the lobby. 'It's a lovely drive and the beach scenery is excellent. You'll probably see some sea lions sunning on the rocks. They love to pose for pictures. Let's get started."

The route north on Highway One took them through a lovely town named Whangarei. From there all the way up to Russell featured a most scenic coastline. They were ready for lunch by two o'clock, and Clive had them booked at this lovely restaurant that overlooked the bay. After they ate, they drove out to the end of Cape Brett and photographed the Hole-in-the-Rock at the tip.

Clive took his time and gladly pulled over for photos when they asked him to. He also took them along the coast to Doubtless Bay, where they turned back toward Highway One and then return to Auckland. Clive told them to be ready to go at seven o'clock the next morning as a long day lay ahead and there was much to see. They ate a wonderful dinner of New Zealand prawns and a large salad, along with a delicious bottle of local white wine. Gerry and Bill hit the bed by eight o'clock and slept deeply and dreamlessly until the alarm clock jarred them awake at five o'clock.

Thus began the routine for their stay in this beautiful country. That first full day began with a drive down to Waitomo to visit the glow worm caves. They stayed at a lovely little bed and breakfast lodge nearby and dined with the proprietors. They chatted happily for an hour or so before the owners had to begin preparing for the next day. They obviously knew Clive, and the couple enjoyed listening to them gather some wool and tell stories while they ate.

While driving, Bill was struck by the narrow, twisting highways. "Clive, how long does it take to learn to drive these roads? I'm still getting used to seeing us drive on the left side of the road, but, man... These things are narrow and winding. When that big truck passed going the other way, it felt like we had maybe six inches, er, fifteen centimeters clearance. I know I flinched."

"Not to worry, Bill. It was more like thirty centimeters. I've been driving these roads since I was a lad. Never hit anything yet. Always a first time, though," he said, laughing wickedly.

"Very funny, Clive. I'm sitting back here clutching my seat belt like I'm on an amusement park ride. How long before we start feeling more relaxed?" Gerry said.

Clive just laughed. "You'll be fine, mum. I've had tourists screech, groan and whimper for the first two or three days. You lot have been true and brave soldiers. Right. Here's our turn-off toward Rotorua. Notice all the roundabouts? We think they're more efficient than having traffic signals or stop signs everywhere.

"We'll visit the Maori Village later. The Maori are our indigenous peoples who came here from the east, probably Tahiti or Bora Bora. These people were—and still are— excellent sailors. Imagine traveling a couple thousand miles across the ocean in a dugout canoe. Tonight, after dinner, I'll take you to a lounge where Maoris perform the *Haka,* or chant.

Each *Haka* has a different story or message. I think you're gonna love it.

"This whole area around Lake Rotorua is a bubbling cauldron of hot springs and mud pools. We're going to be staying at a lovely old mansion that overlooks the lake. The lake, of course, was formed from a collapsed volcano many millions of years ago. Indeed, all of New Zealand was formed by volcanic activity. We still get the odd earthquake and eruption up and down the country. It must have been very exciting around here millions of years ago."

The mansion, named after its long-dead original owners was indeed lovely. Their room was small but tidy and very comfortable. They had drinks on the terrace before dinner, and as the sun was lowering to the west, dinner was served. There was no menu, the inn simply made wonderful dinners for its guests as if you were family. Their dinner companions this night were from Argentina and Belgium.

Clive took them to the little club where the *Haka* was performed. The amount of energy and passion exhibited from this "dance" was astonishing. They stayed long enough to see two of them performed by different teams of "dancers". Everyone applauded loudly for each performance.

Back in the room, Gerry and Bill commented on how easily they were accepted by everyone they met or saw.

"I didn't see any glances or frowns, or anything but cordiality from everyone," Gerry said.

"Yeah. It's like nobody cares that we aren't the same skin tone. I think there used to be some friction between the Maoris and the original European settlers here, but after New Zealand cut the golden umbilicus from London, all that petered out. Racial harmony seems to be mostly the norm here. Imagine that. Racial harmony. What a concept."

"Yes. The Maori people really are handsome ... and large.

I'm sure there is some sort of segregation, but I haven't seen any so far. We'll have to ask Clive about that later."

It took two more days of easy travel to reach Wellington, the southernmost city on North Island. They took the ferry across the Cook Straits to Picton, South Island. The scenery along the way to Wellington was bucolic and even spectacular in spots. Clive said the trout fishing in the streams throughout the country was wonderful. "It's not unusual to battle a five-kilo trout here. You Yanks are happy with one kilo fish, but we throw them back or use them as bait for a marlin," he laughed.

"You're making me drool, Clive. We didn't sign up for a day of fishing, did we?"

"Nope. More the pity. Then, I probably wouldn't be able to get you back into the car."

As they traversed the straits, Bill remembered reading about a unique reptile found only here. It is the *tuatara*, the only member of the order *Rynchocephalia*. The scientific name is *Sphenodon punctatus*. This unique species looked a lot like an iguana lizard, but its skull was more closely aligned with those of extinct dinosaurs. The San Diego Zoo recently acquired some specimens for display and research. Bill mentioned this to Gerry and showed her a picture of one in a brochure.

"Very interesting, darling. I love it when you go full expert on me." She said that with a big smile, hugged his arm and laid her head on his shoulder. "So how big do they get? Do they eat people?"

"No. They grow to about a meter long over their sixty-year life span. They are vegetarians, so not to worry. You are far too much animal to interest these guys." That got him a punch in the gut.

"I'll show you some animal later, big boy."

To say that South Island was long on incredible scenery and friendly people would be the same as saying that the grass was green. The entire country of New Zealand is about the same size as California and has widely varying but unique scenery, as does that state. Clive was a wonderful guide who took them to lovely cities and towns like Christchurch, Dunedin and Queenstown. They stayed at very comfortable inns and lodges everywhere. Perhaps their favorites were the Wilderness Lodges near Franz Josef Glacier and another at Arthur's Pass. The landforms were magnificent works of glaciers, erosion and volcanic activity.

Then there was Doubtful Sound.

They had to take a boat across a small lake to get to a coach that drove them over mountains to the head of the sound. Clive bade them farewell at the boat dock and said he'd be there for them in two days, when they returned from their cruise in the sound. What made this part of the tour so special for Bill was riding over a mountain pass with sheer drops on both sides of the narrow road. Along the mountainsides were arrays of plants and trees that he'd never seen before. They learned that many of these species occur nowhere else on earth.

The atmosphere was a misty mystery of wispy tendrils that coursed through the valleys and ridges. It was a cloud forest of unimaginable beauty and elegance, as far as Bill was concerned. They finally descended to the dock, where their Doubtful Sound ship waited. As they queued up to board the small vessel, they looked up at the sheer cliffs of the fjord to see the mists covering the pass and the mountains they had just traversed. It was like entering a place that time forgot. The water in the sound was perfectly glassed off, without a breath of wind to disturb its compelling tranquility. Nearly everyone seemed to share feelings of reverence, as conversation stopped and they all just stood looking at the cliffs covered with dark green plants that allowed the infrequent peek at the ochre-colored rocks beneath. Bill knew these rocks were made of *tuff* lava, or volcanic ash that layered and cemented itself into soft, easily eroded rock. He imagined the glaciers that went through here many centuries ago had little trouble carving out this incredible place.

It was getting late in the day, so they had dinner in the ship's dining area before leaving the wharf. The captain told everyone that they would be sailing just a short distance to a scenic cove and anchoring for the night.

And, oh my, what a spot to stop!

They were surrounded on three sides by sheer cliffs festooned with that variety of plants known only to South Island. Several delicate waterfalls cascaded down those cliffs but fell into the sound so quietly, that it sounded as if they were just whispering to everyone. Just as the sun was about to set, it broke through a hole in the clouds and lit up one of the waterfalls with golden light. The water drops glimmered like jewels as they fell. Fortunately, Bill recovered enough from his reverie to take several pictures before the sun ducked back into hiding. Gerry clung to his arm, murmuring little "oh, oh" sounds as she gazed at the scene. They walked all around the observation deck and leaned on railings until dark. No words were necessary. They shared knowing looks that this was one of the most spectacular days of their lives.

The slow boat ride out of the sound took most of the morning and early afternoon. The scenery in the sound just got more beautiful as the light of day changed. At the mouth of the sound, they motored out into the Tasman Sea and around the corner to see more of the sculptured tuff cliffs. Dolphins suddenly appeared and frolicked in the ship's wake. The ride back into the sound was kind of saddening in that this special place would now have to be left behind. Only their memories and, hopefully, enough good photographs, would serve to conjure up the magnificent, awe-inspiring land forms juxtaposed against the waters of the sound.

When they got back to Clive, they both started trying to unload what they felt and saw.

"Relax. One at a time. Pretty special place, eh? I've never seen anyone come back from that excursion unmoved. You two are obviously more sensitive than most to the magnificence of this beautiful place."

"You're right, Clive," Bill said. "We'll never be the same again. So, where do we go from here?"

They drove back through Te Anau and headed up the west coast. They stayed at a nondescript hotel in Franz Josef Glacier that night, ate some good lobster and drank really good local beer with dinner. Clive previewed what lay in store for tomorrow.

"We'll drive up the coast to Pancake Rocks for more picture-taking. Along the way, we will stop in this lovely little beach town called Hokitika. There's a kind of jewelry crafts family working in a marvelous shop there. They're friends of mine from years past, so I always bring my guests by. Nobody is ever disappointed. Right. Let's be off, then."

Hokitika was indeed quaint and lovely. It reminded Bill and Gerry a little of Solana Beach up the coast from San Diego, but without the ostentation. Clive recounted a story from a previous visitor: "There was this bloke from Kansas, I think, who stopped here with his wife. We toured the town and walked on the beach for a while, and then he turned to me and said, 'Clive. Where is there a telephone?' I asked him why he needed a phone. He said, 'Because I want to call home and tell them to send all my stuff. We're not going back.'

"I just laughed. He told me he was serious. Well, he didn't

exactly make the phone call, but lo and behold, a year later, he and his lovely wife appeared here. That's their little gift shop over there. Interesting people. His family had run a large cattle ranch since the 1860s and then they found oil on his place. He told me he just sold the ranch to a big oil company and brought himself, his wife, and his money to Hokitika. You Americans... I couldn't imagine any Kiwi doing that."

They did buy some lovely jewelry from the shop Clive took them to. The artisan was a very nice and interesting guy and he and Bill chatted about many things while Gerry and Clive looked at some of the larger pieces. "Darling, could we have this lovely inlaid conch shell shipped home? Isn't it wonderful? We could mount it on the wall opposite the couch."

"Wow. Let's have a look." The shell was about half a meter long and two-thirds of that across. There were pieces of what Bill presumed was mother-of-pearl inlaid on what appeared to be alabaster. It was a perfectly detailed conch shell, but the inlays made it almost sparkle.

"Gerry, this is absolutely beautiful." Bill asked the price and whether or not they would ship to California.

Mack Lowell, the owner and artisan said, "Sure, we can ship it. It'll cost upwards of two- hundred dollars American to crate and ship. Takes about a month to get to the U.S. You're on the west coast, so that'll cut a week off the shipping time. It'll be too big to fly, so it'll have to go on a freighter. Oh. And the price I'd like for that beauty is fifteen hundred dollars... American. You still interested?"

Gerry and Bill both said "yes" at the same time. They looked at each other and laughed.

"Will you take our credit card?" Bill asked.

"Well, I'd prefer if you went to the bank in town and had a draught drawn against it. I'll charge you two hundred for crating and shipping, so bring back a check for seventeen hundred U.S. and we have a deal."

They paid for their personal jewelry with New Zealand dollars and drove into town to visit the bank.

"You've bought yourselves a beautiful piece of artwork, Gerry and Bill. Send me a picture of it when you have it hung up, Clive said."

"We will. I think the mounting job will be the big challenge for me. Who knows? Maybe we'll just tell Mack to hold it for us. We might return here with all our stuff too." Everyone chuckled at that notion, except Gerry and Bill looked at each other and made "maybe" faces at each other.

On the flight home, Bill took Gerry's hand and said, "After we get our clocks reset. We might want to have a long talk about ... things. I know I'm still in a kind of velvet shock from seeing New Zealand and experiencing some of the nicest, most laid-back people I'd ever imagined meeting."

"Yes, sweetheart. I'm feeling the same thing. I never imagined a trip like this would have such an impact on my imagination and sense of adventure. Right now, let's relax, get some sleep and look forward to repeating this day on the other side of the dateline." They laughed at that, pulled down their sleep masks and tried to dream their way across the Pacific Ocean to home.

Chapter 41

The Best Decision

They were sitting on a bench on Point Loma above the Cabrillo lighthouse. They watched the waves break gently against the tip of land below. The sun was starting to sink into the west... Sinking toward New Zealand and tomorrow. It was a brilliant late January day in San Diego, the kind where clouds simply never had the audacity to appear. It was chilly, but they'd worn their sweaters and windbreakers. The sun on their faces was warm, but their thoughts were anywhere but where they were sitting.

The conch shell had arrived the week before and just looking at the complex crate that prevented any breakage made them pause and ponder. Those other possibilities....

"Darling," Gerry started. "We need to talk and let our thought streams come out. We do so many things well when we work as a team. Maybe we don't want to uncrate that beautiful piece of artwork."

That's all it took for Bill to start his wheels turning. "Gerry, my sweet wife, I too wonder if we're not destined to go to other places. I'm an American through and through, but my country is shifting under my feet. The crazies who voted the current slate of idiots into our government now want to blame that government for their own greed and the politicians' grab for power and money. Whatever happened to helping the poor, or assuring everyone can vote, or really making equal opportunity a thing that can work? What's so wrong with universal health care? Who the hell is Milton Friedman? Did anyone really think that the big money boys were going to 'trickle down' their largesse to the middle and lower classes? What's wrong with regulating businesses so they don't build products that fail or hurt people? What's wrong with everyone paying their fair share of taxes to keep our police happy, our teachers able to put food on their own tables, or having our military standing ready to defend us against our enemies without wondering if their boots will come apart?"

"Easy, my sweet. That's a big bite. I share your point of view. Honestly, I've never trusted so-called conservatives with our budgets, and history shows that they almost always create a national mess that the forward-thinkers have to clean up. I think this time will be among the worst ever. All they seem to do is try to make us a nation on the cheap by denying the public world-class infrastructure, denying less fortunate people a hand up to succeed, or making sure our children get world-class educations. They want world-class everything but don't want to pay for it. They even want to abolish the Department of Education."

Bill followed with: "These right-wingers rail about socialism, but do they want our military to be a privately owned, for-profit organization? Our military is, after all, the largest socialistic organization in the country. No, of course not. Add to that, when have you heard any conservative talk about civil rights, racial justice and integration? I'm still waiting to hear any of it from that group of silk suits."

"OOH. I've never heard you be so adamant."

"You know," Bill said, "being married to you these many years has made me more conscious of those things you just mentioned. Teaching school and seeing what parents were doing to their children added to my thought development. I'd say that just under half of the kids come from homes where parenting is either lacking or not helping the kids to understand what's going on in our country. Hell, half the kids don't know what the Constitution is or how many branches of government we have. And, add to that, they don't care to learn it. I think that lays the groundwork for a self-absorbed, self-indulgent and self-centered populace.

"Why should a white kid grow up trying to do justice for brown or black kids? They don't see that in *not* doing so, they weaken our national fabric of society. Makes me crazy."

"Yes, my darling. We agree on all those points. As a black woman trying to feed two kids after having her husband violently killed, I didn't pay too much attention to the other stuff. But after I met you and we were married, I started to play back all the memory tapes. What I saw in those memories was the discrimination, the unfairness, the unequal wages for the same work, the racially vectored policies in housing, and the lack of opportunities for integrated neighborhoods. The fair housing and lending laws are being flouted and ignored with no part of the justice system addressing the designations by banks and lenders of certain neighborhoods in our cities, for example. One of my fellow teachers tried to buy a house in Euclid. But the covenants and extra loan fees were so high and restrictive that he had to look elsewhere. Turned out that the same bank that denied him a loan in Euclid eagerly approved one for virtually the same amount of money for a home in central Cleveland where the citizens were mostly black. Another of my colleagues tried to do something similar only to find out that the bank charged higher interest rates for a loan to a black family, or denied them a loan due to them being 'too risky'. And this was for a guy with a Masters degree, a tenured teaching credential and a spouse who was a lawyer."

"I never truly saw you as a black woman. You were just Gerry from the moment I met you through your car window. So, when somebody looks at us askance, I take it personally. I have to fight the urge to take them by their shirts and ask, 'What the hell are you looking at?' Of course, I know the answer. And you know, baby, I'm really getting goddamned tired of iterating that answer over and over.

"I want those racial shock reactions to be in my rearview mirror. The more I think about it, the more I want to take our money and ourselves to Hokitika. Our conversations with Clive and the New Zealanders helped me understand the Kiwi culture somewhat. I kept looking for the telltale signs of embedded racism. Yes, he admitted that there were still some difficulties between the Europeans and the Maoris, but nothing like it is here. In fact, the Maoris are hard at work trying to preserve their ancient culture, because they are becoming so few, and so much of that pre-Captain Cook culture is disappearing. Clive said that New Zealand is more worried about Orientals coming to their country. They've established immigration restrictions on different nations just as we have here.

"I guess there will always be human tribalism no matter how hard we try to govern ourselves and our differences. But I didn't see the kind of institutionalized racism and overt hate that we have here. Hell, we still have active Ku Klux Klan and other white supremacy groups raising hell in most states."

"So, my wonderful man, are you saying that you've pretty much made up your mind that we should pick up stakes and move halfway across the world to escape racial prejudice for us? Are you saying you'd rather live in a country that respects and reveres science and justice rather than one that is drawing redlines to make sure white people stay together while excluding black people? Is that what I'm hearing you say? Are you saying that those who say they support our Constitution, then ignore it at their own convenience are making us less of a democratic republic?"

"Yes, that's what I'm saying. My only connections here are you and our two beautiful children. I don't doubt that we both could get jobs in New Zealand as teachers. I've researched that and with their growing population, qualified teachers are in demand. We are so very fortunate to have enough financial resources that we could make and execute the decision to move to New Zealand with little trouble. We both have to be all-in for the move, though. The thing is, we'd no longer be a foursome. It'd be just you and me. But who else have we ever needed? I love you with all my being and never want to be apart from you."

"Yes. I understand. I love you too, with all of MY heart. Nor could I imagine going through life without you by my side. If we are deciding to leave this country for another, we should be sure of our reasons and our commitment. We can't go half-cocked. Yes, if it turned out to be a mistake, we could come back. But somehow, I don't think we would.

"Of the places we visited there, which one do you think will be best suited for us? If we're going to want to teach, it'll probably have to be in a town or city. What do you have in mind?"

"Well, I thought Dunedin was a nice town. They even have a university there. We should call or write to Clive and ask him detailed questions about how to go about moving our stuff and finding a place to live and work. It will be complicated. I'll call their consulate first thing tomorrow.

Besides, wherever we end up ... wouldn't it be a nice place for the kids and their families to visit?"

Epilogue

In 1975, a boy was born to Earl and Kultida Woods in Cypress, California. They named the boy Eldrick Tont Woods. The boy's ethnicity covered the gamut of European, Asian, Native American and African ancestry. Earl Woods was a retired U.S. Army Colonel who fought in Vietnam. One of his Vietnamese colleagues in that war saved Earl's life in mortal combat. The Vietnamese Colonel's nickname was *Tiger*.

When Alice Morgan retired from touring on the LPGA tour, young Eldrick Woods began his rise to golfing fame and fortune. Eldrick's father, Earl, named Eldrick "Tiger" too. But before Tiger Woods became famous and rich beyond any dreams, he paid the price for being not white. The neighborhood in which the Woods lived was mostly white and Tiger went to school with mostly white kids.

The boy often came home from school in tears from being bullied and chased by hateful children. He often took out his rage and frustration by hitting golf balls in the garage netting his father built, or at the driving range. One day, Tiger didn't come home from school when he should have. His frantic parents went looking for him and found that some of the white bullies had taped Tiger to a tree and left him. Kultida begged Earl to move away. Earl decided that they would fight and not run.

Golf was Tiger Woods' salvation from the taunts and abuse from bigoted people. He became the greatest golfer in the world for many, many years. His legacy will be about all the awards and championships he won as a golfer, but his battle with discrimination and bigotry will not be nearly as intensely chronicled as his prowess as one of the most famous people in the world.

The Alice Morgan story is fiction, of course, but it sets the stage for understanding how much race, bigotry and mindless hate affect the citizens of the United States. And yet... This story also demonstrates the strength of the human spirit and what can happen when determination overcomes pettiness and stupidity.

Acknowledgements

This is my seventh venture into novel writing and it seems to become more of a process that goes beyond just creating characters, a plot and some emotional moments for what I hope will be a readership that gets immersed in it all. My editors and publishers along the way have sent me to graduate school for writing and getting published. Suffice to say, they know who they are and will, I hope, take gratification from reading this book in realization that they helped this author produce it.

One of my favorite authors, Mr. Timothy Hallinan, has often stated that his best attribute is that he "finishes the damned book". Those words ring in my head when I get a little lazy or stumble along with trying to properly develop a character or a plot line. We teach each other, and although Mr. Hallinan knows me not, he has taught me valuable lessons in authorship.

That said, if it weren't for my spectacular spouse, Elaine, I wouldn't have been set free from what keeps our household rolling along to pursue my literary adventure. She is a master organizer and makes sure we remain solvent and still able to enjoy ourselves in Denver, Colorado. The other woman in my life is my lifelong friend, Ms. Sally Baldwin Kling. She has been a fountain of encouragement and feedback as a beta reader and a critic after publication.

This story collected tidbits from my personal experience with people of all races. I've lived in that "white bubble", but had great friends from work and in the social milieu, like Lilian Fryar, Claudia Harris and Chris Earles. Their sharing of insights from the African-American community made me a better person and inspired me to write a love story where racial animus was counter-intuitive to the action and characters of *The Foursome – A Love Story.*

The End

Made in the USA
Middletown, DE
03 April 2023

27597135R00187